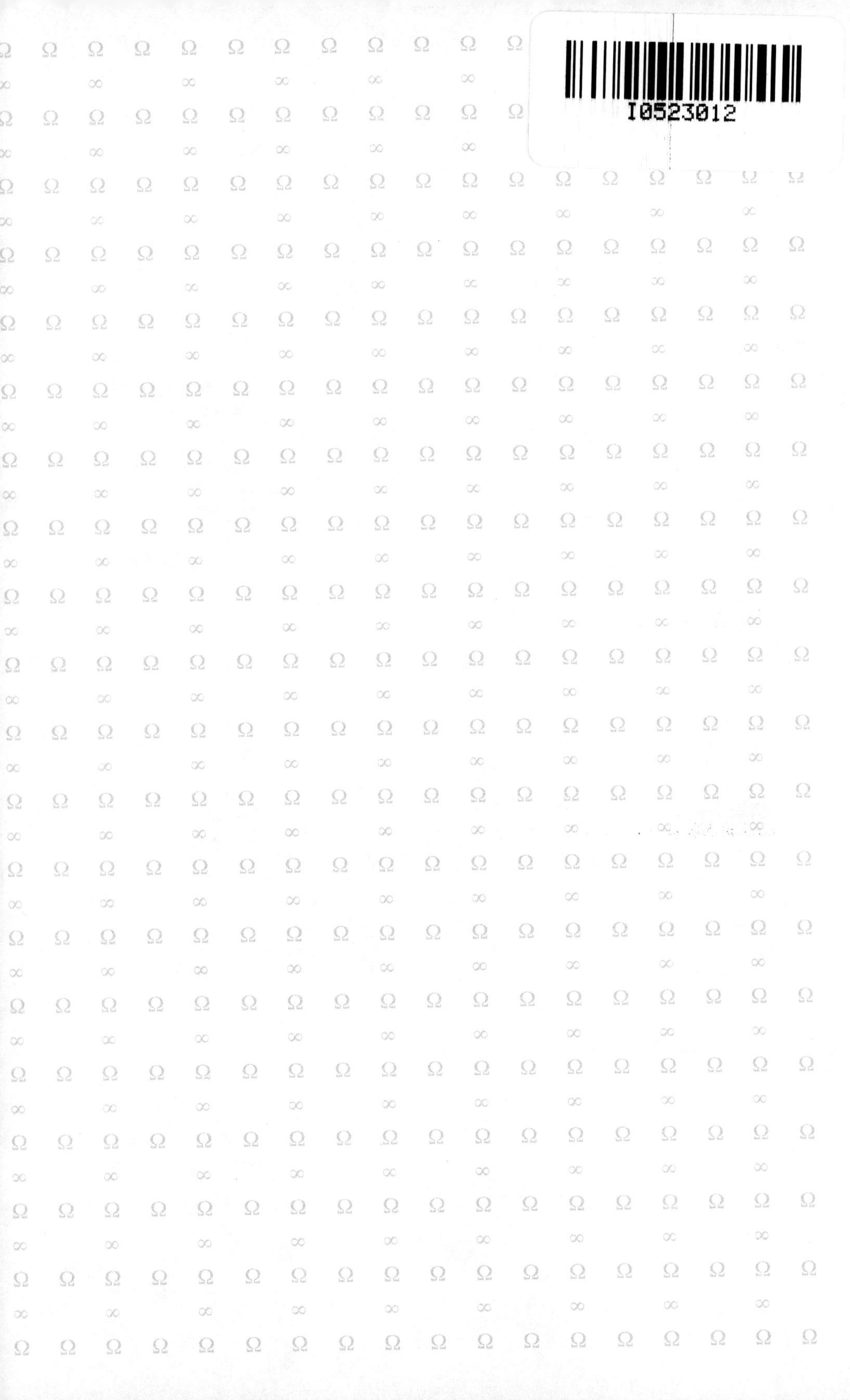
I0523012

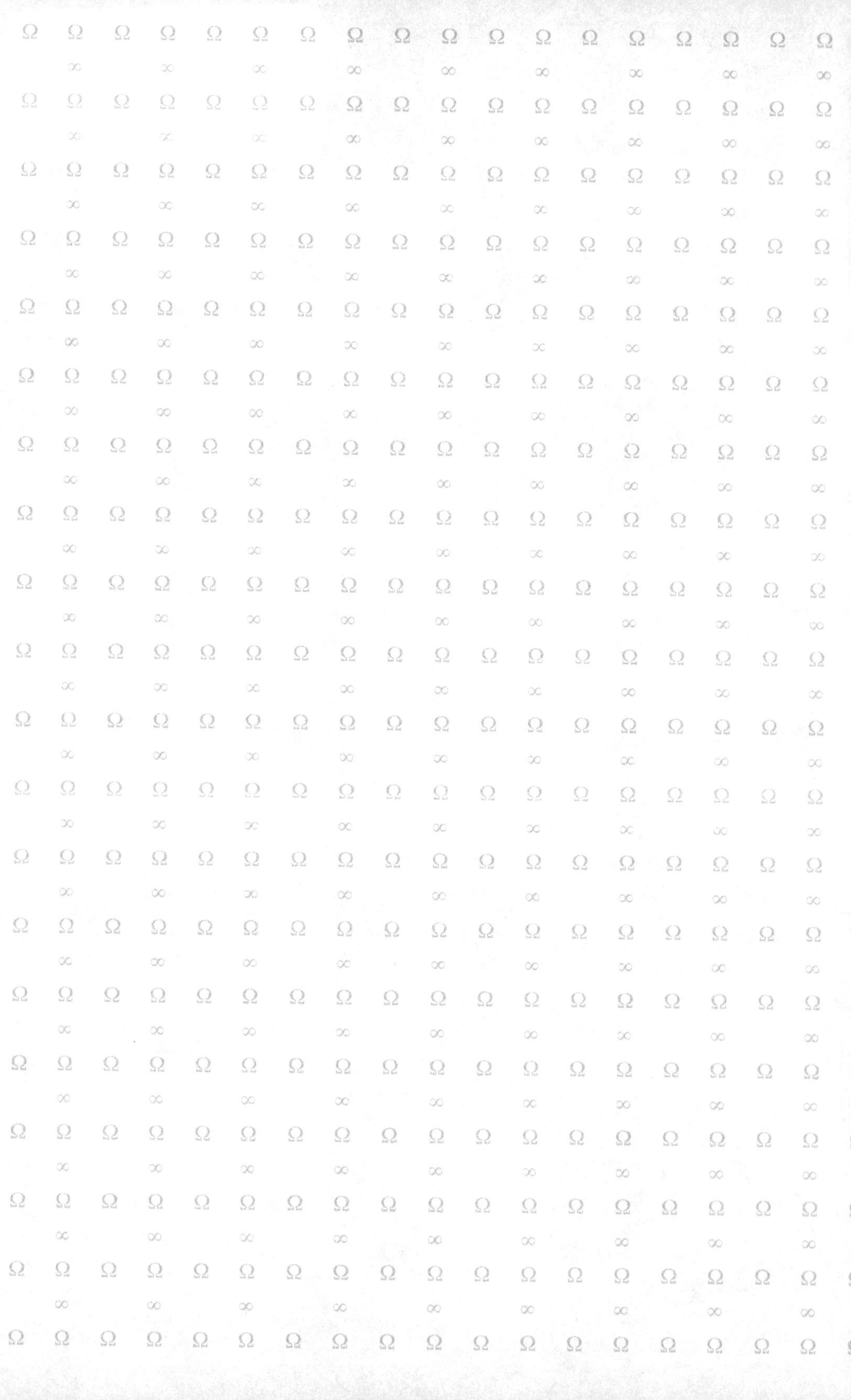

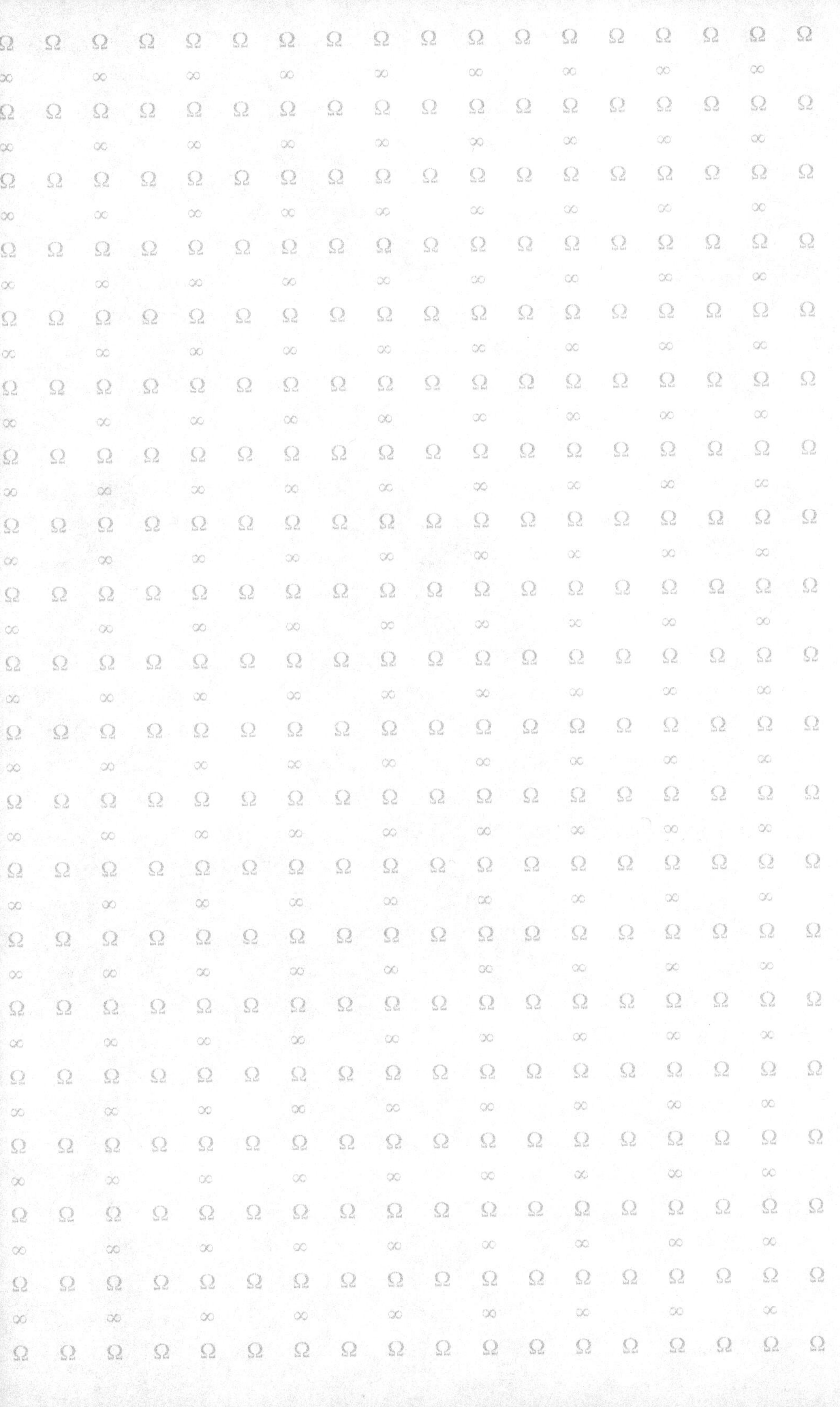

One Surviving Story

Twenty-eight writers select the one story they would like to survive them

Edited by Howard Firkin

in case of emergency press

We are proud to acknowledge the Traditional Owners of country throughout Australia and to recognise their continuing connection to land, waters, and culture.

We pay our respects to their Elders past, present, and emerging.

We support recognition, reconciliation, and reparation.

One Surviving Story

Twenty-eight writers select the one story they would like to survive them

edited by Howard Firkin

in case of emergency press

http://www.icoe.com.au

Travancore, Victoria

Australia

Published by in case of emergency press 2020

ISBN 978-0-9943525-7-6

I will always remember this moment. And I have. It either is or as though I've been granted fifteen minutes to go back, and it's the *smell*—the moldy pine smell—I drink it, my eyes burning, and realize every age signs its name in scent.

Drips in the woods. Distant groan of machines. Thirty years old, home to take my half of my parents' estate (my sister the other), garden trowel, rather ridiculously, in my pocket—just as Kitto said, a survivor. Ah, Kitto. Saw it coming, and declined. Gone, but still there in spirit. Only, I know what that means now. Means gone.

Can't help it, can't help it, can't help it.

John M. Williams, *In the beginning was Kitto*

Table of contents

Introduction v
Good People *Tim Hawkins* 1
Cleaning out the closet *Mary Pomfret* 5
Echoes from the Dolphin *Roger Vickery* 12
An Ex in Provence *Sofia Chapman* 23
The Mummy's Foot *Beth Spencer* 33
Zack *Jill Baggett* 40
Go With Me To That Land *David Shapiro del Sole* 49
The Kiss *Robert Nowak* 55
A Father's Pride *Bill Cushing* 63
Dumpster Diving in Paradise *Jim Ross* 66
Talking Under Water *Ian Jamieson* 70
Satellites *Sharon Willdin* 78
Blood Diamond *Warren Paul Glover* 81
A Steady Drip *Martha Patterson* 85
The Farmer's Task *Deline Skinner* 89
Liberty *Ruairi Murphy* 92
A Letter an Email *James Hannan* 100
Tai Ringal's Tale *Jeremy Gadd* 110
Fish Wounds *Arathy Asok* 118
One Winter's Afternoon *Leigh Swinbourne* 124
Over Your Head *Christopher Ringrose* 130
The Dispatch Rider *Peter Newall* 135
Behind the Glass *Sam McAlpine* 144
Amanda *David Lloyd* 152
Marina *Gavin Mndawe* 160
Through a Child's Eyes *Jo Mularczyk* 165
First Steps *Sara Abend-Sims* 169
In the Beginning was Kitto *John M. Williams* 173

Introduction

This anthology is a companion volume to One Surviving Poem, published last year. That volume arose out of a conversation between poets where it was noted with surprise that each of the poets had personal favourites that had never been published. If poets have found that their best, or favourite, piece had been undervalued, mightn't the same hold for writers of short stories? It was in the hope of preserving some of these cherished stories that we asked writers to nominate the stories they would most like to live on after them, and to include them in a single anthology.

The resulting collection is as diverse as you might expect, with stories from Australia, America, India, Africa, and Europe, but it has a surprising unity. I was struck, when re-reading the collection in its final order, how the first story, *Good People* by Tim Hawkins, sets the tone of the whole collection. Despite the diversity of subject and circumstance, despite the situations and trials, the stories are fundamentally about good people trying to make sense of a world where goodness is not always apparent, where the people they encounter are not necessarily good themselves, where their own limitations confound their attempts to live as they intend. But remarkably, for all the difficulties, sadness, uncertainty, and confusion facing the people in these stories, this collection is one of triumph, of hope, and of love for the wild variety that defines everyday humanity.

I hope you enjoy the collection as much as I do, and I hope you are enriched by stories of strong, stubborn, odd, mysterious, error-prone, *good* people.

Howard Firkin

Good People

Tim Hawkins

Tim Hawkins has lived and travelled widely throughout North America, Southeast Asia, Europe, and Latin America. His writing is widely published and has been nominated for Best of the Net, the Pushcart Prize, and Best Microfiction. His poetry collection, *Wanderings at Deadline*, was published in 2012 by Aldrich Press. A poetry chapbook, *Jeremiad Johnson*, was published in 2019 from in case of emergency press, and a story and poetry collection, *Synchronized Swimmers*, will be published in September by KYSO Flash Press.

Find out more at his website: *www.timhawkinspoetry.com*

Good People

About thirty of us were spending the summer in paradise—on an Alaskan island with 22 hours of daylight and a view of whales, eagles, and boundless sky.

For entertainment we had a VCR and one videotape—*Highlander*—in the common room. Neither the idyllic setting nor the lack of variety mattered much though as we laboured more than 100 hours per week processing the salmon run and loading the bounty onto Japanese freighters.

Any free time was usually spent slumped in exhaustion. During the height of the season, most of us gave up on such social niceties as brushing our teeth, simply because it was too much bother. I took to wiping mine on my shirtsleeve.

My job was grading salmon as they came down the line: one bin for sushi grade, another for canned fish grade, and another for dogfood. After 15 hours at a stretch, one grade blended into another and those salmon continued their turbulent migration even when my eyes were closed for a few hours of troubled sleep. When the freighters pulled into harbour it was all hands on deck for as long as they took to load.

But every so often there was a lull in the action—a 48-hour opening or bad weather—and then we would all crowd in to drink coffee and to watch *Highlander* for the umpteenth time.

"I am Connor MacLeod of the Clan MacLeod," we bellowed as one.

After most had drifted out, Gary would remain, talking to whomever would listen and, finally, to himself.

"I had a friend named Jim once," he might say out of nowhere. "He killed his family and then he killed his dog, but he was good people."

"Good people," he would add for emphasis. "And a mighty fine dog."

Gary's previous employment included a stint stomping the heads off chickens at a processing plant in Arkansas. How he had made it safely to Alaska, off his meds and no doubt muttering to himself the entire way, was a mystery to all.

But now that he had arrived, Alaska was probably the best place for him. There was a general tolerance of eccentric behaviour that might get one beaten, shot, or locked up in the Lower 48.

Of course, there were hazards here as well. In addition to bears, crazy tides, storms, and mosquitos the size of a man's hand, there were human threats. Alcoholism was rampant. I had personally seen two loggers squaring off with chainsaws outside a bar in Ketchikan. And of course, along with a lot of fine, hardworking people there was the usual ration of bullies, bastards, and sociopaths.

One (take your pick), who worked with us, was a supervisor named Del, a scowling, sarcastic brute, who was working off a debt to the owner that summer because, on a drunk, he had driven a hi-lo off the end of the dock, plunging it into the depths of the bay into which swam a mother gray whale and calf each morning.

The whales arrived early, sometimes doing a full circumference of the small bay and swimming back out into the open ocean. Other mornings they would stay and frolic, especially if a small, wiry, bespectacled young man named Peter stood at the end of the dock to spray them with a hose.

I had noticed that this Peter seemed to have a way with plants and animals. Earlier in the summer when we'd had some free time, he had taken out the company's small aluminium skiff and latched onto a halibut large enough to feed us all for a week. After being pulled out beyond the breakwater into open ocean, he had somehow managed to drag the beast back to shore. He had arrived to much excitement and a flock of bald eagles circling overhead.

Later in the summer, when we were on the brink of mutiny due to the rustic conditions, sameness of food, and general exhaustion, he had trekked into the interior of the island and returned with a bag of the most exquisite magic mushrooms anyone had ever ingested. Their effects created a renewed sense of acceptance that most of us were stuck on the island only until our contracts expired in the fall.

One night, toward the end of the season, when things were beginning to finally slow down, I found myself in the common room with Gary and Peter. Connor MacLeod had just defeated the Kurgan and achieved a massive Quickening. Peter and I were speaking in very bad, French-inflected Scottish accents, while Gary grinned and nodded.

"Connor MacLeod of the Clan MacLeod was good people," he said.

Del walked in, grumbling and slamming things around in search of God knows what, just in time to hear Gary's remark.

"You realize he's a fictional character, don't you, dumbass?" he sneered.

"You are a fictional character, dumbass," Gary responded.

"What did you say, shit-for-brains?" Del said, moving surprisingly quickly toward Gary. Before Gary could respond, Del had knocked him out of his chair and onto the floor.

"There can be only one," Del said. "And don't you forget that."

"You are not the one," Peter said quietly.

Del turned toward him with a furious look.

"You want some too, pansy?" he asked, taking a step toward Peter before suddenly dropping to his knees.

Del's look of fury changed to one of incredulity just before he began rolling on the wooden floor, furiously clawing at himself.

"Do you hear me?" Peter said. "You are not the one."

Del, whimpering, staggered to his feet and lurched out of the room, striking his head on the door frame and falling once more as he fled.

I could hardly believe what I had seen. I sat motionless, unable to utter a word. Peter seemed spent.

Finally, Gary got up from the floor, brushed himself off and resumed his position in the chair. "You are good people, Peter," he said.

"You are good people too, Gary," Peter replied.

Cleaning out the closet

Mary Pomfret

Mary Pomfret writes short stories and poems and her work has been published widely. Her debut novel 'The Hard Seed' was published in 2018. Mary lives and works in Bendigo, Australia. In 2016, La Trobe University awarded Mary a doctorate in English for her creative thesis on generational trauma. As a writer, Mary draws her inspiration from the beauty and awfulness of life; she believes that there is nothing so terrible that it can't be hallowed, re-imagined and transformed into art.

Email: *marywriter@live.com*

Website: *www.marypomfret.com*

Facebook: Mary Pomfret Author

Cleaning out the closet

Tomorrow she would paint his room. She gazed at the peeling wallpaper—teddy bears playing drums and trumpets, arms and legs frozen in the motion of marching to the silent beat of a childhood tune. More of it just seemed to peel away each year. Ricky had never asked for it to be taken down. His girlfriends all seemed to like it, but now the teddies were marching their final march.

She blew the dust off the box of Lego blocks as she lifted it from the bottom of the closet. Rose paused for a moment from her task, her back stiff from bending for so long.

"Do you want this old Lego?" she called to him down the hallway.

"And what would *I* do with old Lego, Mum?" he called back.

At breakfast earlier, she'd said to him, "Ricky, just an observation, not a criticism, but I have noticed that you seem a lot more relaxed now that you have finished your degree and you have a job to go to… now that everything's finalised."

As soon as she uttered the words she wished she hadn't. She knew instantly by the furrowing of his brow that she had annoyed him.

"Oh have you, Mum? And who are you? The narrator?" he'd said with a mouthful of toast. "You know, Mum, you have narrated my life for me since I was three. Every time I do anything, you have to tell me about it. I really don't want to hear your version of my life anymore, especially in those plays you write."

She laughed. "Can I have that last line?"

"No… not unless you pay me for it," he said. His frown had disappeared.

He was leaving. He was going to Canberra. He would be back from time to time, but he was leaving. Like the fool in the Tarot card deck he was on his way. If she faced it, he was gone already.

When she scraped off the wall paper tomorrow she would keep one small square and put it in a frame. How Ricky would laugh at her when he saw it. *Mum, you and your sacred relics,* he would say.

She thought about the faded little drawing that hung on her bedroom wall. How she treasured that little artwork. Although she had framed it, the glass pane had not stopped the fading and each year it got a little lighter. Bits of it had faded more than others. It was a simple one-dimensional drawing of a house with one door, two windows and chimney with smoke blowing out—you know the type that five-year-olds do. Across the top of his drawing Ricky had written in his very best printing, *MUM YOUR HOME.* A few months ago, she had decided to take it down to photocopy it before it became too faded. When she'd hung it back on the bedroom wall, she'd noticed that part of it had faded entirely. The stick figure her son in self-portrait, five year old style, who had stood along the side the house, had disappeared entirely. Is that how children fade from our lives? Is it when we least expect it? Then she wondered if she had deceived herself, imagined it. Perhaps he had never been in picture at all.

She glanced again at the peeling teddies and the growing pile of discards in the corner of his room: broken toys, old text books, tatty folders of notes, odd socks, old soccer boots, a broken bike pump, a once-treasured Pokemon collection and now the shoe box full of old Lego. Rose had been cleaning for most of the morning and her legs were beginning to feel stiff from all the bending and reaching into far corners. She sat down on the edge of Ricky's bed to rest for a moment or two. She arched her back, stretched and looked up at the ceiling at the cobwebs in the corners.

Thinking back to a scene from her own disappearance, her own leaving home, she could see her father standing with his back to the open fire in the kitchen as was always his habit in the cold winter. He was standing there like that the night she told him she was leaving. Did he feel then, as she did now?

"I'm going to Western Australia tomorrow, Dad." She remembered he looked down at his feet and he didn't say anything for a long while.

"Well, do you want me come as far as Melbourne with you?"

"No, Dad. I'll be okay."

Did she say goodbye to him before she left? Perhaps that had been their goodbye, those few words in front of the fire. He'd said to her years later nothing can really prepare for that unexpected moment when your child tells you they are leaving. She recalled the final scene of her departure. The tyres of the taxi had crunched the stones in the driveway as it pulled out. She hadn't looked back.

None of us want our childhoods when we are eighteen. It is something we have to leave behind, move on from as quickly as possible, an embarrassment almost; a skin to be shed, to be cast off. How fragile it all is. How fragile, how fleeting and how careless we all are when we are acting our part, taking our turn. How quickly life becomes memory, like scenes in a play with an ephemeral script that can be replayed at will.

"Mum, what have you done with all my socks?" Ricky called from the laundry. Rose laughed to herself. Some things never changed. He had never been able to find his socks.

"Well, maybe you wore them for days on end and then they self-destructed," she called back. By now he would have tipped the laundry basket upside down on the floor and he would be swearing quietly, hunting through the pile of clean washing.

"Very funny, Mum. You must have put them somewhere. You're always messing around with my stuff. Where the fuck…" his voice trailed off.

It seemed like just a blink of an eye since she and Tom had pulled up outside the grey stone-walled orphanage to collect their son. She remembered how the adoption worker had mentioned to them that they might offend the locals with their smell. Apparently, Europeans who eat dairy food have a particularly acrid scent to the noses of Asians who don't drink milk or eat cheese. Ricky smelled like lollies to Rose in those first tentative days. In fact, the whole crowded city had a heavy cloying sweetness which seemed particularly oppressive in the humidity of the late afternoons. Even the nuns smelled sweet.

But Rose remembered that it was the smallness of him which struck her most, at first. For his three and a half years he was a tiny, elegant little person, but so small. He was wearing white shorts with a picture of Homer Simpson on the back, a red and white striped T-shirt and an American baseball cap. The nuns said that this was 'his trousseau'. Had they powdered his face? Perhaps they had, because his face looked so white compared to the rest of him—a pale moon face which seemed too big and round for the rest of his little body. And she picked him up, picked him up for the first time. For Rose, that moment was as if her newborn had been placed on her chest—a *mise en scène*, a still shot, emblazoned in her memory. Rose was amazed how light he had felt. He clung to her without knowing who she was, where she was from or what role she was going to play in his life. It was as though there was some innate optimism or hope within him that she would meet his needs; that she would care for him; that she would be his mother.

Rose returned to the editing of childhood accumulations and pulled out a couple of old soccer boots. Ricky had always loved playing with balls. She recalled that she took balloons with her in her luggage because the agency worker had told her that Ricky's case notes reported that he loved playing with anything that moved. The lightness of the balloons seemed to be so in keeping with the elegance of those delicate little hands. She, Tom and Ricky spent those first early days in a luxurious hotel in Manila and their new son seemed to suffer from disorientation of a kind. When Rose took him to the shopping centre and held his hand, he would tug at her pulling her in the opposite direction crying "Dun tay uu." (Let's go this way). Rose realised later that he didn't have the words for "Let's go home," and she was sure that this was what he would have been trying to say. The home he would have meant would have been the stone grey building: the orphanage.

Memories seemed to be tumbling over one another while she was down on her knees retrieving the last of the Lego pieces. She thought now of the first time that she heard Ricky cry. He banged his head on the poolside table, not hard, but hard enough to make him cry. Rose remembered the sound he had made. The word *cry* was inadequate; it was more like an animal sound, a tearless, low rasping bark. Is that what happens when a child's cry goes unheard, ignored, unnoticed for hours days, months, even years? Does it become a mutated form of itself—a sound of hopeless misery rather than a shrill expectant call for attention? It only came the once, that sound. She had never heard him cry that way since.

And then there was that Friday morning not long after they arrived back in Australia. Funny how she remembered that it was Friday. But that morning was different—there seemed something more intense about his need to be picked up. She didn't put him down to make breakfast. Instead she carried him to the lounge room and turned on the CD player. Pavarotti sang. Ricky tightened his grip around her neck and wrapped his legs around her waist, locking his ankles together. She was very slim in those days and he had long legs. They walked together like this for nearly three hours, up and down the lounge room floor, backwards and forwards, up and down, with Pavarotti stuck on repeat. It was only after the phone rang out three times that she decided to answer it. This time Ricky didn't cry when she put him down. This all seemed like light years ago to Rose now in one way, yet in another it seemed like yesterday.

Another call from the laundry interrupted her thoughts. "Mum, there are no undies either?" She looked at a pile of socks and underpants in the corner behind the chair. Rose had been successful in teaching Ricky many things, but doing his washing wasn't one of them. She had taught him to drive though. Hours of practice, hours of being together in the car, talking, arguing about something or other, and Ricky learning to drive.

She recalled the day they had driven to the Murray River for a long driving lesson. They bought fish and chips and sat on the riverbank watching the river flow and the steamboats paddle by. He sat on one rock and she'd sat on another. Somewhere she had read that the ancients had recognised that certain places are 'thin places'; places where you can feel the past, present and the future; places where the veil between this world and the other is like fine lace. Ricky turned his back to her, messaging his girlfriend on his mobile phone, eating hot chips, unaware of his beauty, unaware of his own fragility, unaware of her overwhelming love for him at that moment. "Mum, they didn't give us any tomato sauce for the chips," he said.

They played Paul Kelly's *To her Door* all the way home. "That song makes me homesick," he said. Was his script the same as hers after all? "I know what you mean," she replied. It was a song that she played over and over when he was little. She would sit on the back porch with a glass of wine on summer evenings, playing music on an old portable tape deck and watch him riding his scooter, amazed at his simple happiness and joy in just being alive.

Tom said once, before he left her for the last time, "Boys love their mums and they hang around for a while, but once they are gone, they are gone. You've got to accept that Rose. Just let go. Boys just go." Rose tried not to think of Tom often; but as she caught sight of the last little red Lego block wedged in a crack on the floor of the closet, she missed Tom. She missed him, and the part he had played in the story that they had shared.

Loud music jolted Rose back to the cleaning of the Ricky's dusty closet. Who was this blasting again? Eminem—*When I'm Gone?* Tomorrow even the teddies on the wall would be gone. Loud footsteps echoed down the hall. His tall athletic form filled the doorway. "Mum, I've got to go in a minute and there's no..." He stopped and looked at her. "Mum... are you...?"

"It's okay. The narrator's just stuck in a tragic scene." She wiped her face with the back of her hand.

"You're weird, Mum."

In just a few hours, after he was gone, she would probably stand in the garden for a while under a tree. Anything to avoid that moment, that moment when she would walk back into the house, bracing herself for the finality of seeing the familiar become unfamiliar, that moment when her home would dissolve into a dwelling, become merely a timber construction with a tin roof, empty of all but furniture and fittings. A strange landscape in which she knew she would no longer fit, no longer have a place. Ricky was still there, he hadn't left yet, but already she could hear the crunch of the tyres on the stones in the driveway. And she knew he wouldn't look back. Tomorrow she would paint his room.

Echoes from the Dolphin

Roger Vickery

Roger Vickery is a Sydney-based writer of short fiction, poetry, plays, scripts and textbooks. He has won over 70 literary awards and his work has been published and performed in Australia and overseas. Roger's stories draw upon his varied working life as a sailor, soldier, community advocate, marketer, barrister and TAFE teacher. Many of them have strong social justice themes.

This story, which won the 2014 Ned Kelly Crime Short Story Award (the Sandra Harvey Award), was inspired by the journals of Ian Hood, an artist who ran an unorthodox youth refuge in Kings Cross in the 1980's. Roger chose it because it captures the laconic voice of that casual street shepherd and the harsh—but not always bereft—lives of his outcast flock.

Echoes from the Dolphin

On my first night at the Dolphin, Curtis takes me for a late night snooker game in a cavernous parlour in the back of the Cross. The TV set above the entrance is filled with a close-up of Hogan boasting that Crocodile Dundee has become the most successful Australian film. Curtis kills the power button with his cue and shows me how to ricochet off a bloodstain near the left pocket.

At dawn we watch a white fog spread across the Dolphin's steep roof like a slowly collapsing parachute, covering everything but some black malthoid patches on the slate shingles and three Victorian chimneys that reach up like lighthouses. Curtis steps through the third floor window. I follow, scrambling and sliding across the shingles and join him at the top, straddling the roofline like a horse.

For a few minutes we sit there, flicking scraps of malthoid into the Elsinore swirl below. Curtis folds his bomber jacket across the spine of the roof and inverts himself, legs bicycling in slow motion, until his shaven skull is resting on the jacket and his headstand rises in the mist like a fourth chimney. Then he loses it and he's sliding. I don't reach out. I know already that no-one touches Curtis. He brakes with invisible feelers against the shingles and clambers back—maybe he really was with the Flying Fruit Fly Circus—and leans out, pointing through the clearing fog and I make out graffiti on the Bourke Street flyover.

SYDNEY—A SAWN OF NEW YORK. HAF THE SIZE
TWIS AS DANGERUS.

"Mine," he shouts. "Deadly eh?"

*

'Bob the bird' lives next door in a building that housed Murphy's Bar until it was closed in the mid 70's. I'm standing on a milk crate on the Dolphin side, sneaking a look, when he emerges from one of the three derelict Land Rovers in his backyard and pads towards me.

"Never met my wife, have you?" he asks in a high, soft voice, never dropping his eyes.

I shake my head.

"Chinese woman, doesn't like sunlight, it disturbs her skin." He reaches the bottom runner of his side and pulls himself up. "She walks,"—the Bush Tucker Man on ABC TV has the same bright-eyed look—"through walls. Coo."

Fabian sidles past me, a picture in porno chic. "Bon jour!" he calls, bestowing a languid, long nailed wave in our direction.

Bob glares at him. "That boy recruits for a sect of warlocks," he barks; no trace of birdsong now.

"Black or white?" I ask.

"I cannot say." He steps down and walks backwards to his Land Rovers.

"Come in for tea sometime. My wife and I are Taoists. Coo."
"He's loopy—" Curtis says. "—lives alone."

*

Curtis and Lucy insist I see Brubaker, the 70's movie, where Robert Redford plays a prison governor. When a prison official asks Redford: "Governor, you appear to have a mite too much in common with your charges. Maybe you the same as them…you like making your own rules," I see Curtis nudge Lucy.

At The Illustrated Man near Central we watch Ned K. tattooing drunk. Curtis points a needle guns at my bourgeoisie heart. "Stamp?" he asks. I choose a dolphin for my right shoulder. Next day Lucy gives me a sleeveless T-shirt.

*

The management Committee asks me to schmooze a charity matron. Our potential new patron is blonde and flirty, a 40 something double for Kerrie-Anne Kennelly, the midday TV chat show host. She walks into the Victorian dining room which doubles as my office, sends her two suited minders on an investigation tour and calls me over, patting a place close to her right leg. I remember she won an undisclosed sum from the Sun-Herald a few years ago after their society columnist had claimed she was partial to a bit of rough trade.

"There don't seem to be any spiri-tual or re-ligious foun-dations to your refuge," she smiles and shows a lot of pink tongue. "Aren't your clients badly in need of that kind of struc-ture?"

"I think a refuge should be a genuine haven, a sort of post-modern hollow log… a place where damaged kids can rest up and pant and—" I hit her with a broad, street-savvy smile, "—heal a bit."

She drops her eyes. I must get to the dental hospital. Too late. "Most juvenile welfare agencies operate through rules, curfews and expectations that spit out a socialization program with two goals—employment and a clean nose in regard to the law. Take the Salvos, for example—"

She straightens. "What's wrong with those goals?"

"Our kids need a refuge, not a moral make-over. Oiling points of friction between them and organized society can wait until they've experienced some safe time. You met Fabian on the way in. He was incarcerated when he was 10 for being in a 'state of neglect', 'uncontrollable'. They chucked him, not his mother, in the home. And Curtis, with the shaven head, he's one of the stolens, taken at four."

"Why can't the Salvation Army help youngsters like them?"

"They only take kids who stay clear of drugs and booze. They bombard them with their holy mantras—stay clean, stay quiet, stay down! Any kids who dare to fall off the salvo bandwagon are pitched back into the street, quick smart. That's how they achieve their great success rates and justify their generous funding."

She rises, tugging down her skirt. I think our midday show is cancelled. Fabian is waiting for KK2 and her entourage when they retreat into Bourke Street. As he glides beside one of the suits, I can hear scraps of the pitch floating back to the refuge.

"Mafia—made me hawk my fork at the wall—few dollars—help to reconnect with the living lord."

Our management committee won't approve. But there's no curbing a true artist.

Curtis is restoring 'the bird', a 1962 Triumph Thunderbird. At sundown he walks through the house with another gleaming piece of motorbike armour that has been chromed by someone who knows someone in Tempe and rests it on a baby blue plastic tarpaulin near the back door. The bird's handlebars are angel wings. Its skidbars shoot forward like silver crossbows.

Propping his back against the trellis on our crumbling brick wall Curtis scrubs down a rusted SU carbie under the lights of the starship high rise towers that surround our little home.

*

I agree to ride pillion on the Bird's first test ride from Woolloomooloo to Bondi, a run that offers sharp corners and uninterrupted dash. My old heart sits up as we grand prix through Edgecliff and zip through the curly descent into Old South Head Road. But the bird collapses on the home stretch and I leave Curtis beside the rapids of Oxford Street, leaning over his patient with the intensity of a field surgeon.

A pair of rabbits shoplifted from Paddy's market have materialized. They spend most afternoons twitching and staring at the chattering TV. At night when the front door is open the bigger one hunches up against the security mesh and contemplates the traffic. The alley cats are watchful.

Curtis has begun 'sitting' Lucy when she works her early morning at the bus stop. Lucy slides into the trick's car and guides him to a back alley in Paddo. Curtis follows on the bird and waits in the cover of a jasmine bush with a crowbar in his saddlebag—another buggered young warrior looking for wrongs to come his way. Today when they came home a twist of Jasmine was tethered to his scarred crown.

*

"Are you moving?" I ask Ollie. He's hunched over the snakes and ladder board, scratching at the jailhouse stamps on his neck. When he dropped in from the Palmer Street squat he seemed happy enough to play but he's landed on murder a few moves from home and refuses to take the slide.

"Ollie?" I ask again

"You're crap. A pervert!"

"Why would you say that, Ollie?" Mister Calm, that's me.

"Who else—?" He looks around the lounge room. "—this cunt a place?" It's a fair question. During the Dolphin job interview the treasurer asked me what skills I could offer. I nominated street smarts and fast reflexes and he smiled and that made me overconfident. Then he asked me to sum up my character in a few words and I heard myself saying "Well meaning voyeur would sum me up nicely."

Ollie throws the dice at my head. Curtis reluctantly steps in until Ollie swears himself quiet. For the sake of reconciliation we take a midnight drive in a purple Torana that someone has loaned someone.

As Curtis approaches a set of lights in Oxford Street he steps on the brake pedal. It goes slack. I sigh and bow my head. We glide towards a stationary taxi, hit and watch it slide forward into another taxi. Curtis reverses and we zig-zag through the back streets of Darlinghurst, careening brakeless around corners until he dodgems the Torana into a convenient tree that juts into Rosella Lane. We abandon the poor beast as it billows steam and run.

At the Dolphin I can barely make the steps.

*

Bob is calling from the back fence. "Your warlock is loose with a knife!"

Fabian has a history of suicide attempts. Usually, they don't go too far. But you can never be sure. The truth is, they give us a secret rush.

Someone has a panel van. We pile in and spot Fabian pacing through the Domain, brandishing our only bread knife. We shadow him down Macquarie Street—pursuit cyclists waiting for the final bell.

Every 30 seconds Fabian yells at us. "Gonna see Leah!"

"Leah jumped from the bridge last year," Curtis whispers.

"I know."

"Last year." I can barely hear him. "Last year. Today."

Fabian's eyes are fixed on the Hanger.

A squad car appears. We wing behind hunter and hunted. Sirens!

Fabian freezes and begins crying. After ten minutes of face-saving negotiations the cops release him to me 'on recognizance'.

The boredom of form filling keeps more lawbreakers out of court than one hundred social workers. But they keep the bread knife.

Lucy greets us at the front door wearing a Drizabone over her new working clothes—a spangled bra and G-string that she sheds in one of Saffron's places. "Like a bleach, sweetness?" she asks Fabian. He sniffs and touches his hair. She tugs him by his long fingers into the bathroom.

Word spreads we're having a party. I invite Bob. Curtis offers him a rollie. "And it would contain. Coo?" asks Bob, sniffing it.

"White Ox." The tobacco of choice of street kids and ex-cons—goes down the throat like a rusty razor blade.

Bob nods approval. "The Chinese symbol for strength. Coo." He lights up and draws back. The rollie explodes, removing most of his eyebrows.

"A bitta gunpowder from a .22," explains Curtis, doubled up, tears in his eyes.

Sometimes I forget how young they are.

As I'm helping Bob across the fence, I see a small woman waiting in the shadowy doorway of Murphy's Bar.

Karma balances the books. Later that night Curtis fails to exhale all his petrol during his fire-eating act. They know us well in Casualty.

*

Winter settles over the Dolphin. The corridors and stairwells are dark and gloomy. Ugg boots are dusted off. Kerosene heaters stink up the rooms. The chill of boredom is worse than the sneaky wind.

Sally is killed.

She was our household familiar. Every girl's confidant, courier and messenger, Fabian's harasser, expert visitor, cat massager, the ping-pong ball of Bourke Street. Perhaps she was tripping in the traffic. Perhaps. Fifteen.

*

I have Anubis, the dark God of the Egyptian threshold, tattooed beneath the dolphin on my arm. Curtis checks the red scabs on my arm, pronounces them clean and begins picking at my book.

"In the Book of... Tho-th," he reads aloud. "An..u..bis is the one to turn to for aid. He is the watcher in the twi--"

"Twilight," I suggest and cop a glare from him.

"Cun read...The jack-al God who... stands in double for... form... between the Ways. At his feet... on watch... wait the jackals themselves."

"It's just a stamp," I warn him.

*

Another tower is being completed over our heads. The buildings fuse at night into an apparently invincible luminous-eyed Battle ship Galactica—an all-in-one sentinel, lighthouse and watchtower of the Fantastic City.

Squatters two buildings down are pressing on Ollie's turf. Displacement rules like a dangerous planet. One morning he's waiting on our front steps.

"You're no mate of mine. You toothless weirdo!"

Must get to the dental hospital.

It's 2 AM and I'm pottering in the kitchen when a grey-blue gorilla bursts through the doorway and begins throwing me from wall to wall. There's a sour gritty powder in my mouth. The edges of my remaining teeth feel as if they're disintegrating. I grab at Ollie's throat. He starts choking. I release my grip and try bending his fingers. They just keep bending.

I manage to manoeuvre him through the hallway. We stumble down the front steps into Bourke Street where a fog like the one from my first night has taken over the street. Ollie keeps throwing big clumsy punches. I fend them off like a desperate breaststroker. Curtis emerges and watches us puffing and abusing each other for what seems like minutes. Then he steps in—stiff armed—a balled fist for each of us and we shuffle back and suck in white oxygen. "Shake!" he says.

I put out my hand. Amazingly, Ollie takes it.

Then he runs towards William Street, arms low and loose, disappearing into the mist like a young silverback.

We bar Ollie. He issues death threats. Five nights later someone kicks in the back door and trashes the place. When we arrive home we find the rabbits huddled behind the cracked, still chattering TV.

The last bite of winter is deep. I fillet an old wardrobe and use it to start a good blaze in the lounge room fireplace. Curtis and Lucy huddle close, yawning as the heat and light cast flickers of hope over their weary faces.

Later, as if for dessert, a Holden explodes in the back lane and burns brightly with movie madness. We warm our hands and backsides there, joking with the fireys and two young cops, all reluctantly enjoined by this Guy Fawkes handout.

In the morning Curtis de-bones the wreck.

*

While night prowling I meet a Croatian girl with the tragedies of the Balkan cockpit in her eyes. For her my 'Fantastic Citeee' glimmers like the pair of spangled roller skates that are tied with a bowline across her ex-Red Army pack.

We walk across the Hanger to the north side, kissing and bumping until it's time to part. I catch a ferry back across a wind damaged harbour and puff up William Street and left into Bourke, just in time for another of the treasurer's fiscal breakdowns.

Curtis punches me in the arm after the committee members leave. "Stuff em. You've lasted nearly a year."

We both smile at the surprise of it.

*

Curtis scores some lightweight scaffolding from two Kenyan illegals who have run out of money and are bound for Villawood Detention Centre.

We set the frame parallel to our one free-standing wall and for three weeks, whenever call-overs, bail applications, alibis, affidavits and swearing to good character allow, I play Michelangelo di Bourke.

By late spring a tiger in a jasmine bush is peering out at a she-wolf who suckles Romulus and Remus while a queue of changeling children wait their turn. The boys are stamped with medieval monsters, winged skulls in black cowls and foraging sharks. The girls have shyer pieces—a red-backed spider on a hip; a heart amongst leaves captioned True to only One.

The changelings, their awe of first contact long gone, barely notice the rays streaming down from the Star Ships that surround them.

*

Summer drapes her languid scarves over the Dolphin. Rugs are shaken; the kitchen scrubbed. We spend time in the backyard with our shirts off, spinning moneymaking schemes.

On Tuesday a letter from the treasurer is slipped under the chain across the Bird's quilted seat. "This committee regrets to advise that due to financial exigencies..."

I pack my oils. Sell off surplus goods. My room is spare and light again. A nomad's camp.

*

The committee offers a compromise. If I withdraw my unfair dismissal complaint Curtis can stay as unpaid caretaker until the wreckers come.

The young lawyer who brings around the Deed of Waiver refuses to witness my signature until Fabian stops blowing into his ear.

Afterwards Curtis pokes at the little red seal on my copy and whoops: "Could be years!"

Maybe.

Word spreads. The Dolphin becomes fat with our old kids.

Lucy who has been sacked for 'acting superior with a g-string' flashes an engagement ring from Feisal, a club security consultant. "Maintenance money, sweetness! Maintenance money!"

Fabian is seen to wash a cup.

Haci drops by, tongue rings humming with valued gossip from Long Bay.

"I need just one thing to feel at home," I joke.

Lucy looks up from her spread out snapshots of Feisal's villa in South Lebanon. "What's that?"

"Ollie to come by and rough me up."

"You're safe, eh?" Haci chips in. "Dead—about two weeks ago, eh?"

"How?"

"Needle, eh? Full uh battry acid."

The party dwindles. You feel the sadness but also relief, pride even, that we're still here, scoring an extra day beneath the star ships.

My family moves on, as all families must. I squeeze hands and hug them. They pat my old neck and I walk up William Street, bound for the sea.

An Ex in Provence

Sofia Chapman

Sofia Chapman completed a Bachelor of Arts (Hons) in Modern Languages at the University of Tasmania before running away with the piano accordion to play on a theatre barge on the Rhône, Avignon, France. Sofia returned to Australia to study playwriting and is now a professional accordionist with the band Vardos. Sofia has written and co-produced numerous plays at La Mama, Carlton, and also features in La Mama's 50th anniversary book. Sofia received the 2012 Melbourne Fringe 'Best Emerging Writer' Award for the epic 'The Four Accordionists of the Apocalypse'. Sofia's début short story, 'The Cave of Dr Cayla', written during a residency in France was published in Gargouille Literary Journal in 2016.

An Ex in Provence

Provence is the best place to break up with a lover, as lavender helps one sleep. Provence is the worst place for a break up, as the wine is cheap and cheese and croissants always close by, so the general geniality of the lifestyle can make a couple enjoy themselves too much, which masks their marital problems. That summer, lavender was banned in Provence because of allergies. As we approached Aix en Provence, I knew our relationship had come to a standstill. Oh Reggie, when did it become tedious? I remember your Wedding Day poem:

I was waiting,
laden in offerings,
stupidly, good faith having gone wrong,
for we know foolish tasks of love henceforth must be stemmed.
Towards you, lovely one, my thoughts are unchangeable,
and to you I bequeath
a rôtisserie of white goat.
Woman throws peace into confusion;
hormones toil uselessly.
Mind tries to calm, sits down,
gracefully green,
but come, my friends, grind coffee!
-for the limo is near.
I must for to speak finally,
sing of the bride with her beautiful
shoes which match the cake,
and her bridesmaids in sadistic
banana yellow.
Stem the violet-robed daughter of Bridezilla,
forbearing friendship, putting aside anger;
stamp on violet robe hems.
Hither, holy Graces and Pierian Muses,
help when a song taunts the mind, emanating from
a wedding band,
the bridegroom
and his annoying companions.
A long awaited love caresses her hair,

putting down the synth and other instruments,
until golden-sandalled dawn stomps on our impossible love.

You had just completed a thesis on Sappho and styled yourself a feminist, which I thought at the time was sweet but like the car, it backfired. You tried to silence me if I showed you up by pointing out, for example, that George Sand was a woman.

Our getaway car was festooned with 'Just Married' and heaps of tins, plastic bottles and other recyclables which you had insisted everyone bring and attach to the back of the vehicle.

I thought it romantic when you adamantly dragged the noisy, tinny entourage over the border to South Australia to our honeymoon destination.

It wasn't long before I realised that you'd suggested South Australia because of its recycling laws: you get a refund on beverage containers, and it was with these 10 cent pieces that you'd hoped to subsidise the honeymoon.

Stingy.

That's one of the things that has distanced me from you, removed you to the third person.

Reggie never bought gifts. He would say, 'Do you remember last month when I bought you that hairpin? That was your birthday present.'

Once for revenge I bought and served him that coffee which has been pooed out by monkeys. He unexpectedly liked it and it ended up saving the marriage.

For a while.

I remember when the subject of unbirthed, unreared children first raised its head. The discussion went something like this.

Moi (Therese):	If you work like a man you're more likely to have boys.
Reggie:	I do work like a man.
Therese:	That's debatable. No, I mean if one is a woman.
Reggie:	What of it?

Therese:	Darling, make me director of the company and I'll give you a son.
Reggie:	You? Director?
Therese:	Directrix. I'll tickle the boxes.

I don't know that I ever wanted kids, perhaps just wanted to direct the company. It was a canny way to get my foot in the door. I had been finding it hard to elicit responses from potential employers. I had eventually resorted to underhand tactics to gain their attention, with creative cover notes such as

'Dear Anastasia, thanks for our lovely evening in front of the fire. '

or,

'Dear Sasindu,

I saw your wife yesterday, does she usually wear her hair like that? Her heels were incredible, although I was worried she might fall if she didn't have that dashing young man on her arm. Is that your son?

Yours faithfully'

etc

which prompted certain responses, but not of the sort I had sought.

Why should they?

I didn't even get back to me.

Finally, the note I had been waiting for.

'Unfortunately the standard of applications has been extremely poor, which is why you've made it through'.

Proudly I waved it in front of Reggie. He sneered.

Reggie:	I engineered that, remember? You're losing your memory.
Therese:	I'm more worried about your memory. You have forgotten that I've always had a bad memory.'

My ploy worked, but after the kids were born the novelty wore off.

Reggie and I bought two funeral plots next to each other in scenic Provence so that we could camp there. After all, the word 'cemetery' does mean 'sleeping place'. We thought we should go there before the kids noticed, and perhaps rekindle our relationship. We put the baby monitor on while in France.

I had learnt French so well that I started teaching it to the French. Reggie was jealous because I did better at it than he. Wouldn't speak to me for two weeks.

In French? you ask?

In any language. Yes, his silence was in French, if you will.

Until the shouting.

Have you ever seen an empty car with its doors open at the traffic lights, apparently abandoned? It was possibly vacated by me and Reggie, one of us traipsing after the other, screaming through some continental streets.

Reggie was jealous of my literary leanings and accused me of having an affair with the renowned but now chubby author Alain de Bottom, who occasionally sailed past our 'Pension' on his big seated bike.

I hit the absinthe after the rift. A deliberate choice. To be more French in my misery, more *fin de siècle*[1] and historical. I read what I could stomach of George Sand, and wrote a poem of my own.

I sold you and you sold me,
Beneath the weeping willow tree.
I told you, as you told me,
'You know such things are never free.'

Sky was blue the tree was green,
the things we said, they were quite mean.
I sold you and you sold me,
Why can't we both be free?

I sold you and you sold me,
into some kind of slavery.
I bought you and you bought me,
if only temporarily.

I was blue and you were green.
The things we said, we did not mean.
I sold you and you sold me,
Why can't we both be free?

---

[1] *End of the century. Usually refers to the end of the 19th Century.*

One should never reignite things with an ex. Even some *'conquête de passage'*[2].

Reggie said that in Latin, 'Ex' was ablative. I called it, 'A blot I've' tried to forget.

It started with a text message.

Reggie:	Wanted to talk to you soon. One night stand sounds… miss your face. I mean yes! Meet me in Paris. I will see you painted in the footlights.
Therese:	I hit the floor and work my abs in the Moulin Rouge, *tous les soirs*.[3]
Reggie:	You seem to me lazy done well. At last, the green light—this is a new footloose with you.
Therese:	Let's head to Provence! Wineries without driving… It will be a wonder, full view.

We headed south. Dusty Cézannes without end.

The aforementioned dangers of Provence. No glutton-free food here, and one who loves cheese risks becoming that gorgon Zola described in *L'Assommoir.*

Reggie had a plan to trade in illegal lavender, to set himself up as an Herb Baron.

Struck with eczema in Provence, I soon became edgy with Reggie. I tried to indulge us with cultural activities but he became distant. He was sitting fully dressed in Marseilles one night and toying with a Panama hat when I came downstairs.

Reggie:	What are you doing up, what are you doing?
Therese:	I fell awake. Now I can't sleep, even had time to go to bed, that's probably why I can't sleep.
Reggie:	Guess what I was thinking about?
Therese:	Sleep? Terrible to happen here, do this to myself piece by piece. I need lavender.
Reggie:	I don't believe I could help you.
Therese:	Please Reggie, sheesh!

---

[2] *One night stand*

[3] *Every night*

(I was hoping this gangster talk would appeal to his new Herb Tycoon persona.)

Reggie: Ok. Hot lavender, a straight shot. Cheap.

Therese: Cheap? It's good shit.

Reggie: Yes, exactly—exactly like out in the country.

Drugged with lavender, I yawned.

Therese: Hear that? Back to the bedroom.

Sprawled on the bed, we spotted a speck on the map. 'Île de If'.

Perhaps there and only there we might mend things; could 'If' hold unknown possibilities for us? We headed out over the water, to the Frioul Archipelago, lured by this 'Island of If'.

Reggie: Where's the beach?

Therese: It's about 200 metres away in the rain. Well it's not always in the rain, I suppose.

He dragged out two deckchairs. I was frustrated. Why not sit on the sand? We bickered in a random and disconnected way at Grand Soufre beach, o aptly named place of great suffering.

Reggie held out handfuls of stuff.

Reggie: Can you carry my phone please, and my keys and wallet?

Therese: I swear if you had your own bag you wouldn't need me.

Reggie: Why did you insist we go to that performance of 'Pictures at an exhibition'? It was like listening to paint dry.

Therese: O but your expression—I thought you were enraptured—it inspired me to write. I was immediately out of ink after the concert because of you.

Reggie: Your hair looks awful.

Therese: You idiot! Don't you know everyone is wearing their hair awful in Paris this year?'

I broke off, climbing away from tourists, children, Reggie, safety.

As I ascended the *colline*[4], a magnificent *calanque*[5] came into view.

I was entranced. Transfixed. Sold. These were the rocks, the stability I sought.

Therese: Who needs Reggie?

The appetising creamy stoniness, the tactile smoothness of those rocks, peppered with shrubs. Some disdain the shrubbery of Provence, preferring grander, taller forests of the interior, but I adore this semi sparse and low level scrub. Up on those higher rocks, an almost lunar quality, its own terrain. You can see where you are, that there is no-one around but herbs.

Oh, except for, in the distance, the silhouette of Alain de Bottom struggling up a hill on his x-large saddled bike.

I felt I could stay forever. The company was practically running itself, and now that the kids were grown up and free—or were they only three?

In the morning, I could enjoy the sunrise from the vast rock on the left, looking out towards the… East? South? Spain, Tunisia, Corsica, Morocco? Anyway, I would find out.

Towards lunch you would see me scavenging for eggs on the next massive rock, with its own slightly different texture and ecology, perhaps descending to the shore in search of pipis and mussels.

Late afternoon, I would range the next outcrop, warmed all day by the sun, cooling into sunset, when I would traverse leaping the gap to the final rock, with its mysterious distant human made structure, perhaps for shelter or dancing. (I later discovered this to be the Fort Ratonneau. A fort against Reggie.)

I stayed there far too long, discovering that my wedding ring had disappeared during the scrambling. I was glad to leave it in such a place.

On my way back to Reggie, through a small island market, I contemplated what could become a parting gift. If he had a man

---

[4] *Hill*
[5] *A rocky inlet*

bag he wouldn't need me anymore. I handed over my euros and strode on.

In the apartment, we sullenly watched the English language channel.

'And today's news brought to you by…' followed by some car ad. I tried to make light of it.

Therese: What does a car know about news? It just goes on about itself.

Yet Reggie noticed that car. Perhaps all this penny pinching was so that he could buy it for himself. I caught him studying the hexagonal map of France, and the Canal du midi, twirling that hat and muttering 'A man, a plan, a canal, Panama.'

I gave him the man bag.

In the small hours, I awoke and wafted downstairs.

On the small fussy table stood a card, ridiculously oversized, with sentimental pink flowers and, in cartoon font, 'Sorry I'm leaving'.

Inside, Reggie had scrawled with abandon: 'Going solo—I've got that Côte d'Azur feeling, want to drive in my Panama suit, in a white convertible with the wind in my hair. You'll find this departure sudden, but remember that little *guinguette*[6] near Narbonne? You had the mussels and I had the lamb's brains? That was our break up dinner.'

Perhaps we'll not meet again until our fateful funeral days.

It's time to pack. There's much I don't need, so I depart with just a small backpack and appropriate knives.

As I stroll down Rue Vie Neuve towards the port I sense a goodbye to provenance, to everything which has gone before. *En avant, pour une vie neuve.*[7]

He's sent another text.

'My last days would be made had I not lost that certain-T. Therese. Send me some woman of the house. Moves—mostly

---

[6] *A kind of restaurant, often by the water, with music and dancing*

[7] *Ahead for a new life.*

women become like you to hit on—amazing. Miss you, you. Be kind to the vine my love… '

(I guess, don't drink too much? Don't abuse alcohol?)

Keep your Island of If. Give me Frioul—her *calanques* are more dependable. I think I can live there forever. Or at least, for an indefinite amount of time.

The Mummy's Foot

Beth Spencer

'The Mummy's Foot' won *The Age* Short Story Award and was first published in *The Age*, and then as a 'prose poem' in *Things in a Glass Box* (Five Island Press New Poets Series, 1994). An audio version was produced as part of a program based on *Things in a Glass Box* for ABC-RN's *Poetica*, December 2004. Text in italics in this story is adapted from Mildred Place, *Wrapped for Eternity* (Guildford: Lutterworth Press, 1977).

Beth Spencer is an award-winning author of poetry, fiction, essays and writing for performance. Previous books include the verse memoir, *Vagabondage* (UWAP), a bilingual collection *The Party of Life* (Flying Islands) and the short fiction collection, *How to Conceive of a Girl* (Vintage/Random House). In 2018 she won the Carmel Bird Digital Literary Award for *The Age of Fibs*, now a Spineless Wonders ebook. She lives on the Central Coast, NSW and at www.bethspencer.com

The Mummy's Foot

(This Girl is Missing)

1969: Beggars Banquet is released on the Decca label. Boris Karloff dies. A $5000 reward is offered for nine year old Vicki Barton and the State Library refuses entry to a man without shoes, he writes a letter to the paper.

My brother's accident occurs somewhere just over Bordertown. The green car and the white car collide. In the white car a child breaks her leg and is motherless.

In the hospital we wait in the hall and as the walls slide I rest my cheek against the floor, which is cool and solid like so little else. I focus on a sheepskin rug, a bent straw in a cup. Later I walk out into the night air along a ramp, holding my father's hand. We take great mouthfuls till our lungs hurt. He steers his bulk like a ship and I lean in to his wake.

My brother's accident is like a small furious hurricane, lifting us up in little shocked groups and transporting us, windblown and dishevelled, over the dotted lines on the map. Unseating the wedding plans and the savings for the new car.

We find a motel, but it is too expensive. My father spends a day searching while we wait at the hospital, and after that we sleep fitfully in the unfamiliar dark of the People's Palace Hotel.

We visit the museum in the mornings, and in the afternoons we sit by the white bed. My mother says it is rude to ask questions.

I get bored with the water fountain, even the tiny cups.

A specialist, highly skilled in his work, approached the head of the corpse. In his hand he held a long, slender hooklike instrument. Deftly he pushed this up one nostril, and working in a circular movement, he broke through the ethmoid bone, up into the cavity of the brain.

In the museum I visit the Egyptian Room, while my mother knits in the park. The room is dark with lit tables. Long gold boxes with smooth serious carved faces and black-rimmed eyes. The Egyptians, says a sign, were 'great sensualists and lovers'. Under glass on the table is an unwrapped mummy's foot, withered and yellow. *Note* the painted toenails: says the sign.

The People's Palace Hotel is four storeys high. The back stairs are long and precarious. In the Ladies' Room there are two baths, both of them deep and stained, with clawed feet. We wash in the basin. All night long there is a shuffling and moaning in the hallway and in the mornings we purchase tickets for breakfast—sausages and toast. I feel like a queen as I buy opal chips in a street stall and thumb my way through brown paperbacks at ten cents each.

For fifteen days we sit by the white bed. It is necessary, this idleness, like too few seats. A penance for our guilt.

The nurses come and stand by my brother and smile. They hold his wrist in their hands, count out his pulse against little watches pinned to their breasts. He opens his mouth and they press a thermometer between his lips. They touch him deftly as they shift the sheets around his body, as if they have known him all their lives.

In the afternoon my mother takes a photograph of me dipping my hand in the fountain at King George V Square. I am wearing my bridesmaid shoes and my second best dress. I wear my hair like a model and smile up at the camera.

Withdrawing the hooklike instrument, he chose another. This one was a narrow, spirally twisted rod that had a small spoon-like tip. Pushing this up into the cranial cavity, he began, slowly, bit by bit, to draw out the brain through the nose, discarding each piece as he went along.

One day, instead of the hospital, we take a taxi and search among the tall weeds at the Adelaide cemetery for my grandfather's grave. My mother has a photo and a number.

My parents move rigidly and carefully in this city, on the alert for danger, always careful to brush the dirt of the city off their clothes at night, to wipe the rim of the glass, to keep wide of building sites.

Adelaide is a city of death and accidents and close shaves, a cursed city. My grandfather's pneumonia; my baby sister's camp bed split by a fallen branch. We repeat these stories to each other as we drive across the border in a convoy of concerned relatives.

City of museums and hospitals, city of churches.

In the hospital, the doctors stride swiftly through the wards – their white coats, their stethoscopes. The bodies laid out for them in rows. We leave meekly at the sound of a bell.

We photograph each other in parks and beside the river and in the Square, and we wear our best dresses on weekdays, because there are not enough second-best to go around.

In the great hall of the museum there are hundreds of stuffed birds in bits of trees from their natural habitat. In another section the white bones of dinosaurs fill whole rooms right up to the roof. For twenty cents you can hear the sound of bats in a cave.

Next to the mummy's foot is a small parcel of rags which x-rays have revealed to be a cat.

We take back cartons of freshly squeezed orange juice to our room and drink it from the tiny vegemite glasses on the dressing table that taste of dust.

The man who was to perform the next task stood outside the tent waiting to be called in. He held in his hand a fairly large, flat black stone, one edge of which was honed to razor sharpness. His job was not a pleasant one, and gruesome to watch. Hence the other workers and the priest held him in abhorrence.

The sign outside the church says it is the same as ours, but inside they drink the communion wine from the little cups one at a time as it is passed around, instead of all together at the end like we do.

Somehow this flaw in the familiarity we seek is even more upsetting than the traffic noise and the shuffling in the hallway at the People's Palace.

More upsetting even than the woman with the withered yellow skin who called to us from the steamy depths of one of the baths while we were washing in the basins. "Pass some soap, love"—her voice dry and cracked. My mother and sister stiffen, and say nothing, but I take the soap to her and get to see the brown patch of hair between her legs and the way it ripples and moves when she reaches across to take the soap from my hand. Her toenails are painted red and there is an empty glass on the floor.

In the watery green corridor of the hospital after church, we pass quickly by a grieving family outside a closed door.

My brother tells us stories about the other patients. The handsome motorbike rider in the corner, asleep now, after being smuggled out last night to a party with the nurses. The wheelchair races up and down the hall at night. The nurses come again and touch him and take his pulse.

My mother keeps her knitting in her bag. We alternate ourselves amongst the too few chairs. We take turns with the water fountain.

My brother sleeps during the day and stays awake at night. Somewhere in the hospital is the little girl from the white car.

The priest wearing the jackal mask approached the body, which had been turned slightly on its right side, exposing the left flank. The tent throbbed with the soft, rhythmic chantings of the priests… The masked priest dipped a small rush pen into a pot of ink, then drew on the left side of the body a spindle-shaped line about 5 inches long.

The whiteness of the hospital, and the yellowness of the museum, this is how I spend my days. And at night, the People's Palace.

In the artificial cool of the hospital we shuffle the days like packs of cards. I spend my time between the water fountain and leaning one hand on the back of the chair to take the weight off my feet.

I pose beside a statue in the Square, tipping my head back and crooking one foot forward like they do in the papers.

In the Egyptian world, the Museum says, Osiris married his sister Isis. The Egyptians took out the heart and weighed it on a scale before placing it back in the body.

At the hotel we watch 'Homicide' on the television, sharing the common room with a group of old men, and my mother cries as George Mallaby is carried out, feet first, covered with a white sheet, from a mine accident. On the news they show another photo of Vicki Barton, and Vicki's mother pleads with the kidnapper to bring her back. Police investigate a lead in Adelaide.

We tell each other how much we hate the city, we are country people. We are just waiting until my brother is well enough to take home.

Every day, the white bed. Everyday the same conversation.

We are afraid my brother will lose his heart. He lies under white sheets all day and the nurses come and wait on him. My brother's foot shrivels underneath the plaster, yellowing at the edges.

We go to church again and this time we drink the wine and replace the cups straight away.

In the museum I put 20c in a slot and hear birds calling to each other in a forest. The stuffed hawk, perpetually swooping over the stuffed mouse…

Only the heart was left in place. It was thought to be the seat of intelligence and feeling, and so must remain intact within the body.

For fifteen days we sit by the white bed, until at last the doctor nods, a nurse smiles, and we are allowed to take him home.

On the tarmac at the airport, waiting to board the plane, two of the nurses come to see us off. Someone takes a photo of my brother sitting up on a stretcher on the ground, wearing a check shirt and a black cardigan, a pillow propped behind him. In the background are the boarding steps, and beside him, a pair of knee-high brown boots, and another set in pink slingbacks; a handbag on a long strap.

We fly him back across the border, pale now and much thinner. Swathed in plaster.

My brother has become soft and white, all his bones broken and reset. He grows darker and paler: his skin bleaches to the colour of the plaster casts on his legs, his hair and eyelashes grow black and thick like the row of stitches that line his jaw.

We talk about the taste of the Adelaide water as the plane hits the runway at Essendon.

March 1969: An Australian soldier is killed in South Vietnam's Bien Hoa province. Susan Atkinson sings her way through the Manson trial. A diplomat warns on coloured immigrants. Lil Abner is appointed official custodian of the statue of Colonel Jubilation T. Cornpone.

Disaster strikes at Violet Town. And the girl seen in Adelaide is not Vicki Barton after all.

(Have you seen her?)

Zack

Jill Baggett

I have always been fascinated with the written word and enjoy creative writing in all its forms.

Many of my published stories, articles and poems are based on real life experiences.

I also enjoy playwriting and seeing my words come to life on the stage.

I have written manuals and newsletters used by the Health Department for adults and children.

Am currently presenting workshops on creative writing, editing manuscripts for friends, judging competitions, hosting a magazine page and a newspaper column.

Zack

I think of Zack often and smile. The smile comes from that warm place deep inside that is reserved for special friends, places and memories.

The day I met Zack was warm and sunny in the autumn of 1968. Kings Cross pulsed with life then as it does now and Victoria Street was still a backwater, an oasis of calm in the stormy sea of glitter, noise and aromas.

Number 209 was a tenement in 1968. It is now a railway station. It had a lot more personality as a tenement and Zack lived there.

Just married, John and I were looking for somewhere to call home when we saw the 'rooms to let' sign. It was hanging lopsidedly from the wrought iron gate of a four-storeyed tenement, a little attic room perched jauntily on top.

An elderly man lounged smoking against the veranda post.

"G'day," he said, moving the cigarette to the other side of his chubby face. "I'm Pappy. The boss won't let me smoke inside. You looking for a room?" We nodded and the cigarette changed sides again as Pappy turned and called, "Zack, customers," through the open door into the dark recesses of the hallway. "She's the boss, you'll find out," he added with a grin.

The sciff scuff of loose slippers on lino signalled the boss was arriving. "Who's coming at this time? Sunday morning and all, a body's hardly out of bed," she grumbled. "I don't think I've got anything."

We prepared to resume our search when Zack appeared in the shaft of sunlight hitting the door. Masses of grey hair stuck out from her head surrounding her lined face, piercing blue eyes looked us up and down and the twitch of a smile at the side of her generous mouth belied the words.

In all the years I knew Zack I only saw her wear two dresses. The first of these she had on now—a tight fitting stretch knit number with alternating hot pink and lime green stripes. A belt crossed her ample hips and pink, worn, slippers on the end of fuzzy grey legs completed the ensemble.

"I'm Zack, and if you're coming in you'd better come, the coffee's getting cold. Bobby! Get out of bed, we've got visitors," she shouted towards an open doorway on the right.

A quick glance at John showed me he was also wondering what belaboured soul Bobby was as we followed the boss down the dimly lit hall.

A brown furry bundle torpedoed into the hall and snuffled excitedly round our ankles. "Dachshund, best dogs there are," stated Bobby's mistress. Through the open door we could see Bobby's place on the crumpled array of bedclothes. One small pillow was set between two human sized ones nestled on either side of the double bed.

A small window sent shafts of sunlight into the large kitchen. We drew up rickety chairs to the wooden table and I looked doubtfully at the thick mug of rich milk coffee put in front of me into which Zack was spooning several teaspoons of sugar. I didn't take sugar in my coffee, but knew John was going to love his. A plate of rich cakes was pushed towards him.

"Why aren't you eating?" Zack asked, pieces of cake blended with milky coffee splattering onto her chin. "I can't abide bodies that don't eat." Morning coffee finished, Zack pushed herself back from the table. "Come and I'll show you the flatette. I'm expecting those folks to leave soon."

"Do they know they're going?" asked Pappy.

We followed Zack down the sagging steps to the basement.

"Number 209 has 16 rooms and two flatettes. The flatettes have their own entrance," Zack informed us as we wended our way down. "Take the flight of steps down from the street."

On arriving at a pink door labelled No 2 she knocked and entered via a master key without further ado and ushered us into a kitchen area.

"Anyone home?" she croaked.

"Just a minute," a startled female voice called from the adjacent room. "It's only me," Zack strutted through the bedroom door. "I know yer leaving soon, so I've brought the new tenants to look over the flatette. I know yer don't mind Ducks."

Zack beckoned us to enter and to my amazement 'Ducks' turned out to be two bodies of foreign appearance sitting up, stark naked, in bed clutching frantically at the sheets and doing their best to look dignified while Zack expounded to us on the virtues of shared facilities but private entrance.

Our first night at Zack's was disturbed at 2 AM by a blast to rock the foundations, followed a few minutes later by Zack's croaky voice admonishing loudly,

"Bobby, get out of the bloody gutter!"

Alarmed at the blast and forgetting briefly who Bobby was, John jumped out of bed, thinking she may need help carrying one of the residents out of the gutter. He leapt up the stairs from our basement entrance and was amazed to see Zack, matted hair blowing round her face, torn nightdress flapping round the old pink slippers, dragging relentlessly on Bobby's lead, the little dachshund, four feet clinging desperately to the pavement, happily sniffing at an enticing morsel of food dropped by a thoughtful passer-by.

"What blew up?" I called, pulling on my dressing gown.

"Bobby, get out of the bloody gutter or I'll job yer," croaked Zack's voice. Someone must have been hurt and fallen into the gutter after the bomb exploded, I thought.

"What's happened?" I yelled, exasperated as I tried to hurry up the dark stairs. "They're blasting for the railway, Ducks. Don't worry," called Zack. "Bobby wants to do a pee but I won't have him eating out of the gutter. Go back to bed," she ordered and dragged the protesting Bobby to a nearby tree.

John came back to bed grinning.

We discovered the blasting was to be part of our lives as the Eastern Suburbs Railway Line was in the early stages of construction in 1968. Much of this railway is a tunnel passing right under Kings Cross and more importantly right under Zack's tenement. Where Zack lived for so much of her life is now the entrance to the railway station. Blasting was carried out at regular intervals of the day and night much to Bobby's distress. The fright of waking to the sounds of a bomb blast was too much for his doggy bladder.

We woke to Zack's impatient pounding on our door at 7 AM next morning. "Is something wrong?" I blinked at her sleepily when I opened the door. "What with 16 rooms and all to clean I've got to start early," she griped, dragging a voluminous bucket and mop through the door, a feather duster and broom clutched firmly in the other hand. An emerald green dress, obviously the mate of yesterday's model, and the pink slippers and hair tied up in a red scarf, she looked ready for work.

"Did you get the fridge to work?" she asked companionably as she set to with the feather duster, oblivious to John's scowling countenance. "It's an old Silent Knight, best fridges they ever made." She hummed a few bars of Annie Laurie and John pulled the covers over his head.

I'd pulled on my dressing gown and was wondering where to put myself and if I should offer to help when her next comment made John's eyes appear over the covers in alarm and my pulse start beating wildly.

"I can't abide drink in my house," Zack was saying, "mind you only use the fridge for food."

In the 60's it was fashionable for the bridegroom's friends to give him a cellar tea and John's friends had applied themselves to this task with gusto.

The only contents of the Silent Knight was alcohol—lots of alcohol, everything from whisky to sherry, to beer and wine. We'd put it in the fridge because we didn't have anywhere else to put it in the tiny flatette. To our combined horror Zack opened the fridge with a flourish saying, "Mind you keep it clean and defrost it every w...."

"Mind you a little now and then can do a body good. Pass me that broom, Dearie."

My sigh of relief must have been audible and John turned to face the wall and pulled the covers over his head again.

Thursday was rent day.

"I want no money for two weeks," Zack had firmly announced on the day of our arrival, "I can't abide folks wanting to pay me in advance. I can't get rid of them if I get sick of them then. Pay me in two weeks."

Feeling less than secure, we'd unpacked and I'd wondered how long it would be before she tired of us.

Tire of people she did. Many a tenant would come home to find his belongings on the landing outside his door.

"I'm sick of the sight of yer," was often the only explanation given. Those fortunate enough to be still in possession of their rooms on Thursday were expected to produce their rent promptly between 5 PM and 6 PM. As each one handed over their remittance they would be given a small cardboard box. In each box were either six fabulously rich rum balls or six delightfully fluffy king-size scones, freshly baked and still warm. For those guests with whom the boss was especially pleased there would be a carton of giant eggs. Each had not two but three bright orange yolks. I was never able to entice out of her where she procured such amazing googs.

"Ah, that's my little secret Dearie," she would cackle gleefully and shut her lips tightly, adamantly and firmly.

Zack's rents were about half the going rate and while a paying guest in her house, each tenant was treated as a family member. The sharp edge of her tongue and her abounding kindness were distributed to each in liberal amounts. One week I was ill and taxied off to hospital amidst the pandemonium of a Kings Cross rush hour. That week Zack would only accept half the rent from John.

"Ye're only half here, Ducks," was her reasoning.

Tramps would sometimes wander down the steps of our basement entrance and sleep curled up in the sheltered corner under the potted rubber plant.

One Sunday morning John found two bottles of beer nestled in the mulch around the base of the tree.

"Hey, look at this Darl! We've been left a present."

Looking like Bobby after a stolen piece of cream cake, he brought the bottles in and placed them in the fridge to cool.

"Just what we'll like after lunch," he grinned in anticipation.

Cooling time duly over he placed bottle number one on the table with a flourish and went to retrieve the opener from the bottom drawer. The day was a hot and humid January scorcher and Sydney baked. I was looking forward to the icy bitterness when we heard a scrambling rustling sound from outside our door and an exasperated, "Well, wouldn't that rock ya?"

Salivary glands drying quickly we went to the door and there was Pappy's comfortable form scratching his head in bewilderment. He looked at us and reddened noticeably.

"Ar… Um… you wouldn't have seen a couple of bottles of ale here, would you?" he stammered.

"Yes," said John, pointing to the table. "We were just about to… are they yours?" he added miserably.

"I hide them down here from Zack," he looked like a guilty toddler. "I wouldn't like her to find out," he added eyeing us sceptically.

After that he came to our rooms for a clandestine hour most Sunday afternoons. Zack and Bobby had their afternoon rest oblivious to the whereabouts of the third member of their family.

Tuesday was washing day.

Each tenant would put one sheet and one pillowcase on a pile at the bottom of the stairs.

Zack's Tuesdays began at 5 AM when she and Bobby would bustle down to the old tin shed at the bottom of the little inner city garden. There, Zack would fill the ancient copper with water. Wood appeared weekly as if by magic, I guess Pappy's work.

"I can't abide new-fangled washing machines when it comes to linen," was Zack's stock answer. "There's nothing like a good boil to whiten sheets." Boil them she did, stirring and punching them with the worn copper stick, the sweat pouring from her brow adding to the potpourri in the copper.

She'd never let me help. "What would you young ones know about boiling linen?" she'd grumble. "Go and get me a nice sweet coffee, there's a Dear."

I'd go up to the kitchen and there would be Pappy already making the sickly brew.

"Tuesday washing will be the death of her. Why can't she see reason?" He'd nod to the automatic washing machine in the corner of the kitchen. "She uses that for everything else."

There was a rotary clothesline for ordinary washing and tenants' use, but the prized sheets had to be hung out to flap gaily in the breeze on the old prop lines crisscrossing the yard especially for that purpose. With 16 sheets and 16 pillowcases from 16 tenants, this was no mean feat and we'd hang them out together. One lot dried while the next boiled.

"What if it rains?" I ventured eyeing the venomous grey sky one Tuesday. "It never rains on Tuesday," barked Zack into the copper. "It wouldn't dare," she added ominously—and it never did.

Innumerable trips later up and down the creaking staircase to turn the sheets on the half hour eventually saw them all on the kitchen table, dried, aired and sparkling white. Soup size cups of the sweet rich coffee and a small mountain of cream cakes were placed on the sideboard ready to provide the sustenance necessary for the next part of Tuesday's ritual.

Zack would take one end of a sheet and Pappy the other and each would walk to opposite ends of the kitchen. A mouthful of cake and coffee was obligatory before the first cry of "Pull," issued from Zack's lips accompanied by splatters of coffee soaked cream cake. Pappy would spring into action and pull with all his might on his end of the sheet.

"Fold," more cake and coffee came with the second cry, and Zack and Pappy, working with a unison that would not have shamed Fonteyn and Nureyev, would stretch and fold the sheet in perfect timing and exactly in half.

Again picking up both ends the cry "Pull" could be heard all through the boarding house, but this time Zack, fortified by another sip of coffee, would give a pull to be envied by an Amazon and Pappy's tubby body would fly halfway down the kitchen desperately holding his end of the sheet.

"Fold," Zack would cry again and back he'd totter to his end of the kitchen. This process was repeated until each sheet was a perfectly folded, creaseless envelope of spotless linen waiting to be delivered to the lucky tenants' doorsteps the following Tuesday morning.

One day the following winter Zack asked me to help her clean her flat. We worked in companionable silence for a while, each with our own thoughts and Zack occasionally humming a few bars of Old Black Joe.

"It's a strange name 'Zack'," I said, thinking aloud.

"My first husband was Mr Isaacs," Zack surprised me by volunteering. She was dusting a photo of two young girls dressed in the style of the 30's. She looked at it tenderly and a cloud passed over her face.

"I'll tell you one day," she said placing the photo back in its place. She never did tell me, so I still wonder.

Zack was rich. That day we cleaned her flat she showed me several bundles of bankbooks.

"You can only have $10,000 in an account without paying tax on the interest," she said. "When I go I'm leaving me money to them that needs it." She slammed the books back into the drawer.

True to her word, years later we received a solicitor's letter to say we were to receive $5,000 from Zack's estate—the rest went to a children's hospital. Zack and Pappy never talked about their past. I could never draw them into a conversation that involved their lives before they'd come to Kings Cross thirteen years earlier. Who they were or where they'd come from is a mystery.

But I think of Zack often and smile.

Go With Me To That Land

David Shapiro del Sole

I live in Launceston, Tasmania, where I work part-time as a counsellor in private practice and play games with my granddaughter.

Go With Me To That Land

Heavy clouds brood over the city. Jimmy watches them while he stands in the front doorway of his home as if he has been abandoned there on an island of time. He has just said good-bye to Lisa, his partner, who is heading off to work while his five-year old daughter, Rita, is playing with her favourite doll on the living-room carpet. He feels the morning's weight as a bank of clouds, which is nearly blanketing the sky, proclaims unpromising news. Then he turns, walks along the hallway into the lounge and sits down beside his daughter on the floor.

"Molly has been a bit naughty," the child says looking down at the soft, floppy doll that she holds in her hands and then up at her father.

"Not again."

"She doesn't want to have a bath today."

"Why not?"

"She doesn't like baths. I told her she has to have one."

"Because?"

"She'll be stinky if she doesn't."

"Oh... does she want to be stinky?"

The child laughs. "Noooo. She just doesn't like baths."

"I see."

She lifts the doll's face so that it is against her ear. "She says she is okay to have a bath, now. I told her that after her bath she could have a story."

"Nice."

"But first she has to get some clean clothes."

She begins to mime choosing clothes.

"She's picked out her clothes. Okay, Molly, let's take off those old clothes and put them in the wash."

He recognizes that his daughter's words and tone belong to his partner, now being channelled by the child's play. There's a pause in their conversation while she goes through the motions of helping the doll undress and then placing it in the bath.

Smiling down at her, he watches admiringly. He marvels how his daughter's capacity for make-believe creates an alternative to an imposed, take-it-or-leave-it reality. He considers that what she imagines is as important to her as what she experiences through her senses. She plays and mixes with both. As he contemplates how naturally she travels between these distinct worlds, he encounters an uneasy feeling that he has lived too cautiously, like a mouse poised at the threshold of its shelter, sniffing the air to assess what danger awaits it.

When Lisa arrives home at the end of the day, the three have dinner together, and afterwards Lisa puts Rita to bed. Jimmy is reading in the lounge or, more accurately, is trying to. In truth, he is impatiently waiting for Lisa to finish and to come and sit beside him on the sofa.

When finally she enters the lounge, she carries a mug of hot tea for each of them and a small plate with Lebanese pastries balanced on one of the mugs. They are sitting on the floral-patterned sofa bought on Gumtree five years ago from a young couple living in the inner city. The husband borrowed a trailer onto which Jimmy helped load the sofa. It seemed an important purchase back then when they were setting up house, irrefutable evidence they were a family. The sofa's weight and solidity reassured him that all would be well in spite of his jealous disposition, his fears that whatever was good in his life could not last. And those fears, of course, only grew stronger after his and Lisa's separation when Jimmy had to move out and lived with his grandmother for almost a whole year. Those were dark days.

"How was your day?" he asks.

"A mixed bag. Sometimes I feel I'm going round in circles. If it's not the clients, it's the bureaucracy of the place."

Jimmy hears the burdened tone and feels the undertow of her weariness. His own mood begins to sink while he listens as though it were tied tightly to hers with a knot he has neither the power nor desire to undo.

In an effort to break the downward pull, he asks, "Do you wanna foot rub?"

"That would be lovely."

He rises from the sofa, walks to the bathroom and returns with a small bottle of lavender-scented massage oil. He pours a few drops into his left palm, rubs his hands together to spread and warm the oil while he sits at the end of the sofa by Lisa's feet.

"That's really nice," she says gazing gratefully along the length of the sofa at him.

The sensations in his hands coming from their warm, lubricated movements over the vulnerable recess of her arch, the cushioned roundedness of her sole and her toes, each with their small, contained, individual character, travel along pathways of his pleasure and affection. His measured breathing anticipates the moment of their retiring to bed, and he feels himself already within the wonder of their bodies meeting.

After a couple of hours—during which time Lisa's receptiveness grows, her easy laughter beginning to flow as the evening progresses and she gradually relaxes—they rise, take their cups and dishes to the kitchen, pee, brush teeth and head for the bedroom. Once under the covers they follow a familiar ritual: talking idly, eventually dropping into silence for some moments and then he reaching into the darkness for a thing as undefined and endless as the darkness itself, the sum of all his longings. His fingers find the soft firmness of her flesh. It is warm and responsive, surprisingly so as if his surprise were due to his having found a gift left on his front steps by an unidentified benefactor.

His hand roams instinctively over the rises and falls of her body recognizing each contour and variation of texture as an expression of his own dreaming, as though he himself has contributed in creating what he is now meeting. It is not long before he finds himself in a rush of sensations, his awareness tumbling, spinning wildly in a pool of crisscrossing currents before he is carried beyond his fear and jealousy, exultating in the sense that his body is eternally flowing forward.

Their daughter, Rita, sleeps untroubled a couple of metres away. The darkness of the room holds them, contains and in turn is contained by them. It is a part of them and they belong to it. Its presence is alive, a pulsing body less substantial than their own, like a shadow when the sun is behind, that goes before as a scout on a mission to gather intelligence on an uncertain future.

When their love-making runs its course, each of the them stretches out along the other, Lisa's back to Jimmy while Jimmy cradles her head with one arm and the other drapes across her belly as they peacefully slip into sleep and bid good-bye to the day.

When Jimmy awakes briefly in the night; he thinks he can hear coming from the small bed in the corner of the room his daughter's breathing. He listens. He isn't sure, perhaps he is only imagining, attributing to his daughter a sound woven of silence solely because he wants, even needs, to hear it. In his half sleep, he imagines he is holding her. Or is it her breath he holds? He cautions himself about making any move that might compromise the breath's fine and fragile crafting. Then his body shifts, turns and rolls over on its side, and, barely conscious, he thinks he hears a reassuring voice as he drifts back into sleep.

The next morning, driving to uni for his class, he is tired. He can still feel the warmth of Lisa's body mingling with his own, his limbs rescued from uselessness. His chest holds an aching for his wife, his daughter and for that which makes all of them, including him, more than who they are. His ribs, like fingers, encircle it in a hard, bony grasp. He promises not to let go, not to let it fall from his clasp. He repeats his vow, invoking the magic of words, to strengthen his resolve. He recalls Rita mimicking her mother's words as she played at her own version of mothering, and suddenly—witness and protector of an intimacy that, often against his will, has brought him closer to himself—he finds he is engulfed in a mix of grief and responsibility. The possibility, however small, of losing what is inexpressibly precious both haunts and goads him. He must gamble everything, he tells himself. He cannot hold back. The feeling in his breast reaches a pitch of intensity so great it seems to vaporize his insides, so that soon there is nothing left of him except the empty air he is moving in. He feels himself only as an absence, as someone who has left, leaving behind not a memory of who he was, but a kind of weather one experiences when the air is remarkably still.

He parks the car and makes his way along the campus walkway to the large, gray building where his class is held. Above him, smooth, heavily muscled branches of non-natives arch toward the light. The trees are silent, perhaps in the face of their forced relocation and of having to put down roots in foreign soil. Their broad, dark leaves flutter in a breeze, each looking like the palm and fingers of a hand gesturing direction to a wayfarer.

The Kiss

Robert Nowak

Robert Nowak lives and works in a small, country town. Sometimes he lives in a small-country town. Sometimes he drives to Melbourne, which is a big city in a small way. He is a valued commentator on the Australian political scene and there is scarcely a politician living who is not indebted to him for the advice he has given and continues to give, freely and often.

The Kiss

There's not a lot to a rustic hamlet.

It was five o'clock on a Sunday afternoon in late autumn. The valley was dry for this time of year.

From behind the venetians in the store you could see the bridge, a few scattered houses with plumes of smoke curling up towards the overcast sky, some road signs, the hotel across the pot-holed road and a crow calling 'more' repeatedly as it flapped laboriously over the hill behind the pub. And right close up was a man wearing a pair of boots that would make Vincent van Gogh weep.

It was Larry, sitting on the bench outside the store, which was shut. They close at noon on Sundays in autumn and winter. The pub is open till eight, but mostly pretty quiet.

As usual, Larry had started an argument about nothing.

"Ya didn't know what was going on and ya had to butt in and that's what caused the misunderstanding. I just wish you'd mind your own business. Frank is a great guy but he takes these things personally."

"Well, it's my money that's paying him," she said, just quietly enough.

"That's right. That's right. Stuff it, I'm not going through this again."

He walked three kilometres down the road to the pub.

It was a windy, annoying day. As he walked along a car went by. No one he knew. Interstate plates. As they passed, he looked up. The children stared at him through the side and then the back windows.

"What are you bloody staring at?" he thought. His hair. His clothes. His walk. Especially the fact that he was there, walking, in the middle of nowhere. The clothes he wore were the sort of things the old ladies in the Op Shop threw into the rag bag without a thought. But so what? He was comfortable. Who cared anyway? Fuck 'em. He knew who he was. He had plenty of good gear in the wardrobe. Leather pants. Sequinned flairs. Orange taffeta ruffle-fronted shirts with incredibly long collars. Winkle pickers with chrome toes. Fuck 'em. He knew who he was.

Another car went by. He looked up to see the car slow and the whole family craning their necks towards him. The father and mother waved. The kids made peace signs. Larry quickly picked up a clod of dirt and hurled it and roared at them,

"I am not an animal! I am a Genoa resident!"

Most of the time it was a joke but not always.

The temperature was dropping. He crossed his arms and walked on.

When he got to the pub he saw Frank's old bomb parked out the back. Frank's old EH, held together with wire. Frank had been driving ten years without a licence. Not only that, but the policeman from Wallabong was there, too, with a couple of his cronies. They spilled out onto the verandah momentarily and then spilled back in, their guffaws accompanied by shrieks of female laughter.

"That's just great."

Country life had never really appealed to Larry, though for nine years now he had been fairly stuck in it. He liked trees, and animals, even snakes though he had to kill them once in a while, for his kids' sake. If it was just him he wouldn't have killed them. They were beautiful, snakes. Scary, but beautiful. He liked the river and the hills and cows were ok and even fresh air was quite nice in moderation.

Country people, though, he was not so sure about them. Though he got on well enough with most of his neighbours there were some—men generally, at least they were the ones who made their cheap and nasty opinions obvious—who made it clear that being a househusband was despicable.

Nevertheless, he tried his best not to let this cramp his style. He enjoyed himself at the pub and as far as possible he was himself wherever he went, within reason, of course.

Larry and Frank had been friends, bar acquaintances and then friends, for several years. Frank was a carpenter and sometime timber worker. Frank. Frank of Frank and Carol. They lived in sin—enough said, Champion!—on a block of land owned by his son-in-law a few miles out of town. Frank had worked hard all his life and owned nothing. Carol grew large quantities of wonderful vegetables but she had no teeth to chew the bastards with. When you met them, Frank would declare warmly that it was always nice to meet nice people and Carol would start talking to you and never stop for as long as she knew you. Once upon a time Frank had been married to Carol's sister who was still around somewhere.

Despite ten years in the bush, Larry remained an urban person. He had been an dealer in antiques, but nowadays he looked after the kids and did some of the housework and not much else. After they had had their house floated in, Frank had helped them at various times hanging doors, building the chimney and so forth, and the day before they had had this misunderstanding and Frank had gone off very cold and formal which was about as bad as it got with Frank, this side of fighting.

"Well, you please yourself, Champion. I am not a man to argue," he had said, ominously.

A troupe of choughs lit briefly in the moulting peach tree in the yard of the store. Larry turned to look at them and they cocked their heads and regarded him with their big, yellow eyes. Old von Bockholdt called them 'apostle birds'. Thelma Brownlie, formerly Sievers, called them 'happy families'. George Johnston, Thelma's brother, called them 'turd turners'.

Larry looked back at them, and said to the birds, in a voice that could have been venomous had it the energy, 'Fuck off!'

And they did.

Larry considered Frank Meehan to be the most decent man in the district. They both liked to drink, to bullshit and to laugh and they both liked to treat people decently and they were uncompetitive. Sometimes Frank made remarks about 'Coons' and 'Slopes' which made Larry wince, but no-one was perfect. Larry himself often referred to 'Abos', but this he said was just normal English and not abusive.

"It's how you say it. If anything, it's a term of affection."

It was about six o'clock and starting to get dark. Larry was tossing things around. The company of the policeman and his friends was not an attractive proposition at the best of times. Their hard laughter and the hysterical shrieks of the woman continued depressingly. She was the storekeeper's wife. She was a good woman. Larry liked her. She was witty. But she was bored stupid. The pub door flew open and she ran out and vomited over the balcony. More laughter. Larry felt even more depressed.

Ideally the bar would have been empty and he would have been able to prop there and talk about nothing to the barman for a couple of hours and get half cut and go home and apologize. It's always me, he thought ruefully, almost bitterly, it's always me who says 'sorry'.

But, then, it was inevitable because, despite the things he sometimes said, he really believed that his wife was perfect.

Not only was there the damn stupid policeman, there was Frank, too. Possibly a painful encounter. Frank was a patient man, but when he got dark, he got really dark for a long time. The pity of it was not that there might be a stand-off or even an argument: the pity of it was that he was really fond of Frank. Frank, full of stories and sayings. Good-natured, Irish, sentimental, three sheets in the wind, decent, good old Frank, the scaly bastard. You're evil, Champion, evil! It wasn't just the joking. Frank understood. Soft hearted, Irish Frank understood and forgave like Jesus Bloody Christ. Once he knew the facts, Frank was a man of compassion, and it didn't matter if you were an Iti, or a Fishhead or even a friggin' blackfeller for that matter.

He thought of Frank, late in the evening, already underwater, the way he would lean slightly (a lot) towards the bar, grip it firmly in both his hands and demand, ominously,

"Rum, Champion! Rum! One for the road. Oh yes, we must be making a mile!"

And his earnest explanation that you could tell good Guinness if a rat could run across half a dozen pints without getting its feet wet.

Larry smiled to himself. He could have gone home, of course, but his saving grace if he had one was that he was always himself (within reason) so he thought 'stuff it!' and went into the pub.

Just inside the door, at one end of the long bar, the policeman and his two mates were joking noisily with Denise. Her husband was nowhere to be seen. They were all fully charged, especially the woman. They glanced at him indifferently and then paid him no attention. Frank was at the far end of the bar nursing a beer and reading the newspaper.

Frank turned as Larry approached and after a moment's hesitation turned back to his newspaper. The publican came in and without being asked served Larry a beer and held up his hand to indicate that it was on the house. Larry was a regular customer and on Sundays he always got a free one.

"Thanks, Bill," said Larry.

"No worries," said Bill.

Then Bill went back to the lively end of the bar.

Frank and Larry were standing quite close together. They had never before been on poor terms with each other. Either could hate, but they couldn't happily bear a grudge.

They were watching proceedings at the far end of the bar where the cronies were goading the storekeeper's wife to further excess in a game involving pickled gherkins. Having watched this spectacle for a minute or so, they looked at each other and both began to apologize at once.

Frank stood humbly but surely on his old time country manners and extended his hand and shook Larry's with much warmth and at great length. Larry almost cried himself when he noticed the difficulty with which Frank managed not to let his big Irish tears run down his face.

Frank was surprisingly upset, even for a sentimental fool. Larry was hardly his born and bred, tried and true type of countryman. Larry was a city boy who had stood out like dogs balls since he had arrived but he was the only person who hadn't… I mean, well, your mates would back door you or siphon your petrol or borrow your socket set and lend it to someone else and forget who or not do something you relied on, kill your dog at night for no apparent reason, whatever. Frank would have been hard pressed to say exactly what it was about Larry he liked—unless it was that Larry was, well, somehow, fair dinkum. He was a battler, too, and he had some heart, the bastard. What you saw was what you got. Even if he did only pretend to be a Collingwood supporter, it was obvious pretence.

Larry put his arm around Frank's shoulder.

"Hey, Frank, Champion, it's ok."

Frank returned his hug. And then, without thinking what he was doing, Larry kissed Frank on the neck.

Then he remembered where he was. He glanced over Frank's shoulder. At the far end of the long bar the policeman and his mates were dancing with linked arms around Mrs Umback whose eyes stopped rolling when she saw what Frank and Larry were doing.

She stared at them in brief amazement but said nothing.

Cursing himself for a fool, Larry said,

"Oh shit, sorry, Frank, I think I might have done the wrong thing…"

The policeman dropped a gherkin down the front of the woman's dress, and, pretending that it had been an accident, or that he was making amends, he tried to retrieve it.

"No, no, son, that's quite alright, thanks…"

They remained for a moment in their embrace. Tears ran down Larry's face. He smiled weakly at Denise and shrugged his shoulders.

Maybe it was the time of year, or maybe sunspot activity. Not realizing that she was preoccupied or unresponsive, one of the friends poured something after the gherkin.

"What hope is there, Frank?"

"None, son, none. No hope at all, Champion."

The woman's sudden, broken, sobbing surprised the men.

"What's wrong?" asked one.

She burst through their arms and went out the door, saying, "I've got to go home." The policeman ran after her.

"What did we do?" said one of the friends. "I thought she was enjoying herself."

The barman shrugged his shoulders.

They looked down at Frank and Larry as if for support. They had disengaged, but the tears glistened on Larry's miserably smiling face.

"Jesus, it's contagious!"

"Ah fuck off," said Larry, quietly and distinctly.

Larry couldn't fight, but if a fight had started Frank would have backed him. Not that Frank could fight.

Larry said to Frank, "Hey, Frank, don't worry about it. We still need a hand with that hot water jacket. Can you come around on Tuesday?"

A Father's Pride

Bill Cushing

Bill Cushing lived in numerous states along with the Virgin Islands and Puerto Rico before moving to California. Earning an MFA in creative non-fiction writing from Goddard College in Vermont, he has just retired after 23 years teaching college English in the Los Angeles. He now lives in Glendale with his wife and their son (and subject of this piece) Gabriel.

His non-fiction has appeared in print and online in *Birders World*, *Cargo Lit*, *Drunk Monkeys*, and the *San Juan Star*. His collection of poetry, **A Former Life**, was recently published by Finishing Line Press.

"**A Father's Pride**" was a finalist in the 2016 Pen2Paper competition, an annual event dedicated to writing about those with disabilities.

A Father's Pride

This is definitely a father's "attaboy" story.

Gabriel was a tad over six years old and deeply involved in the numbers he had, since infancy, shown a fascination for. Although restricted to a wheelchair and unable to speak because of a stroke he suffered in the womb, he was in kindergarten and quite active despite a professional diagnosis of "developmental delay." On this occasion, he proved just how incorrect that assessment might be.

About a month after his birthday, Val, a teacher's aide in his classroom, was testing Gabriel's mathematics skills. She had a stack of the old-style flashcards, those laminated handheld boards with a problem on one side and the solution on the other, and she held up the cards to show Gabriel the problem he was to solve. He, in turn, would respond through the digitally synthesized keyboard he used to communicate. The exercise began tentatively: he would answer some of the problems correctly; others he was either off base or refused to answer at all.

Soon though, Val noticed that Gabriel was slowing down in his response time, meditating on the situation. He would look at the problem in front of him, lean over in his wheelchair to cup his sharp chin in a small, meaty right hand, and then type in his answer to the question. It worked.

By taking his time, thinking over the problem in front of him, and deliberating on the answer, he began getting them. One after another, Val would show Gabriel an equation of some sort, and one after another, he would stop, lean—chin in palm—to answer the question correctly.

The progress she saw encouraged her. Gabriel was answering mathematical problems, each successively more difficult than the last. She marvelled at how thoughtful and measured each response was, as well as how comfortable he was in handling the task.

It was almost too good to be true, which in fact, it was.

Val noticed that Gabriel's ritual became more regular, almost predictable. She held up a card; he stopped, leaned, and answered.

Correctly.

Every time.

Without hesitation.

That was the "tell." Val picked up another card, and this time, rather than listening for Gabriel's response, she watched him. As he leaned to the side, she saw his eyes fix on a point behind her. She laid down the cards and swivelled her chair to find herself staring at her own reflection in a large mirror mounted on the back wall.

Gabriel had been peering into the mirror, reading the reflected answer to each problem, mentally reversing the exposed information, then answering the question. Here he was, gaming the system at six years old.

Like I said: "Attaboy."

Gabriel Cushing with his communication device

Dumpster Diving in Paradise

Jim Ross

Jim Ross jumped into creative pursuits in 2015 after retiring from public health research. He's since published nonfiction, poetry, and photography in over 100 journals and anthologies in North America, Europe, Australia, and Asia. Publications include *Barren*, *Columbia Journal*, *Ilanot Review*, *Lunch Ticket*, *Kestrel*, *The Atlantic*, and *The Manchester Review*. Forthcoming includes: *Granta*, *Roanoke Review*, *Typehouse*. In the past year, he wrote and acted in his first play; and, a nonfiction piece led to a role in a soon-to-be-released, high-profile documentary limited series. Jim and his wife—parents of two health professionals and grandparents of five pre-schoolers—split their time between the city and the mountains."

Dumpster Diving in Paradise was previously published in *Gravel Literary Magazine*, 2018.

Dumpster Diving in Paradise

The online ad for our beach resort read, "*The facility abounds with exotic tropical flowers, fresh fruit trees, song birds, and the sweet scents of Hawaii.*" It talked about "*crescent beaches and Lava rock tide pools... only steps from your front door.*" All the ocean view rooms had already been booked, but the online reservation portal reported that one partial ocean view room remained available. When I called, the reservation agent said, "I'd call it more of a garden view. It's a very partial ocean view."

When we arrived, we saw she was right. From our first-floor deck, we couldn't see a speck of ocean through the rooftops and palm trees. A dreamy fragrant white plumeria overhung the steps to our deck. Other flowering trees were in clear sight; hibiscus, red ginger, and other plants native to Hawaii dotted the grounds. But what dominated the scenery was the blacktop-covered parking lot. That wasn't mentioned, either on the website or by the reservation clerk.

From our deck, we could monitor the comings and goings of three victory red 2017 Camaro convertibles, all rentals and smacking new. Our beige midsize without sunroof kept them company. We also had a clear view of the two sheltered trash receptacles marked "kitchen waste/general trash" and "recyclable paper/glass/cans/plastics" alongside a small dumpster marked "reusables". Our unit was better described as a full-on parking lot/trash receptacle/dumpster view, bounded by an incidental array of native tropical plants.

After we'd been there a few days, one of the red Camaro convertibles was replaced by a black Ford Fairlane circa 1970. We didn't immediately notice who the owner was. Indeed, we almost never saw the occupants of any of the twenty-odd units. One morning we saw a man around thirty-five, wearing a white t-shirt and tattered brown shorts, getting into the Fairlane with a boy around seven, dressed in shorts and sport shirt. The man had a long, pointed beard, longer and pointier than a duckbill, a mix of grey and brown. He wore a smirk that suggested he knew something we didn't. He moved like someone who earned the right to feel humble.

One afternoon I returned from a walk and found the boy standing at the foot of the steps to our deck. He looked up at me and, as if surprised, exclaimed, "George Washington."

I told my wife a moment later and she said, "Maybe he's telling you that you need a haircut."

"Maybe he thinks I look Presidential," I replied.

"More likely," she said, "you reminded him of the Revolutionary War."

The next morning, my wife was up early and saw the man out tending to the dumpster. He wasn't contributing to it; he was sorting through and selectively extracting items he then deposited into the trunk of his car, mostly clothes: shirts, shorts, socks, sweatshirts, sundresses, flip-flops, running shoes. He'd almost passed by when she said, "Your boy was out last night and called my husband George Washington."

The man looked embarrassed. "I'm sorry, I'm sure he didn't mean anything by it."

"My husband took it as a compliment," my wife said.

Her impression was that the man and boy were occupying the basement unit in the rental complex—the only one lacking a deck and views of plumeria and other flowering trees.

Over the next few days, we noticed father and son hanging out at the nearest park, a wide grassy strip abutting a rocky shoreline, with a crescent baby beach on one side, and a children's surfing beach on the other. Visitors maintained a respectful distance from a pair of giant green sea turtles who washed up at one end of the crescent and from a monk seal deserted at the crescent's arid opposite point. The man and boy weren't playing Frisbee, body surfing, building sand castles, or wading in the water. Instead, they were unobtrusively inspecting the trash receptacles that lined the beach and dropping any choice discoveries—mostly clothing, but also beach gear like flippers, goggles, snorkels, body boards—into a huge sack. I usually take photos to capture moments that move me, like a girl who looked lonesome standing guard by the sea turtles, or the red male chameleon that puffed his throat before aggressively subduing a smaller, rosier female. But I didn't take pictures of the man and boy as they continued their ritual dance with the trash cans.

The man kept investigating the dumpster at our resort complex, morning and evening, when the sun hung low in the sky. One morning, Ginger was out and he approached.

"I have something I want to give you to give to your husband," he said.

"Sure," my wife said. "What've you got?"

The man reached into his jacket pocket. "I can't believe somebody threw these away. They're perfectly good. Please give 'em to your husband as a sort of souvenir of this trip and of meeting my son, something to remember us by."

A moment later, my wife handed me a pair of balled, brown Banlon socks.

"These are from our friends with the black Fairlaine," she said.

"These are the kind of socks my Dad was buying thirty years ago. Why would he think I'd want a pair of old socks?"

"Just open them," she urged.

I unballed the socks. The feet were dark brown. The ankles were more of a caramel colour. And the inner and outer ankles bore the image of George Washington.

Talking Under Water

Ian Jamieson

Ian Jamieson is a retired English teacher; it's a career he settled on because he liked books and reading and figured he'd get to do a lot of both. And get paid. At the time it seemed as good a reason as any, though not an entirely accurate one.

Previously, Ian has been a paperboy in London, a bricklayer's labourer, a fencer, a greyhound walker, a factory worker. Teaching suited him best out of those. Ian has an MA and a PhD, and these degrees, combined with his teaching, have meant that he has spent a lot of time either teaching the writing of others, or analysing and writing about the work of others. He now thinks it about time to concentrate on creating some writing of his own. He may have come to this quite late, but it's a case of better late than never. Definitely. Besides, Google has proven very comforting by allowing him to search for and find lots of successful writers who started when older. 'Talking Under Water' is the first story Ian has attempted to have published and this has encouraged him to polish the numerous other stories he has written and to try and get them published. He has also written a novel which sits, figuratively, in the bottom of a drawer; where it belongs. Ian continues to work on new short stories, as well as another novel, which hopefully will not end up keeping that other one company. If his plans for future publication fail to come about, he will still continue writing, believing that for him each day is made that little bit better when some writing gets done.

Talking Under Water

She was surprised to see him that Saturday morning, but thinking about it later she knew she shouldn't have been. It had been coming.

She was early, well before any other customers came to do their shopping. It was still dark, the morning light held back by the dark clouds of the storm. In the halo glow of streetlights squalls of gusty wind shifted and slanted the rain like the darting schools of tiny fish. Lightning lit the underbelly of the clouds. His palms, she thought. There was electricity in the air. It was her Saturday routine: get there early, avoid the busy crowds, especially the clusters of mocking, jeering school kids. A group of them would give loud exaggerated yawns, rub their eyes and laugh at what she was wearing. They had called her a dog, a mad bitch, and finally, when she refused to respond, a killer. That last one always hurt the most, though she knew it shouldn't. Pretending not to hear them was always best. Algal blooms she called them. Not aloud, of course.

She would cruise the aisles of the supermarket, shark silent and alert, carrying her empty plastic bag. She could be different people when she was the solitary wanderer: the pregnant woman rubbing her tummy and planning dinner, the lover picking just the right card, preferably with some poetry on it, though it could never be the right sort of poetry. Sometimes, just sometimes, and then only very briefly, she could again be that person grabbing some coffee to make up for their thermos.

She came to get dog food; such variety to choose from, which was good because he would like that. She would flick her plastic bag open and think of all the little cans that could be filling it. Then walking out of the supermarket she would shift the bag from one hand to the other like she would do if the plastic handles were cutting into her fingers. Her hands had been through enough.

Outside the supermarket the wind whipped the plastic bag about, first wrapping it against her leg, then filling it with air and sending it off like some startled squid. And standing there thinking of a little dog, concentrating so as to keep all else at bay, there must have been some dust and grit in the wind because her eyes started to run with tears. It was with this blurry vision that she saw him. There was another flash of lightning and in that frozen moment he was there, hair plastered to his head and water streaming down his oilskin jacket from the rain. Then he was gone. Into the water, she thought. Could not have been anyone else, just had to be him standing there holding out that book wrapped in plastic. Sure, his dog wasn't with him, but maybe that was because it felt guilty that it had not warned them, had not yapped and barked to save them. When she got the chance, she would tell his dog that it wasn't his fault, that there was nothing he could have done. Yes, she would cuddle him and tell him this, not even worrying about the short white and brown hairs that would be left on her dressing gown.

Having seen him she would now take the long way home, down the side street with the second-hand bookshop, where she would always check the changing window display. You just never know. The other way, the short cut, would take her towards the harbour, past the wooden jetty with its thick planks of weathered grey that were warm against their bare legs when they had sat there watching the sun creeping into the ocean. And in those darkening evenings, as the chill crept in, she had still been warm. But going that way she would have to pass the small building of the research facility and the dry dock that held the wreck and she would have to stare at it, even if it was no longer there. Best to take the long way, especially after seeing him. Mustn't push your luck.

However, there was that night when she did creep through the midnight dark of silent streets to get to the jetty. It was bitterly cold, but she felt none of it. Along the jetty she had walked, the gentle susurration of the water lapping the pylons lulling and telling her that it was an easy and quiet way to go. The water was icy and after the initial shock she knew she would painlessly slide away. She scanned the shoreline, wanted to be certain there was no one there to bear witness or attempt some clumsy intervention. She was about to step over the edge, about to go to him, when there was a movement, the slightest feeling of a movement, but enough to tell her that she should not do it. She turned around, retracing where she had been, but also thinking where she had to go. Now, looking back at that night, it all made sense, she wasn't meant to do it, because he was out there, trying to get back.

*

It was only a small boat, barely adequate for the work it had to do. But the cabin, cramped as it was, made up for it. Each morning, fog sitting damp and moist around the jetty, cloistering them, they would set out to monitor the winter migration of humpbacks. Some coffee each from the thermos she always brought, then the rhythmic chugging of the diesel as they set out for the open sea, his Jack Russell like some figurehead leaning forward on the prow and barking at the mist and spray. Mid-morning and the fog had melted away and the sea was glass smooth and glinting in the warming sun. I need a coffee, she would say. Me too, he'd reply. Leaving his dog, a sentinel that barked at anything that drew close to their boat, they would go below deck and into the cabin, a breach of official protocol, but it never entered into their thinking. Lying there after, never wanting to leave that cabin or that moment, he would reach for the tattered book of poetry he'd found in the second-hand bookshop and each time he would read two poems to her, always concluding with something from Donne, all poems she barely understood. But his voice and the burning clarity and truth of certain lines kept her rapt.

Such huge and powerful creatures. A breaching whale and their small boat is overturned and the water comes in so quickly and he is pinned, pinned against a diesel engine that should never have moved and there is blood clouding the clear blue water, and all that there is begins to darken as they are pulled under. He looks at her, holding her eyes for just a moment and forever, and indicates with frantic gesturing that she must escape, she must swim out of the opening to their cabin. She tugs at him, but he cannot be moved, tries to shift the engine, tearing her nails. He mouths some words and pushes her away and with lungs bursting she leaves him there.

A sightseeing charter boat had seen the sinking, and two of their crew dragged her out of the water. They wrapped her in an old blanket smelling of petrol, hiding a nakedness she gave no thought to. And the sea was again glass smooth and glinting in the warming sun.

People say how so-and-so could talk under water, supposed to be impossible. But it can be done, he did speak under water. And it echoes. She knew the three words that he said to her, and it made things better and it made things worse.

*

She volunteered at the research facility every school holiday. She was a maths teacher, so four times a year she would arrive at the small coastal town. She was passionate about the environment, her one and only passion, until the volunteering. She'd been through a series of relationships, some disastrous, but most just fading away to colourless blandness, like the bleaching coral reefs she read about. It was the documentary Mission Blue that got her started. She had loved it, despite being with a fellow teacher who loudly crunched lollies and wanted to either talk to her or feel her up throughout the film. She read as widely as possible about all things to do with the natural marine world. The science baffled her, some books bored her, others told her nothing new, but like all newly addicted autodidacts she persevered.

She'd ordered a book online and when it arrived the padding was some pages from one of the weekend magazines. And there was the advertisement looking for volunteers. She held no hope that she would be accepted, wasn't even sure if she should apply. But she did apply, and her world was changed. It seemed all too improbable to her, a lame narrative at the start of some light-hearted romantic comedy; it defied probability, wasn't logical, but by the time of her first arrival at the research facility the maths teacher in her no longer held any sway. She arrived late one afternoon. There was a weight of humidity in the air and it smelt of salt and change. Distant clouds, beautiful in their roiling darkness, promised a storm. She was shown into her cabin, a small wooden structure, one of several that lined the shore beside the jetty. The cabin was neat and comfortable and when the storm broke it creaked and groaned, melded sounds of agony and ecstasy. She thought a small wooden ship moving through the waves might sound like that and she wondered if her first night there might bring dreams of new journeys.

The storm was at its peak when she first saw him. He stood in the doorway to her cabin, frozen on the threshold, hair plastered to his head, water streaming down his oilskin jacket. A small dog, a Jack Russell, stood beside him. Only when a gust of wind whipped the door out of his hand did he attempt to say something, but it came out as a stutter or a mumble. He then reached inside his jacket and took out a paperback that was wrapped in clear plastic. He held the book towards her, shaking it and nodding his head as if it was this book that explained everything. He then left, leaving the door open.

He seemed to always have that book of poetry with him. Each time one of her stays at the research facility came to an end he would read her one of the poems, always the same poem. She could never tell her friends in the English faculty about that time he first appeared, or about the poetry. They would laugh and say she'd been reading too much cheap romantic fiction, they'd find it childish, affected and saccharine. So, initially she told her friends very little about any of it, but eventually found herself telling them little bits and pieces. It was as if she could not contain what was happening, and in the pleasure of each telling she became more and more certain. When she came to show them photos she no longer cared that they fell silent in their surprise.

By the time their relationship had been going for just over a year he knew the poem off by heart, though, as if it were a necessary part of some benediction, he would always open the book to the double page where *A Valediction: Forbidding Mourning* was. Leaving, to go back to her teaching, became increasingly difficult, but each time his whispered reading of the poem, as if spreading some soothing, gentle balm, put her at ease. There would be no 'tear floods, nor sigh-tempests', they would have to move away from each other, but 'like gold to airy thinness beat' never separated. Besides, they had plans. He couldn't leave the area, too many deep ties, but she would leave her teaching and maybe they could buy a little farm, or run an oyster lease, or whatever, the details weren't important, things would work out, she knew they would, in the end she just knew they would, had to.

Late afternoons, in the windless and quiet lull just before sunset, they would walk around the narrow bush tracks that followed the shoreline of the bay, the Jack Russell running ahead, barking at any movement. They would often stop on the narrow strip of land that jutted out into the bay. He would ignore the wooden seats that the local Lions Club had put there, preferring to sit on his haunches. He would fall silent, a silence of sadness as if he were visiting a grave, and stare at the midden. He went to a different place and at first she could not follow him; other walkers passing by were ignored and someone fishing in the nearby shallows called out his name, but got no reply. She thought he stared as if he were trying to peel back the layers of the midden, first removing the cigarette butts, the shattered glass of VB bottles, tangled fishing line, used condoms, until he was stripping away the decades, the centuries and millennia. Slowly, in snippets and single scenes, he told her what he was seeing, until she too could imagine their talking, their laughter, the sound of cracking shells and the circle glow and warmth of a fire they believed could keep away the dark. She had glimpsed a part of the world he lived in and she thought there just might be magic in it.

A few months after the sinking she started walking the shoreline tracks alone, always stopping at the midden, waiting and hoping. Often, she thought she could hear a rustle in the undergrowth, and sometimes the distant barking of the dog and she would smile, think of a poem and touch her belly. It was their love, that poem and her rounding belly that would bring him back.

She had been allowed to stay in her cabin, not indefinitely they said, but as long as you need. This was meant to comfort her, ease things, but it scared her, 'not indefinitely' scared her; she didn't want any limitation, couldn't bear to think of the finality of it ending, of all hope being severed. She was hanging on, but it was hard, so hard, and she didn't want anything that might loosen her grip. And having seen him outside the supermarket, having heard the barking of his dog in the bush near the midden, meant she had to stay, she must be the 'fixed foot' for his return.

She never ventured too far, never away for longer than necessary: the supermarket early Saturday, the second-hand bookshop and the shoreline paths to the midden were her places. She would start each trip slowly, arming all her senses, looking for the slightest sign. She would always hurry back, pushed by an urgent fear that she could be missing something back at the cabin. And in her cabin she would close her eyes and take a slow, deep breath, feeling for his presence. And there were those times that she was sure, absolutely positive, that there were signs. It was never anything too loud or obvious because she knew that would be 'a profanation of our joys'. She would then stand in the middle of her room and let her dressing gown fall from her and onto the floor, a swirl soft nylon like the seaweed that drifted around his feet in the shallows near the midden. She would stand there naked, all the better to let her belly take in the memories, soak up his lingering aura. She liked it best if it was cold and her nipples would harden; she would cup her breasts and tell herself that they would do an excellent job.

Then there was that time, well after having seen him outside the supermarket, when she was coming past the bookshop that proved to her that she was most definitely right, that all others were wrong, but that she was absolutely right. Pre-sunrise, on her way to the supermarket, plastic bag in hand, when she looked in the bookshop window. And there it was, right in the centre of the display. It was his book, sitting there with the pages open to their poem, their John Donne poem. He must have annotated the poem, something she'd not noticed before, and the last two lines were highlighted in green marker pen, something he would never have done, unless he wanted to say something important, just as if he were holding her face, looking into her eyes and telling her 'thy firmness makes my circle just, and makes me end where I begun.' The book was a little larger than she had remembered, but memory can be wrong and the mind can play tricks.

She turned and ran back to her cabin, dropping her plastic bag as she ran. She could get another bag at any time, when she got a dog, Jack Russell of course, she could get another. In her room she let her dressing gown fall to the floor. It was then that she realised that the three words he had spoken to her under water were not the ones she had thought. Of course, he loved her, of course, but he was telling her, See you soon, he was saying, See you soon. He was mouthing it from his soul and she could finally understand it because 'our two souls are one'. She gently rubbed her belly and cupped her breasts. It was then that she felt the slow snake slide of blood down the inside of her thigh. Like clockwork they were, always heavy and always on time.

Satellites

Sharon Willdin

Sharon Willdin is an award-winning writer who was raised in Goulburn and currently lives in Sydney's Inner West. She began her writing career in 2015 and since then her stories have been published internationally in journals such as Hemingway Shorts, Brooklyn Review, The Weekend Australian, Spineless Wonders, Antithesis Journal, Anamesa Journal, Chaleur Magazine, Open Thought Vortex, Chicago Literati, Esthetic Apostle, and more.

She was a finalist in the Hemingway Shorts Award, the Joanne Burns Microlit Award, and the Woollahra Digital Literary Award. Sharon won the Olga Masters Short Story Award. Further information can be obtained at her website: *www.sharonwilldin.com*

The inspiration for this short story is parenthood and the value of each moment in time.

Satellites

Pebbles press into my back as we lie to dry on the banks of the Shoalhaven River and wait for satellites to cross the night sky. The thrill of the unknown lurks in the dark water next to us but it's no match for a kaleidoscope of transient celestial bodies.

"Mum, there's one!" Caleb boasts, as if he's discovered the rarest gem. He traces the fragment of light with his finger as it glides above us, hundreds of miles away, on its journey to scan the continent. "Can we go now?"

I stretch my arm out to touch his seven-year-old hand. He gently presses the tip of my finger and turns back to look at the sky. "I *said,* can we go now?"

*

I know a place where freesias grow wild on the side of the road and each spring we drive there in our van to pick them.

Caleb sits in the front passenger seat with the windows down while paddocks of bleached wallaby grass pass behind him. Ephemeral rays from the sun flick his hair and skin and bounce off the curve of his nose. He is focused on deciding which songs to play. He chooses *Songbird* and selflessly brags, "See mum, I don't like this song, but I know you do."

Loose gravel grates under the tyres as I pull off the road and on to the shoulder. Caleb realises why we are stopping. "No. Can't we just go?"

I jump out, slam the door, survey the clumps, and begin to pluck the trumpets, one by one, from the earth, inhaling their scent, taking care not to dislodge the bulbs from the ground, and leaving a scattering for others who may follow.

"Mum!" Caleb screams. I turn and see him, nine-years-old, through the insect spotted windscreen. His jaw locked with anger.

I stretch my arm between the wires on the rusted-barbed fence and gather a last few.

"*Now!*"

*

The back-burning of gums on the other side of Tarago infuses the air with comfort. The van shudders as we cross the stock grids and reverberate along the potholed dirt track to our weatherboard home.

Dusty the kelpie skirts around the outside of the van as we stop and get out. He nudges Caleb and races off to continue his vigilant guard on the bullnose veranda.

I am drawn to the sunset at the top of the hill. Caleb reluctantly wanders behind. Cicadas chant waves as we weave through patches of rye grass and phalaris. I pause and examine a stringybark tree, pull off a small piece of its bark, separate the layers, and rub its fibres between my fingers and thumb. Caleb cautions, "Mum." I place my palms on its trunk to feel the warmth and life inside. "Come on, that's enough."

We continue to the top of the ridge and take rest on the family boulder. Magpies gurgle and kangaroos bound across the clearing as dusk begins to settle and the moon begins to rise. I sneak a sideways peek and see the serenity in his fifteen-year-old eyes and witness his spirit blend with the land. We sit in quiet contemplation for a moment.

*

I visit him in spring, where he lies, lined up, decomposing, in single file, next to my ancestors at Jerrara Creek Cemetery, and I place a clump of freesias into the cracked porcelain vase.

Kirra, his five-year-old daughter, circles the headstones, impatiently kicks up the dust and declares, "Nan, *I'm bored!*"

I grab her hand and we look above to see if we can catch a glimpse of a satellite crossing the evening sky.

Blood Diamond

Warren Paul Glover

Warren Paul Glover is a British-Australian screenwriter, playwright, poet and actor. Warren's short fiction and poetry has appeared in journals such as *The Blue Nib*, *Plum Tree Tavern*, *The Sea Letter*, *Sentinel Literary Quarterly*, *Tuck Magazine*, *Metafore Magazine*, *The Relationship Blogger*, *Moon Magazine*, and *Down in the Dirt Magazine*, amongst others. His plays have been performed in Britain, Australia, and the United States. Warren lives in Sydney and is represented by the TCM Agency. You can follow him on Twitter: https://twitter.com/WazMan01

Blood Diamond

He came to the farm after dark.

I had spent another long day working the land, only ceasing my toil when the sun set, bathing the veldt in glorious orange.

Seventeen days had passed since my husband left me alone with the cattle, my thoughts, and God to join the Boer forces laying siege to Kimberley, that giant ant hill of depravity.

I begged him not to go but he was determined to be with our brothers from the Transvaal and the Orange Free State in attacking the British in their enclave.

"Eliza," he said, caressing my cheek with his large calloused hand, "we have to defend our way of life. Our fathers didn't make the Great Trek, surviving the Zulus, for nothing. This is war. We fight for our freedom and our future."

"I'm sick of war," I said as my heart sank into my boots and I tried not to cry. "Why can't we be at peace?"

Johannes lifted my chin so he could search my face.

"They are not like us," he chided. "I must go. But I'll return. Just you see."

I watched him as he climbed onto his horse. He looked handsome and noble in his broad brimmed hat, jacket, and scarf, an ammunition belt strung across his chest. As I wiped away a tear, I thought how proud our pioneering forefathers, the Voortrekkers, would have been of Johannes and the other men. I waved him goodbye with a smile.

As I lay on the bed nursing my aching back that eighteenth night, wondering whether I'd ever see my husband again, I heard the dogs start up into a frenzy of barking and growling. I got to my feet and reached for the rifle.

"What is it, boys?" I asked as I cocked the gun.

The dogs had heard or smelled something; their tails were up. I grabbed a lamp and wrenched open the door. The dogs flew out barking and I followed.

The sound of snarling led me around the house towards the chicken coops. When I got closer, I could see that the dogs had a black man trapped in the corner, cowering in the dirt.

I set the lamp down on the fence and with trembling hands aimed the gun at him. "We shoot poachers on this farm," I shouted, trying my hardest to sound resolute. The black man raised his arms in surrender. My eyes, having adjusted to the light, could see his fear and fatigue. He looked half dead. His clothing was tattered and as I stepped closer I could see that he had already been shot. I lowered my gun and corralled the dogs into a pen.

"Shush, boys. It's all right," I said in my soothing voice as I tried to quieten them.

When I turned back towards the man his dark eyes were watching me closely. I spread out my arms and tried my soothing voice on him.

"Ok, my poacher friend. I won't harm you. Let me take a look at your wounds."

He recoiled as I tried to examine him, but his eyes were wild with pain and we both knew that he was in no position to argue.

"Easy," I said. "There's nobody here but me. I have some food inside and I can treat your wounds there. Or I can shoot you here. Which will it be?"

He nodded and allowed me to put my arm around him. It was a struggle to lift him to his feet but together we did it and shuffled inside. The dogs were still barking in their corral and I shushed them as we passed.

I laid the man down on the rug before the fire and left him groaning gently as I went to fetch some water and cloths. When I returned he was drifting in and out of consciousness and I could examine him without protest.

He was a young man, thin but muscular. His whole body was filthy and his hands, knees, and arms were calloused and covered in cuts and scratches. I took a deep breath as I dipped a cloth in the water and prepared to wash his wound, a gunshot to the shoulder.

"Now what's your story?" I wondered as I dabbed at the caked blood.

The bullet was still inside him and I decided to take it out there and then. I had once extracted a bullet from Johannes after one of the skirmishes and I knew what to do.

The black man came to and gasped in pain as I pulled it out. He surprised me by the strength of his grip as he grabbed my wrist, forcing me to look him in the eyes. We saw into each other souls then, native and foreigner. I felt hollow, like I had intruded on his judgement with God. He knew that I had seen his death.

I began to wash the rest of the blood and dust and grime from him. When I got to his legs I saw he had a bloodied bandage wrapped around another wound. As gently as I could, I unwound the dressing. This time it was a gash, not a gunshot, as if he'd been slashed by a knife. But there was a large lump under the skin and as I probed at the wound my mouth fell open in shock.

My mind flew to Johannes.

The man groaned and started to shiver. I stared at the jewel nestled in the ruby pouch of his blood and muscle. I reached in and plucked it out.

I dressed his wound, wrapped him in blankets and kept vigil through the night. But the day's toil had taken its toll and I fell asleep. When I awoke, he was dead.

As I buried him, I hoped to God that Johannes would come home safely from Kimberley. He would know what to do with the huge diamond that my poacher friend had smuggled out of the mines.

A Steady Drip

Martha Patterson

Martha is a much-produced and oft-published playwright and fiction writer whose work has been produced in 20 US states and eight countries. Her work has been published by the *Sheepshead Review*, *Silver Birch Press*, *Pioneer Drama Service Book*, *Applause Theatre & Cinema Books*, and the *Afro-Hispanic Review*. She has a B.A. from Mt. Holyoke and an M.A. from Emerson College, and lives in Boston, Massachusetts, the USA.

A Steady Drip

Why hadn't she heard the buzzer? She kept missing deliveries and had to walk to the Post Office to get packages she'd missed when the delivery guy came.

She'd ordered a copy of James Joyce's *The Dubliners* for her friend Sue Ellen's birthday party last night—Sue Ellen had almost miraculously, from Joan's point of view, managed to get through *Ulysses*, but unaccountably—also from Joan's point of view—had never read Joyce's collection of short stories. Sue Ellen had celebrated her 50th birthday. She was the same age as Joan.

Now, a day later, sitting in the hospital with the I.V.—she was getting infusions for rheumatoid arthritis she'd recently developed—she'd been nearly unable to walk when it started, but her condition had improved—Joan blamed herself for being late with a gift.

It started when Nicholas dropped by two evenings ago. They'd had six dates. They'd met online and he lived nearby—and he'd spent the night. She liked him; he was gentle and kind, and, unlike her last boyfriend, didn't talk too much.

But they didn't have sex. Instead, they spoke in a friendly way about how their relationship didn't seem to be progressing and they played Scrabble.

Nicholas won—he had a gift for remembering obscure words, which Joan didn't—she always spelled out the first word that came to her when she played Scrabble. Her family hadn't played board games competitively, but Nicholas said his family had.

Afterwards, Nicholas curled up next to her in bed—they kept their clothes on—but he made no moves. He had tried to once before, clumsily, and she'd rejected him. Nicholas wasn't offended. He said to her, "Women don't go for me. One of them called me effeminate."

In the morning Joan poured juice and coffee and served Nicholas a croissant. They talked again about how nothing was "happening" between them.

"I'm not an asshole," Nicholas said.

"I know. I know you're a nice person. But it's not enough."

"Am I really effeminate?" he asked.

"No," she lied. "It's not that."

But she thought that he was indeed too "soft", had a feminine-sounding voice—clearly he wasn't gay, though—and he acted too timid. Even his clothes bugged her—he wore badly-fitting jeans, too short, and the corduroy shirt he wore that night was laced up the front with a suede thong. It looked like something his mother had bought him.

"I'm sorry," she lied again. "I just don't want to be with any man right now."

"Are you mad I beat you at Scrabble?" He smiled. He was too forgiving and accommodating, she thought. Most men would have tried to kiss her anyway, or otherwise convince her they were worth having.

"Of course not."

He finished his breakfast and left, but not before she told him she liked having him spend the night. She said it made her feel protected, hoping he would "man up" next time and act more macho.

But this was why she hadn't heard the buzzer—because she and Nicholas were eating breakfast with Enya playing on the CD player, and the music drowned out the delivery guy's ring.

So she'd been late with James Joyce for Sue Ellen's birthday. Her friend had shown disappointment last night when Joan brought no gift, though Joan apologized.

She sighed and gazed at the silent TV in the hospital room while the I.V. in her arm dripped. She squinted at the scrawl of dialogue that flashed at the bottom of the screen and couldn't have been less interested in the soap opera. Her own life seemed like a soap opera. She was late with a birthday gift, her would-be lover would never be attractive enough or good enough in bed, and she had an auto immune disorder that required regular medical visits. She sighed. Could Nicholas be turned into a real boyfriend? Maybe, with sympathy and coaching and encouragement. Was it even worth trying? She looked at the skinny tube attached to her arm and wondered at modern medicine. The infusion bag suspended above her head was almost empty and soon she'd be able to leave the hospital and pick up her package at the Post Office.

But right now her life seemed like a steady drip.

The Farmer's Task

Deline Skinner

Deline lives in the southern reaches of Victoria, Australia. She enjoys her unruly garden, and nurturing her expanding patches of indigenous wallaby grass. Time spent walking, tree planting, weeding, exploring, reading and patting her big old Labrador allows for ideas to flow into, and sometimes out of, her head. Magpies make her smile, the smell of a flowing river excites her, as do bushlands, bridges, tunnels, trees and windmills. She writes on a variety of subjects, in varied styles and to varied audiences, even the occasional hand-written letter. She has written a history booklet, *Seventy Somers*, been published in *Balnarring Highways and Byways* and *Somers Paper Nautilus*. She dabbles in short stories, children's writing, verse novels, poetry, essays and other pieces that jog her interest. She is establishing a blog that will be an outlet and motivation to share her words and thoughts.

delineclayre.com

The Farmer's Task

He throws his grubby old hat on the hook by the door. A tail thumps on the wooden floor. Old Woman looks up red-eyed from where she sits next to Old Dog.

Old Man bends to pat the dog.

"How's it goin' mate?" he says stroking the head, the fur, his friend.

"No better eh?" farmer says, knowing.

The kitchen is filled with the smell of dinner simmering on the wood stove. Old Man washes his hands and they sit by Old Dog and look at their plates in silence. Old Dog has not eaten for two days, has lapped at some water. Old Dog sighs as they pick at their dinner.

They put the television on, not to watch but to fill the silence, each in their own thoughts. The night passes.

Old Woman prepares for bed. Flannel nightie, long and worn, soft and comfy. She bends to kiss her husband.

"I'll leave you with him, Love."

Old Woman turns in bed, hearing Old Dog and her old man sighing, breathing, sharing whimpers.

Magpies chortle the dawn in, and the cocky's screech brings her from sleep. She's surprised she has slept. She comes in to the kitchen, stokes the fire and draws the kettle to the hot plate.

"He asked me last night," Old Man whispers.

She places a cup of tea next to her husband, kisses him on the head, bending to pat Old Dog.

"Well, I guess it is time then," she says softly. And swallows.

Old Dog's face follows the farmer as he heads to the door. No longer seeing, but knowing. The backdoor creaks open, bangs shut. Old Dog tries to rise, to follow his man to the paddocks as he has for over eighteen years. He whimpers, lays his head on his paws, his long nails scratch on the floor.

She hears the shed door open, the rattle of hand tools as he chooses. "Do you want me to help?" she calls

"Nah, you stay with him."

Under the big old gum, the one under which he'd had lunch with his mate and the missus many times, he sighed and stabbed at the earth, foot pushing the spade through the compacted soil.

Ravens moan while magpies chortle softly.

She has an old sheet bundled up when the backdoor creaks open. Grief already hangs in the air. Old Man picks up Old Dog, so heavy, and pushes the door open with his back. Old Woman walks beside him, feet heavy, and lays the sheet beside the hole. She stands like a soldier, watching her husband bend, rifle erect beside her. A small glance to each other, click from the bolt, then the sound, loud, reverberates between them.

They fold two corners over Old Dog. They lower him as gently as they can into the grave while a raven's slow cry croaks out above them. Then silence fills the yard.

Liberty

Ruairi Murphy

Ruairi Murphy is a librarian and writer based in Hobart. In 2017, he was shortlisted for the Tasmanian Premier's literary prize in the category of unpublished manuscript and was a finalist in the Tasmanian writer's prize. His fiction has appeared in magazines and anthologies, most notably the 2017 anthology 'Seven Stories'.

In his writing, Ruairi likes to explore themes around identity, memory, and the boundaries between human and animal.

Liberty

Hobart Town, May 27, 1832

My dearest Rebecca,

I write to inform you that the life arranged for me out here in the colony has come apart. My employment as governess at Brinley House ended last year when Mrs Chester used her dressmaker scissors to shred my underwear and nightgowns, the tatters of which she let flutter from the second storey window of the servants' quarters. As the rest of my belongings followed to the French garden below, Mr Chester remained in the sitting room, reading 'Around the world in eighty days'. He had described the first half of the plot to me the previous week while defiling me behind the nursery screen. Such was the frequency of this act and his diminished ability to crest with only a few thrusts, he had taken to talking, first from the gutter, then about anything that alighted on his mind. I have since learned that this is not uncommon in high-born men.

We had finally been caught by Charles, the eldest of his two sons, a soft-headed boy who unbeknownst to us had been watching from within the adjacent closet. He had, however, been doing more than just watching, and his own vigorous attentions to himself caused him to spill from the door and onto the hardwood floor before us. We all momentarily joined the surrounding wax dolls in a state of frozen stupor, before father and son engaged in a frantic race to see who might button their breeches the quicker. A comical end to my time at their estate, but one which yielded two important lessons: in the world of men, my body is worth far more than my mind; and it is possible to entertain two paying clients in concert while servicing only one.

There is no way to dress up the harshness of living with the houseless poor. The anti-vagrancy laws that you and I once championed so that our walks through London might be free from harassment by these piles of rags led me, for a time, to become nocturnal. I slept during the day, always upright and always in churchyards, and tramped at night, gathering with other vagrants on the flags by bakery ovens or in doorways, or any place that afforded the slightest warmth or reprieve from the wind. What little I ate came from charity, either from the Salvation Army or a cripple who grew apples on the side of Mount Wellington. If the cripple was flush with apples and in a pitying mood, he would gift me a bag, which I would keep hidden in the hollow of a dead tree and make last the week. His kindness, while begrudging at times, is a reminder to me that the most generous among us are often those with the least to give.

For a time I lived at a workhouse, seated alongside other ruined women as we unpicked strands of old rope for use in shipbuilding, our nails cracked and broken and the tips of our fingers cleaved with cuts that tore afresh each day. Rather than push through that bright pain until my skin hardened to stone and my touch became like glass paper, I left and took work at a rag factory. The work was easier and I minded neither the flea- and lice-ridden rags nor the rats that moved freely among our feet as we sorted. But fourteen hours a day of this toil bought only a crowded sleep in the cheapest lodgings and a thin broth of potatoes and cabbage poured over stale bread. For man and woman alike, to live this daily life is to live like the bull tethered to the cart, only with a mind capable of music and art and a body not a tenth as strong.

After fewer than four months on different industrial lines, I fell into a paralytic melancholy, resistant even to the goading of a police truncheon. Disease quickly followed, the tilt in my equilibrium leaving me without defence against the miasma that lies heavy and unabated over inner Hobart Town. Here is yet another burden borne by the wretched poor; with humours already frail, they must endure their factories and their shanties backing onto a putrid soup of discharge and dead animals, an open sewer officials have the indifferent affront to call a rivulet.

Having no home at which to receive treatment, I was admitted to the fever ward of a charity hospital. There I lay alongside a rotation of other poor souls, each of us writhing in damp sheets and crying out against the ghosts of our personal delirium. Amid the nuns' constant murmur of prayer, we coughed down meadowsweet and powdered rhubarb and breathed in the spirits of ammonia, lavender and camphor that burned on every shelf and whose smoke hung in the air as a thick haze. Whether by the grace of God or a constitution strong enough to survive the disease as well as its remedy, I endured, and was eventually moved to a recovery room while the remaining impurities resolved themselves.

It was a curious reawakening for me. I had long-since resigned myself to following my personal belongings into the fire pit that burned day and night at the far edge of the hospital's estate. I had not seen this pit, but it had been described to me by the boy who changed our bedpans, who always spoke through a cloth soaked in vinegar that he pressed over his mouth and nose. Many times my mind had taken the trip across the sodden field and over the stone lip into the glowing pit below, and while ultimately free of that fate, I still felt as if I had actually passed through the fire, before rising, like the phoenix, reborn. When next I gave my name, it was one befitting of the new life I had resolved to now lead: Liberty.

One can, of course, live as freely as one wishes within one's mind, but to do so outside requires money, or at least the means to obtain it. I held little hope that my education would bring prosperity, at least not directly; even had I been an attached woman with a respected name and good references, my education would have still only been prized as a tool for polite conversation, little more than a pretty dress worn to signify that I was a proper little representative of my husband. And so if it was to once again be the labours of my body by which I might earn my independence, I no longer saw any reason not to sell it to the highest bidder. Propriety is merely the stick with which the moneyed thrash the poor, a fancy cane they hold forever above our heads lest we be allowed to raise them long enough to see that the only true path from poverty is through the wages of sin.

My first few nights on the streets, I only watched the other women work; or rather I discreetly observed, with varying degrees of success, their movements, their mannerisms, and their interactions with those who approached them. They were largely confined to the Wapping district, an unimaginative name for the waterfront area north of the docks whose concentration and collusion of pubs, hotels, brothels, and gambling houses mark it as the city's unofficial capital of entertainment and vice. The women rarely spoke to clients and almost never to each other; their language was instead one of subtle shifts in poses and lengthening of glances. And while the police were quick to move on any who strayed too far from the shadowy laneways, their temporary banishment from public view was no different to the treatment of any vagrant. All in all, they practiced their trade with impunity.

To my initial dismay, however, this open license, in company with the fact that so many of this island's women are convicts on unpaid assignment work, meant that Wapping was flush with prostitutes. Age was no barrier, women of sixty worked alongside girls no older than twelve, and neither did appearance seem to hinder one's prospects, the very pretty enjoying little if any more success over the plain. It was clear that to compete with these women I would have to distinguish myself in some other way, beginning, I thought, with location.

It was always my intention to try to find work in one of the brothels; not only did I believe myself incapable of wresting payment from a dishonourable sailor, but I had already proved myself especially vulnerable to cold and foul air, chief among the latter in Wapping the whale oil that lies atop the harbour water thick as pus atop a wound, a horrific stench not only tolerated but openly celebrated as the smell of Hobart Town's success.

I approached six brothels, the madam of each content to give me a room within the week. This auspicious beginning I took as proof of my possessing qualities hitherto unknown to me, until informed by the lady of seventh house that turnover was high because of rampant venereal disease. I was taken aback by this, aware that my new profession would put me in the path of syphilis and gonorrhoea and thus almost certainly render me infertile, but wholly unprepared that I might encounter these diseases with such frequency as to risk progressing to their late stages, whereupon I would almost certainly surrender to wasting and paralysis of body and mind. It was largely this fear that led me to choose a house frequented by a medical student, a young Irishman of meticulous observation and note-taking, who, while charging a small fee and unashamedly experimenting on us as he might caged rodents, distinguished himself by never passing judgment on us and, most crucially, exercising the faculty to prefer iodine over mercury.

That desire had thus far not once played any part in my intimacy with men might have made it easier for me to adapt to the idea of fornication as currency. This is perhaps to unnecessarily preface my saying that what I did inside those brothel rooms was work, no more or less.

At first I was frightened of being alone with a man, but they are generally not the beasts society or even they would have you believe. Disarmed of clothes and the gaze of others, most become shy and gentle, requesting to be held long after the act, sometimes even in place of it. In close company with these men are those who relinquish all control in the bedroom, whose insistence on handing over the reins of power and dominance is a perverse but no less welcome departure from the female subservience that otherwise pervades every part of our culture. Unpleasant men abound, of course, but when faced with them I merely reminded myself that it wouldn't take long, and should that unpleasantness turn violent it was within our rights to scream, whereupon our sitter, another Irishman, this one with arms like a ship's oars, had permission to throw the offending animal out on the street without restitution.

I remained in the brothel through autumn and winter and near the end of spring, when quite suddenly our madam was expelled, the reason for which was never disclosed to us. Profit became the likely motive, however, when her replacement immediately forbade the medical student from visiting and dismissed our sitter; this in addition to a new policy of ongoing expulsion of girls for minor indiscretions and the active discouragement of any kind of friendship among those of us that remained, all presumably done on the basis that steady turnover of girls and competition between us drew more clients. I could have moved to another brothel, but my mind had by that time already settled on a different course, one that involved neither the streets nor surrendering half my earnings before I had even laid eyes on a client.

There was also Lulu. Several months before our change in management a black girl named Lulu briefly roomed with us. Lulu was from India but when we paraded before men she would dress only in a leopard-skin loincloth and hold erect beside her a great spear, a genuine assegai whose shaft reached almost to the ceiling. Rarely was she not the first chosen, even fought over, and her popularity quickly led her to be bullied from the brothel by those girls whose business she had near defeated. Lulu's experience taught me a valuable lesson: with a little initiative one can climb high in this profession, but only if one remains out of reach of those who would tear them down.

Since that time, I saved more aggressively, darning my clothes until they resembled patch-work quilts and eating again as the vagrant does, little and infrequently. When finally the brothel expelled me, I had enough money to rent a mud and brick hut on the edge of Battery Point, an area increasingly popular with the mercantile classes. I also rented a sewing machine, ostensibly to join the sweated industries to do needlework for a penny an hour, but actually as a means of allowing men to visit, beginning with those with whom I had enjoyed regular and respectful contact at the brothel.

It is from this hut, a dilapidated dwelling but one nonetheless closed to the elements and prying eyes, that I now write to you. I have a client arriving in a few minutes. Each man must bring and take with him a bag of clothes, and I encourage them to include garments they wish for me to wear. While I have not yet dressed as a savage, I have reprised many times my role as a governess, a pleasing reminder to me of just how far I've come since Brinley House and the Chesters.

That's my client at the door now; a banker, a fastidious man whose mind undresses along with his body, leading him to divulge to me the most terrible secrets about himself. He knows to wait, but I'm afraid I must be quick now and close this letter to you.

My dear sister, I want you to know that I am happy. I still must visit the doctor each week and be ever vigilant not to draw the attention of the actual police as well as God's police, those prim wives who would seek to rescue me back to poverty. But I am warm and gaining weight. Surrounding me are several nice things and I am saving well. Next Spring, I believe I may travel.

This island at the bottom of the world is not the open-air prison we imagined. While it aspires in so many ways to be Britain's beloved child, there is almost none of the class-consciousness of home that indelibly shackles one to their roots. Instead, Van Diemen's Land is a place of opportunity, of re-invention, of rebirth. Under its auspices, that frightened and defenceless girl to whom you waved goodbye on the docks last year has graduated to become a brave and independent woman, one who knows now with absolute certainty that the autonomous life, no matter how difficult, is the only kind worth living.

Have the goodness to write to me. I shall be glad to hear from you if it is but one line to know whether you received this letter.

I remain your ever-loving sister,

Liberty

A Letter an Email

James Hannan

James Hannan is a Victorian-based writer of short fiction. His work has appeared in *Styluslit* (styluslit.com/), *Prole* (www.prolebooks.co.uk/), *Literally Stories* (literallystories2014.com/), *Braindrip* (braind.rip/), and the *Wild Goose.*

A Letter an Email

"Well, when you look at it, when people are in groups of friends, there is always going to be a risk of someone going on," Cath said.

She never should have told the truth. It wasn't like what she did was earth shattering or anything but Ben, like the child he was, hid out of sight over on the other side of the bedroom, next to the dresser, in the space where the door swung open. It was like he was guarding the entrance to the room. It was weird and Cath couldn't work it out, but she couldn't stop thinking about opening the door, swinging the wood onto his legs; at least then he would have to get up and face her.

"When you look at it? When you look at what? What the fuck are you talking about?" he said. It was such a Ben comment.

"Well," Cath responded, starting to get cranky, "I didn't mean it to happen but it did. I mean, after the party, you were off having one of your moods and he was still here. It was really late, everyone else had gone and you hadn't come back. I don't know, we were drunk."

"We were drunk," she said again like Ben might not have heard. "Nothing happened."

He was forcing her to relive that night with another of his little moods. Typical. His moods were what started the whole thing in the first place. She had a fair bit to drink but she wasn't pissed. She had tripped over, spilling her drink on one of Ben's friends. Ben got the shits. He didn't say anything but she could tell: he wouldn't look at her, talk to her, and if she came up to him, he feigned being interested in something else, ignoring her. Then he took off. Well, at least she thought he did.

It must have been about two in the morning that everyone started to leave but Brent was still there. They started talking, just drunk talk, silly stuff. Then something was funny, she couldn't remember what it was now, and they both started laughing. Then for some reason she had something and he was trying to get something from her but she wouldn't let him have it. She held it behind her and fought off his attempts to get it. They couldn't stop laughing and somehow they started wrestling and then he had his arms around her.

"I mean, he passed out so nothing could have happened anyway." Oh, why did she say that?

Cath imagined Ben picking at his nails. She couldn't hear it but she was sure he was. He would be slouched too, his shoulders wedged against the wall, his bum against the floor as his thin torso sagged toward the floor. He would have his head on its side, seemingly disjointed to the rest of his body. It was his standard look and he was good at it.

"So, what you're really saying is that if he hadn't passed out, you would've fucked him, right?" Ben snapped out suddenly.

Cath inhaled sharply.

"No, if we hadn't been drunk and you hadn't been off somewhere sulking like a child, we wouldn't have been in that situation in the first place," she said.

She could have ripped up the sheets on the bed. She could have smashed the window. She wanted to yell at him, stomp on his toe, get the vase and smash it on the floor.

"But didn't you just say stuff will always happen when people are in groups of friends?" he said.

Cath inhaled again.

"Look, can't we get over this? It was just a fucking drunken kiss," she said.

BANG! Ben hit the dresser with what seemed all his might. It scared her but she yelled back, "Grow up will you, you child."

She thought back to last weekend. Ben must have come home and found her and Brent asleep on the couch together. Brent wasn't there when she woke up but he must have seen something because now, a couple of days since that night, he suddenly wanted to know what happened. She could have got away with saying that they were just talking and then they both fell asleep, drunk, and that would have been that. She was sure they weren't draped over each other or anything like that. Even so, she wanted to tell the truth; she didn't want to lie to him.

Ben seemed really nice about it at the start. He seemed to accept her story that they just happened to be alone together and because of the drink had forgotten themselves for a minute. It didn't last long. He started to get moody, and that's when the questions began. How long did they kiss for? What was it like? Did he touch her? Cath found herself in tears but it didn't stop him asking more and more. Did she kiss him back? Did they do anything else? Did she like it?

It was a just a kiss, that was all it was. She wasn't going to sleep with one of his friends. She wasn't like that. She wasn't.

"Well, what are we going to do, then?" Cath said breaking the silence.

"What do mean?" he said straight back to her.

"Well, we can get over this can't we?"

"There's no *we* anymore," he said.

"What's that supposed to mean?" she said.

"What do you think?" Ben said.

"Right." Cath said, a little confused.

Next to the bed on the side table were the remnants of the morning's breakfast. Like most mornings, she drank coffee and ate toast in bed, waiting for him to stir. Before she met him she had never eaten breakfast in bed, but since he had moved in she wanted to be close to him as he would sleep long and loud, grunting and snoring. Mornings were her favourite part of the day. She liked the patterns on the walls and ceiling of the room as light bounced off glasses, belts, plates and other things lying around the room. She liked the way he would wake and find his way over to her; sliding his hands around her body, between her legs, his lips caressing the back of her neck, his body nestling around hers, enveloping her. Sometimes she would find herself underneath him, sometimes on top. Most times she couldn't remember how it went; it never seemed to matter. It mattered this morning. He wanted to be behind her, he wanted to push her face away from him.

***

The sun was overhead and the morning almost over. She felt the air in the room starting to go stale: her teeth weren't clean; she was still in her bedclothes. Ben sat still. It was hard to work out what he was doing or trying to do.

"I think I am going to move out for a while," he said suddenly.

Cath didn't believe him. "What's wrong with you?" she blurted out. "It was only a drunken kiss, nothing happened. Get it? Nothing." This comment echoed around for a moment and then died.

Suddenly he appeared from behind the dresser, standing and putting his hand on the latch of the door.

"Where are you going?" she asked reflexively. Again he ignored her.

"You can't leave." she said. The desperate tone in her voice made him stop, momentarily. She ran to him, throwing her arms around him, squeezing him tightly.

"Don't go," she said sweetly.

"Can you let go of me now?" he said. She felt contagious and released him. He walked out.

***

Ben turned up at what was his and Cath's house. He paused before going through the gate. The front was the same, still overgrown grass in the yard with the Boston ivy turning red now that winter was coming on. Ben took his keys out of his pocket and strode to the front door. The garbage and recycling still hadn't been put out. Oh well, he thought, not his problem now. Entering, he checked for signs of life, looking in the two front rooms they used for a bedroom and study. She didn't seem to be home.

He went into the bedroom and began packing a bag. After a few minutes he heard Cath's familiar step coming from the back of the house. She was home. Walking in and seeing him she tensed, smiling crookedly.

"G'day," she said.

"Hi," he said, but wished he hadn't. He turned his back on her.

He tried to focus on what he was doing but she was dressed only in a towel. It made him uncomfortable. She went behind him to the dresser, about a metre away. He heard the drawer squeak as it slid open. He heard clothes thrown on the bed. He heard the towel drop to the floor. He kept packing. When he had finished, he turned and headed for the door.

"Um," she said, "before you go, I've got something for you." Ben turned but didn't look at her. She handed him a letter. He took it but scrunched it into his back pocket and turned again to leave.

"Can you please look at me, please." she said.

Ben tried hard to act like he'd hardly heard her and kept moving.

"Ben, talk to me, will you? I still love you, can't you see that, can't you see that you're giving up on one of the most special things that could ever happen between two people?" Her little speech made Ben quiver inside. He hoped to God that she didn't see it.

"Yeah," he said, still not looking at her, "it was pretty special."

"Yeah," he continued, "it was pretty special realising you were with someone else." Ben said almost losing his cool. Cath's mouth dropped.

"And it's sooooo special now that I think about all of the other guys you must have been fucking along the way, I mean *when you look at it* that's what you were doing, weren't you?" Cath slumped onto the bed. Ben left.

Back at Tom's, Ben took Cath's crumpled letter—trust her to write a letter—out of his back pocket.

My dearest Ben,

I know I have hurt you deeply and I also know that you may never get over what happened and things might not ever be the same again between us.

Oh, how pathetic can she get? He threw the letter on the coffee table in front of him. He got up and turned the telly on. Slouching back in the couch a few minutes passed and then the news came on. Ben flicked from one channel to another. Nothing on the box caught his attention but the letter still sat there in front of him. He picked it up and looked at it. She had written on both sides, her huge sloping running writing left hardly a blank space on the page. Without even thinking about it he was reading again.

This is something that I will always regret. I will regret that look on your face that morning when I told you what happened. That look is forever etched in my mind. I will also regret the anger that I have caused you. But I wish you would come back to me, I wish you would share our bed, even if we are still working things out. At least you will be here and at least I can try to make you happy again. It's funny, it's only been a couple of days but already it feels like years. I miss you so much.

You might not believe it but I consider you one of the most amazing people I know. If anyone can see that I did not plan to do what I did and have committed a terrible mistake I know it will be you.

I've thought how you must be hurting and how angry you must be. But then I also thought that you, of all people, would see the truth and be able to understand that sometimes people make mistakes that are silly and they wish they could get back.

When you come back to me, I know that we can be happy and that I can make you happy, like before. I keep thinking about when we first moved into our little house and that day when you kept running up the hall coming to kiss me and then back down again to watch the cricket. And then that one time when you ran up the hall I made you stay. The way you kissed me that day inspires me to write you this letter today and makes me hope that soon you will forgive and come back to me.

Yours forever,

Cath.

Ben shivered, screwed up the sheet of paper and threw it in the bin. He looked at the ceiling as the television crackled in the background.

***

It was Sunday and Ben parked the rented ute outside Cath's place. The day was grey, cold and windy. Winter felt like it had set in already.

"So, you ready for this?" Tom said, with a wry smile from the passenger's seat.

"That's why you're here, mate." Ben shot back.

"Okay then, let's get it over with," Ben said taking the keys out of the ignition and opening his door.

Entering the front door to the house, Cath was in the living room, reading. He hated her in that pose, seated perfectly upright with the bookcase directly behind her. She could sit there for hours, cooing, sighing, exclaiming quietly to herself about some dumb book she was reading, about how soooo well written it was.

"Oh, hello," she said. Ben had the distinct feeling that she must have been sitting there for ages waiting for them.

"Hello," said Tom from behind.

"Let's start in here," Ben said to Tom going into the study.

Ben and Tom got to work. An hour passed as Tom helped Ben move his stuff out of the house and onto the back of the truck. Cath went out and when she came back, locked herself in the bedroom. Maybe she was over him, Ben thought.

It was late afternoon and Ben and Tom had just come back for the last load. They got the last pieces loaded and Tom was going out the door when Ben suddenly said, "I am just going to be a minute." Tom shrugged his shoulders and went outside.

Ben went to the bedroom. Going inside, Cath lay on the bed, reading. He stood there for a moment looking at her.

"Here's the key," he said.

"Is this what you really want?" she asked. "What?" He said, disinterested, looking away.

"Is this what you really want? Do you really want to move out? Aren't you over reacting just a little bit?" Cath said.

"Not really," Ben said.

"Okay then." She said back, going back to her book.

He turned to go but as he did she stood up and said. "Look, don't go. You've made your point, you've made me feel like shit, you've made me miserable and maybe I deserved it but really what I did is no good reason for you to move out, for us to end," she said, starting to cry.

Ben just stood there and then started moving again for the door.

"Fuck! Will you not do this? Please stay, please. Jesus Christ, what do I have to do?" She said, bawling. Ben walked into doorway, where Tom had just walked into the house. He must have heard everything.

Ben stood in the doorway to the bedroom for a moment before he said, "Let's go before my slut of an ex-girlfriend goes into hysterics."

When they got back to the car Tom looked over at Ben.

"You're a real arsehole, you know that, don't you?" he said.

"Shut up man. Anyway, she deserves it," Ben said.

That evening, Ben got an email. It was from Cath. He clicked on it, so it wouldn't show up as unread, then he clicked away again. He wasn't in the mood for dealing with her shit. Every so often as he would trawl back through his messages, he would see it, think about reading it but then move on.

About three months after Ben had moved into Tom's house, he moved out again and had to apply for a new place. He was scrolling through old emails looking for rental references. Then he thought he would search under Cath's name. The email she had sent on the day he had moved out popped up first in the feed.

He looked at it, unsure of what to do next. He was tired of packing his things so he sat down and opened the email. After months of avoiding Cath, he was looking forward to reading what he was sure would be another stupid piece of her writing. He slouched forward, putting his elbows on knees, holding his phone out in front.

Ben,

I have tried to write this a thousand times and I still find myself, against all my best intentions, saying the same thing: I guess this is how it's going to be.

Ben, I thought you were a good person. I believed in you. I thought I could trust you with my hopes and dreams, I even thought of you as the future father of my children. But somewhere along the way things got messed up and I got to know the true you. I'm glad.

It's funny because I know heaps of couples that have had bad times and even, god forbid, have lived through infidelity. I don't think though, any of these people who have been through hard times in a relationship have been as cruel as you. Sometimes I think you're doing what you're doing because you never really loved me. Other times, I thought you're just being cruel to me because that's what you needed to do to get over what happened. But after today, I couldn't care less what's going on with you or that you will never forgive me. I will never forget what you said or how you said it. I never thought that you could be such an arsehole. I know I did a drunk and perhaps stupid thing but what you have done is much worse.

I know now that things do happen for a reason and even though I have endured considerable pain, I know that I had to go out with you to learn what a real bastard looks like. Before I went out with you I had fairly good relationships that ended because of one reason or the other. With you it was love. But I guess it goes to show that you can be in love with someone who is not only cruel but someone who is sadistically cruel, hurting others because he likes it. I don't know whether it's because you're stupid, or it's because you have low self-esteem or something but whatever it is you need to see someone.

I firmly believe now that if I didn't get drunk that night and end up kissing Brent my life would with you have turned out to be horrible. It may have taken a month, it may have taken a year but the true you—heartless, stupid and cruel—would have eventually come out. You have broken my heart but, strangely enough, I am glad. And with my eyes wide open I can say in all honesty that I hope I never see you again.

Cath.

Ben was silent for a couple of minutes, deep in thought. Then, he laughed.

Tai Ringal's Tale

Jeremy Gadd

Jeremy Gadd has published fifty short stories in periodicals and literary magazines (several of which have won competitions, such as the Billy Blue Magazine/John Clemenger Advertising Short Story Competition and the inaugural Refugee Week Short Story Competition).

A selection of eight previously published short stories, titled Country, was published by Ginninderra Press (Canberra) in 2008 and a selection of fifteen previously published short stories, titled Under Centauri, by Anaphora Literary Press (USA) in 2013. He has also published two novels (Escaping the Triad—a novel for young adults, Holy Angels Publishing, Melbourne, 1998 (2nd print and online edition Custom Books, Hong Kong, 2013) and The Suicide Season—a novel published by Moon Willow Press (Canada), 2015, reprinted Stormbird Press (Australia) 2019. He has also published several volumes of poetry.

Tai Ringal's Tale

Tai Ringal chased the melon flavoured mouldy men from the uncharted wastelands of head, and when they returned, reinforced, advancing out of the peripheral gloom, jackboots jogging in the night, dragged on taut leashes by baying hounds, taunted in turns by crying sores, he let go of the reins of sleep and slipped lightly from the saddle, leaving his nightmare to canter blindly ahead. He woke, and waking was a solitary moment. His eyes, like shuttered Venetian blinds, clicked to open, and daylight washed into his mind; cleansing and soothing the putrescent zones of darkness that pricked and plagued him in the night. Tai Ringal welcomed the day. He welcomed the day because day brought light and outside seeing, and a momentary end to the horrors that happened in his head.

His eyes blinked, focussed, then grasped at and caught his elusive consciousness. He raised a hand and scratched at the itch that paddled with hob-shod feet between the stubble on his skull. He hiccoughed. The hiccough was followed by a yawn as Tai Ringal eased himself into the luxury of the day's first muscle-flexing stretch. A stretch cut short by a length of rope. The rope was knotted at one end to his wrist. It looped away. The other end was tied to a contraption, waiting patiently on the ground beside the loading dock where Tai Ringal had spent the night. Tai Ringal's right arm, above his hand, was chaffed red-raw where the rope had had gnawed at his skin as he tossed and turned in his sleep. Better to have a rope-burnt wrist than risk losing the cart to pilferers whilst asleep.

Some little boys had once taken his cart. They were short-trousered boys, boys in grey blazers armed with school satchels. He had been looking at an aquarium on display in a shop window, watching goldfish blowing bubbles at one another with puffed-out cheeks. The boys had snatched the cart while he was not looking. His nose had been pressed flat against the glass. At first he thought they wanted to play games. He often played games with children, in the playgrounds and on the swings and slides and things. He Sometimes he gave them rides on his cart. There were too many boys. They had run around him, screaming and laughing and making horrible faces. They got underfoot. Tai Ringal had been knocked to the ground and then had to chase after them for city blocks. But they were faster and kept just ahead, teasing him, jeering and abusing him in boys' shrill voices that hurt his head, laughing at his funny shambling run.

"My cart! Give me back my cart! Please!" He had pleaded between hiccoughs.

When the boys were too far in front to see the pain etched on his face, they rested and waited for him to almost catch up; then ran further, spitting spiteful words and kicking his cart to urge him on. Tai Ringal had struggled on in his funny run until his thumping heart leapt with pain inside his chest and his scalded lungs almost burst. And when the blood pounded in his brain, he had fallen over his feet, exhausted, rubbing the skin from his palms. He again asked the boys to return his cart. The boys replied by throwing stones, while pedestrian passers-by had their boredom allayed by the scene; a break from the humdrum routine of their lives.

A rock gashed Tai Ringal's temple and he bled. The blood ran warm and welcome into the neck of his shirt, a crown of thorns about his hanging head. Perhaps frightened by the blood, the boys now left, emptying the cart's contents onto the street, leaving echoing taunts and lying school mottos. But most of all, Tai Ringal remembered the girl with the pimply face and tears in her eyes her who offered him her handkerchief. She dabbed at his bloody scalp as he stood agitated in the gutter, his ribs heaving, his eyes fixed on her face as he nervously hiccoughed. The girl helped him collect his possessions together. The crowd, subdued, almost silent, drew back and drifted away to their offices to search for lives lost in filing cabinet drawers and databases. But that all happened a long time ago thought Tai Ringal.

Tai Ringal plucked to one side the newspapers that had covered his body through the night, insulation from the dankness and dungeon-dew that precedes the creamy coming of the morning light. He swung his legs over the loading bay. Pausing for a moment with his weight resting on his forearms on the dock, he dropped the last few centimetres to the pavement. He checked his belongings with care: his cart, its contents, his coat and shoes—for holes and wear. Then, placing a grape-red fez on his bare and prickled head, he set off, trundling his cart in hobbling, wobbling, cobble-clanging gait, down the building-dwarfed lane that led into the awakening city to find breakfast and to get away from the loading bay and its stone-dead-end streets before the working men came.

Most mornings, Tai Ringal could be found prodding his life down a drain with the aid of a stick, or sorting through garbage bins in the down-town part of the city, in search of coins or peppermint sticks or something for his cart. This morning Tai Ringal was content. He had eaten a breakfast. Found by wafting with the early morning cooking smells until he discovered an aroma he liked. He had let his nose lead him through the backyards and lanes to a café kitchen door he then haunted, smelling the good smells that seeped from between the floor and door and through the keyhole. He was given a bowl of soup and a nugget of bread, earthy and black. He had eaten bread like that a long time ago. He remembered sometimes—whenever his head left him in peace. A remnant of the bread was now inside his fez, to eat later.

Tai Ringal wheeled his cart to the park. He loved the park. He loved the sounds made underfoot as he trud-trod along the park's pebble pathways. He loved the trees and their rusty wheezing in the wind, like asthma-ridden old men, each with a nameplate tacked to its bare bark breast. Name, rank and serial number only, mused Tai Ringal. And wondered where the thought had come from. Most of all Tai Ringal loved the park for its birds. There were hundreds of seagulls strutting to and fro on rolling sea-legs. The gulls chased each other, in and out among the slatted benches scattered about the grass: bench-boats loaded to the gunwales with sitting, slumbering, paper-reading cargo, floating on lawn seas. Central Park was also where the pigeons lived. All the pigeons in the city seemed to pass through the park. Tai Ringal thought it must have been fashionable to do so.

Tai Ringal took the lump of bread from his fez and broke it in two. He ate half himself, then chipped the uneaten half into a hundred pieces with his fingers and threw them one by one to the birds. The air around Tai Ringal grew dark as it filled with the heavy shapes of the pigeons. The birds whirred and clapped the air, cooing and clamouring for the dough he tossed to their demanding beaks. Tai Ringal saw their impatience and loved them. He knew some of the birds by name and he coaxed and clucked and cackled with them. Sometimes one or two of the pigeons he knew more intimately would sit upon his shoulders, and he would smile his lopsided smile and hiccough happily, telling them about the old country, what little he could remember. They in turn would tell him how much they liked his cart and how they admired the style with which he pushed it about the city. And they would perch on his fez to show their affection. The morning was eaten by the pigeons with the bread.

In the afternoon, Tai Ringal began to polish the cart in which his world lived. It wasn't an ordinary cart, like a wheelbarrow or a handcart or a sulky. It was a long steel toolbox, suspended at an angle between a pair of large pneumatic tyres. Inside the locked box, with his extra boots, beneath his spare shirt, Tai Ringal stored what he treasured above all else in the world. For all his years Tai Ringal had collected things. But he had only kept five. They represented a yardstick of life's worth.

Tai Ringal opened the box, took out his spare shirt and spread it on the grass. He did not often look at the objects. Only when his head hurt a lot and the sight of them lent him a peacefulness inside—or when he felt something was about to happen. He delved deep into the box and drew out a brown paper-bag. From the bag, he place in the centre of the shirt his talismans: a round brown opal that smelt of the earth; a sea-shell the shade of the sky; a gnarled stick of driftwood, shaped like the sea; a peacock's feather that trembled in the breeze, light as heaven and, lastly, his father's grey eye that cried to the sky for the soul of his long lost son. Tai Ringal rocked back and forwards on his knees, his hands gripped together in pleasure. He gazed in rapture at his joy, shining gladly in the sunlight. And he hiccoughed with glee to the clouds.

In the late afternoon, when the shadows of the office towers crept furtively into the park like Manhattan muggers skulking behind trees, in wait for five o'clock, Tai Ringal's head began to sing: a pleasant song at first; mermaids singing in a void of sea-thought, beckoning him further into his head. Tai Ringal wrapped his joy in his shirt and replaced it in his box. The singing swelled inside his skull, became high-pitched and resonant. His head filled with sound until it seemed unable to contain the volume within its confines. Tai Ringal began to tremble. His eyes showed white and grew wide. His skin grew cool and clammy. And then came the mouldy, mouldy men, in shapes of sour lime. Tai Ringal knew what to expect. They had toured through his head before. The singing changed to a chant that hurt as the mouldy men began their run. They ran in ranks four abreast, chanting the march-time for their slow-motion steps as their leper-like bodies shed flesh. And they ran and they ran, and they ran; hailing heels, toe-heel treading in the puerile pulp of his brain. Tai Ringal cried alone in his pain. He fled the park in his funny shambling run, consuming distance while pushing the cart with both hands. He ran through the chasms of the city streets, but the buildings were unsympathetic brick and concrete. The empty windows pulled their blinds and, through his mind's mist, two dark shapes loomed. He knew them from long ago. He knew he should stop and he did, saying 'no, no' to his run-will.

They stood arms folded, waiting. Tai Ringal shuffled uneasily on the pavement, warily watching their movements, shifting his weight from one heel-less, wire-laced shoe to the other. They did not move. They examined him. They noted he wore a tattered overcoat, once grey and now smoky brown from continual use as a groundsheet. It trailed its frayed hem on the ground. As if by request, in a whirly of wind, the coat flopped back to reveal a hunger thin ankle. His trousers reached only below the knee. His skin was the colour of factory funnel soot; grime a second sausage skin. And on his muddy cropped cranium sat a jaunty red fez with a long black tassel that swung. Tai Ringal's eyebrows twitched and he hiccoughed. The uniforms were smart. He had a uniform once with white webbing, brass buckles and a gun. But that was in another world, the other place inside his head. Then he heard the hounds bounding into his brain, their saliva seared lips curled back, speeding paws in film of red dust and stabbing lights flooded his mind.

"It hurts," Tai Ringal said.

They put Tai Ringal into a van and shoved his cart in after him. The ride was rough and Tai Ringal was thrown about inside, bruising his back and shoulders. The man sitting behind the steering wheel thought this amusing. He kept twisting around and peering through the wire-reinforced glass window to watch Tai

Ringal's discomfort, making the van swing around the corners so that Tai Ringal was flung by the momentum, striking the steel walls with great force. When they finally stopped, Tai Ringal was too slow in extricating himself from his cart on the floor of the van, so the men dragged them out, entwined together, and dropped them both to the road. Tai Ringal was then frog-marched into a foyer, held at either elbow, his feet out of touch with the floor. The men thought it amusing. As he climbed a flight of stairs, Tai Ringal was tripped from behind and he fell.

"You don't mind a little fun do you?" asked the uniform standing on the fingers of Tai Ringal's right hand.

When his legs were pulled beneath him on the stairs, he had cut his chin. Some blood dripped to the floor as they pressed him into an office and Tai Ringal tried to wipe it up with his sleeve. The lights felt hot and pulsated, making his head feel worse. Elsewhere the pain did not matter. Tai Ringal asked if the light could be taken away and, although he may have been mistaken, thought he heard the mouldy men laughing in reply. He was officially charged with vagrancy in the name of some God or queen.

The cart was wheeled in and the long steel box forced open, and the contents tipped on the floor. Tai Ringal watched grins crawl across their faces. The man who drove the van began to sift through his joys.

"One shirt, one pair of old boots," he recited, making an inventory of the contents of the box. "Three newspapers, evening edition; one brown rock, one stick of wood, one feather, one shell and one false eye."

Then he wrapped Tai Ringal's joy in the newspapers, stuffed the package into the waste bin and pressed it down with his boot.

"I don't think we need to keep that!" he remarked, and Tai Tingal's head exploded in agony, an opening bud, and the falling petals were trodden into the floor.

The man who had driven the van gripped Tai Ringal's neck and steered him from the room. He propelled Tai Ringal along a bewildering series of corridors, driving him as he drove the van. A cell was chosen at random. A barred door opened and Tai Ringal was hurled into the opposite wall. The impact of his collision with the muscle-bound far end of the cell sucked the breath from his frail body. He came to rest slumped against the wall. In the midst of a fit of hiccoughs, he cried for his now destroyed joy. Someone eased into the cell. His companion leant outside the cell door. A silhouette in Tai Ringal's night.

The mouldy men were everywhere. Tai Ringal could not believe they had finally cornered him. They moved around him in a semi-circle, with splayed, long, spidery legs and snow on the toes of their boots. One by one their molten faces spewed sickly grins, and they swayed and sang in unison, in perfect balance on the balls of their feet, moaning their mare-songs as they closed in. Tai Ringal could hear their hounds in the distance, their paws scrabbling on the polished surface as they savaged their way down the corridors of his mind. Coming closer. The hounds coming closer and closer. Tai Ringal found himself shouting over the din. Then a door burst asunder and the hounds and mouldy men were upon him. Somehow, through his torment, his nerve ends registered blows and the popping of bones and the shredding away of his flesh. As the queasy faces of the mouldy men melted and their laughter cracked and rang in his ears, Tai Ringal rose upon a rearing pain. He rose and rode towards the star-bright brilliance coming to greet and envelope him, smiling, for the pain in his head had ceased.

And his father's grey eye closed in its search for the long-lost soul of his son.

Fish Wounds

Arathy Asok

Arathy Asok's debut collection **Lady Jesus and Other Poems** is described by *Journal of Commonwealth Literature* as "Resistance poetry with a sharp edge" (2019, Vol. 54(4)). Her most recent work was the poetry installation titled **Word Me Out** that was showcased at the fifth edition of the South Indian Poetry Carnival at Pattambi, Kerala. She is a bilingual writer and was featured poet at *The Blue Nib Magazine* (Issue 37, Ireland). Her poems have appeared in national and international journals, in print and online (in *Samyukta, Poetry Chain, anti heroin chic, Poets in Nigeria, Blue Nib Magazine, Door is Ajar, Womaword Press* and *Culture Cult*). They are included in an Anthology called Native Petals, Nocturne and Iliyali (USA). Her short stories in Malayalam have appeared in *Madhyamam Weekly* and English short stories in *Rupture* (Pakistan), *Credo Espire* (USA) and have been translated to her mother tongue and published in *Indian Express Malayalam Online.*

Fish Wounds

I was named Scarlett.

I am dark oil and gnarled fingers.

I wait with the fishes in the morning heat rising to afternoon drowsiness.

The fish stink of me.

Touching the slippery body on the ice-cold wood, I touch again the flakes of his skin riding beneath my arm. I hear his hissing sound before he plunges into my silvery depths bursting night stars.

When I saw him first walking in with his hair afloat, I thought about the mischief in the curled lashes, the lips wanting to smile away the afternoon sun. I saw him talking to Gabrielle and Veronica and then shaking his head. I was sitting in the dark corner of the market. My fishes were almost sold. I thought he would not come around to me. He would not look at my fishes. He would not look at me. Inside me, deep inside me I willed him to turn and I willed him to turn. There was something molten gushing though my veins, slipping through my thighs. My sagging old thighs. And when he turned around to catch my eyes in the dim corner of the fish market, he must have seen the glint in them, for he stood looking into my eyes from the distance and for a second he stopped the sun from descending. The whole market was stunned to pink as the sun loomed down. His hair floated around him and his slender form swayed as he walked. Past all of them whose hands dropped out to call him, he walked towards me and I did not realize when he stood there, so very near, that his broken nose was seen in its brokenness. When he smiled, fresh green waters parted to clutch with force all the weeds that had gone astray.

"What do you have?" he said before he hunched before me. I could see the matted hair on his hand, the perfect hand.

"Sardines," I said.

"Oh but I can see prawns... what about them?"

"They are not for sale. It's to take home," I said. My voice does not shiver. I am as rough as you have seen me all these years. On my hands is the toil and the turf of the sea. My body is short, sturdy, and dark. I have flesh bulging out of my shoulders and my waist spreads around my hips. My face runs oil and my hair is a halo around my forehead.

"For whom?" he says before he gets up.

"To take home." I say. And I lift my eyes to his only to stare at his lips that were still asking me something. I see Veronica approaching though the corner of my eyes. I see her smiling at him in familiarity.

"I sold fish near his house. Newly married now, Scarlett. Wants to buy prawns for his wife. Give him some. Give him some." She reaches out her fingers to nudge him and he laughs aloud.

It is thunder.

It is thunder.

It is thunder I hear around me lashing in thick waves.

"How is she? Started going for work?", Veronica asks.

"Not yet. She's got a week's leave more. I've started though," he says.

"What work?" Veronica nudges him again. She has that lewd look in her eyes that I abhor. He looks at her in wonder as he has not understood what she said. Then it dawns on him and he smiles. It is a slow smile like a caress. It is a slow smile like the soft wind on my cheeks. He looks at her but he looks at me. He looks at the old breasts sagging inside my old white shirt. He looks at the bigness of it. I know he looks. I know he looks. Because I can feel heat there.

"The prawns are not for sale," I say roughly. "It is to take home".

"Scarlett, poor boy here waiting for your mercy. All the prawns are sold but yours. Don't take it home today or give him some from that. He is known to me. Here let me divide."

I thrust away her hands when she touches my prawns. I see the smile in his eyes. I have not looked up. But I will him to stay. I will him to stand there and go on talking to Veronica, to Gabriella, to someone. Only not to let him go. And then I feel his scent in my nose. Male scent like the lily flower at night. I break it to pieces before I open my mouth. He feeds into me. He feeds into me till I am full of him. As they part, when the candles light, I see that Veronica has moved away in anger. Gabriella has disappeared. He still stands there as if willing me to look. My face is defiant when I look up. But when my eyes meet his, I find them fixing in stupor; the endless ways I see open there. My breath is caught in my throat that has suddenly become parched. The whole market is drained of voices. There are only murmurs somewhere far away. When I stand up, my legs had drowned. A short old lady looking up at spring. I barely reach his waist. He has not touched me. He has not touched me. But he has enveloped me to his body, curling his eyelashes to my wide waist and hooking his slender fingers under my armpits. Before he dips into the night, he stoops to my ears in a whisper, "I shall come."

I feel my breath catch in my throat. I whisper back. "When?"

His finger runs on my lower lip and he says, "Day after tomorrow."

When he has floated away, I sit in the candle-lit darkness, my hands busy peeling the prawns. I knew he would come. I knew they would know. The world would curse me for the evil they knew I could do. He a young man and me an old woman. Grandmother of two. The elder girl of whom has come to stay with me for whom I am peeling the prawns. But when he comes, I shall make way. I shall take him to me. I shall swallow him alive so that he cannot leave me again. Because when he walked into the market that evening, he walked into me. He dug caverns in the valleys that I did not know existed. He took me in my oldness and heaviness to the star-clad mountains and he dipped me in the golden seas when the sun set. Newly married indeed. She would be the shell. I will be the flesh. The flesh he will chew and swallow. The flesh he will knead and taste. I am the flesh that will peel on him when he peels. I am the flesh. I am his. When he walked into the market he was mine. When I get up, I wipe my thighs with the roughened cloth I use for the fish. I smear myself in the fish smell because I could feel his lillyness. When I lift my fish basket and put the peeled prawns into my box, I try not to sweat. And when I walk home in the dark, I smile to myself because tonight he shall search for fins on her body, he shall slide his hands and not see any scales. And as she waits to scream, he shall walk away because he will be waiting for the day after tomorrow when I shall deliver him to the pearl oysters and the star fishes. When he shall smell fish in my pores and be witched.

In the night I cook the prawns for my granddaughter. She has cleaned the house before I came, made rice in the mud pot. I do not say anything as I sit on the wicker chair for a second before I go outside to take a bath. I do not let her see the smile that has come to my lips unbidden. I do not feel ashamed that I, the grand old dame feels what this girl now in her prime of youth should be feeling. Oh. I am young now. I float with the wind. The moonlight spills on me when I pour water under the naked sky. When I go inside, the photograph of my dead husband on the wall glares at me with all the hatred he felt for me during our days together. I remembered for a moment the struggle of what I left behind, the whicketty house I put my soul into, the days in which I wanted my children to stop feeling hunger pangs, when I wanted them to have a new piece of cloth rather than the torn and mended ones I could salvage, the days when I took them to the small school at the end of the road where they looked forward to the one meal they would get at noon, where the teachers scolded them for the old uniforms they wore and the torn books they had and the stub of the pencil they held. I then remember how I walk out of the house where he had not let me move, to strange houses to beg for work, the loads of clothes I washed, the loads of vessels I cleaned, the unending rooms I swept, the days and nights I toiled. My youth at his hands that hit me late into the nights and my body battered at his needs in the dawn. My swollen eyes that I tried to hide from prying eyes, my bruised lips and broken cheeks that I lowered my face with. And the days that rolled into months and years when he grew less important when I sat selling fish at the market, when I worked to make my children grow, to put them through what they would feel was life, to give them some words they could pass on to their children, to put little flesh into their bones, to marry them off. And then today. Today when one daughter is dead and the other happily married to a far away land, who I meet sometimes once in two years. The days now that are mine, who looks forward to the granddaughter who would come frequently to stay with me because I brought her up when her mother died young. Her father who was a good man who married again to beget more children and the wife who would spit fire at my granddaughter. The women staying around me in houses that look like match boxes, houses we have built with our own hands and sweat, women who have iron in their soul because they were molten by life. They who chatter aloud on the road as we walk. They who have struggled all their lives to struggle more at old age, who have known happiness like water drops at the desert and who light candles at night to close eyes in peace before him who is on the cross for them.

And tomorrow he shall come to this house on the sand and see me in glory. He shall see the tiny rooms divided by half walls and the small stove where we make rice with wooden sticks gathered in summer. He will not look around though. In his eyes will be the sea he walked past by to reach me. In his hands will be the wind he caught when he rushed to reach me. That would have been his only thought.

To reach me.

To reach me.

To reach me before the big fish waiting at my doorstep with blood red eyes for fins would gobble me whole.

I know then we shall swim the eternal sea he gathered and taste the wind wine. We would touch the sky where it was deep pink. And that he would never return.

Now that he has come. Now that he has come.

Now that he has come.

One Winter's Afternoon

Leigh Swinbourne

Leigh Swinbourne is a dramatist and fiction writer resident in Hobart. His work has been shortlisted for the Patrick White Playwrights' Award, the Varuna Award and The Tasmanian Literary Prizes. His plays have been produced locally and interstate. He has published two critically acclaimed collections of short stories, 'The Shark' and 'Away', through Ginninderra Press, which will publish his first novel, 'Shadow in the Forest', in 2019. More on Leigh's writing can be found at www.leighswinbourne.com.au.

One Winter's Afternoon

Dr. Leonard Fuller M.B., B.S., F.R.A.C.G.P., huddles from the chill into his astrakhan overcoat, hands clenched in pockets, breath pluming before him like a spirit. Directly facing him is a faded weather-board cottage, poor but squarely confident somehow, on a cracked concrete base surrounded by a bare yard pocked with rubbish and spare ashy tufts of grass. This is unexpected, the bareness, solitude. From a stock of working class clichés he had imagined a cramped terrace, squeezed between like: squalling babies, talk-back radio, sharp domestic squabbles in a foreign tongue, spicy kitchen smells... We always assume the proletariat more vital for some reason, Dickens and Dostoevsky probably the prime culprits. He, of all people, should have known better.

For it is very much a working class suburb, but also an old industrial zone, so he has driven past untidy waste stretches and this property is adjacent to one of these, a half-built derelict estate. On the other side, fifty yards distant over a tangle of rusty barbed wire, a decrepit gothic factory slumps silently, windows all eerily vacant like eye sockets.

A factory like the one he worked in forty or so years ago when he'd known this suburb pretty well. Doesn't look like much has changed, now it all gradually comes back to mind. One of a sequence of endless lousy jobs, somewhere near, Taubman's Paints, scouring out recycled vats, dangerous industrial labour, stripped to the waist, poisonous air, hot as buggery. Supporting his older unmarried sister and her boy, and his pickled war-invalided father, all dead now, while powering through a Medical degree five nights of the week. Where on earth had he found the energy, the drive? Belief and enthusiasm now seem relics as distant from him as these presently before him. He digs the ferule of his umbrella into the footpath, uproots a dead weed. Not a cloud in the sky, why did he bring the bloody thing? He feels down, enervated, unusual for him, but probably simply because everything looks so drab and he had such a late night.

"You must come! Don't you care?"

The flatness of the place seems entirely at odds with the shrill urgency of the young female voice on the line that persuaded him out of the fug of his office. He hardly ever makes house-calls now, particularly from the second surgery, and on such a raw day. But Pollock was tied up with the insufferable Mrs. Macallister, the caller was insistent, and actually he had nothing much else to do.

The thought of his assistant makes him conscious of a slight foulness on the back of his tongue. Too much red wine (definition of an alcoholic: a man who drinks more than his doctor), though in this case a pretty justifiable over-indulgence in a vain attempt to ameliorate the dull convivialities of the previous evening. Dinner at the Pollocks was becoming almost a weekly event. He does not like Pollock, brash, opinionated, ambitious, and his perky arriviste wife. Of course, he himself had been much the same at that age, and this is perhaps why.

Other unpleasantries of the evening now crowd in on him. After he thought it was all finally over, drifting off on the electric blanket, his wife had turned to him, the most astonishing thing, they had not made love in well over a decade, and what with this and his over consumption, he'd had to suppress a reflex to vomit. What on earth was she thinking? Had parvenu Pollock turned her on? Parvenu Pollock's priapic prick, bit of a medical legend from all accounts. That last girl, he had to let her go. Pity. To be honest, he wouldn't mind a shot himself at the young wife, enjoyed her bending to the oven when he went out to freshen his scotch, imagined hiking her skirt. Fantasy alright, but in real life you had to endure the bloody conversation.

Not that he can endure any conversation these days. His wife at least respects this, days on end when they literally do not pass a word. What is conversation anyway when you break it down but exchange of information? And what information could they possibly have to exchange after all this time? Yet they had both been great talkers once, sitting up half the night, all that nonsense: politics, religion, literature, matters long since exhausted. These days he never even picks up a newspaper, let alone a novel. People saying the same things over and over to one another down the years. Why on earth do they do it? What is the point? Sometimes he feels that it is only silence that makes life bearable. He could break with her of course, with them all for that matter, but even that seems far more effort than it is worth. Too much fuss, he has always hated fuss. Easier just to keep plodding on, line of least resistance. Gingerly opening the gate on its single hinge, the picket fence is also half collapsed, a good kick would do for it, he picks his way fastidiously up uneven paving past yellow papers and crusty dog turds. The front door could also use a lick of paint; he raps the knocker firmly, importantly. The sound is swallowed, but definitely would have carried. Waits. Nothing. Raps again, louder. Nothing. A third time. The breeze picks up, grit in his eyes and teeth. Must get that bridgework done, he's as bad as some of his patients in postponing the inevitable, old men always the worst. He couldn't possibly have made a mistake; he glances back at the gate. Thirty eight, same as his own house. He hears the woman's voice again, the exaggerated articulation, the hot edge of panic. Wrong street? Maybe there are two. He crosses back over to the Mercedes, glossily conspicuous, tossing the umbrella onto the back seat where he has left the street directory. Street and directory correspond.

He returns to the front door and smashes the knocker repeatedly into its base, bangs the ball of his palm on the wood, shouts into the wind, making a spectacle of himself, if there were anyone around to see. He stops, and the sudden contrasting quiet spooks him. Maybe something serious has happened. He makes his way around the house to the back, which appears weirdly as same as the front. An empty dusty yard, no back fence, the old night-soil lane exposed. A fly-screened back door bangs erratically in the wind, the inside door is latched back open. He enters.

The kitchen. Worn linoleum, dirty curtainless windows. He calls out again. No response. But everything seems orderly, plates and pots and pans neatly stacked on open unpainted wooden shelves. But it also looks dusty, unused. He handles a saucer, an old cheap willow pattern from his youth. There is no food about. The sink is dry, slightly stained, slightly foul. He turns the tap. A hollow sucking sound, but no water. He crosses to the 'fridge, again a design he remembers from the past, the modular-shaped top, once ludicrously thought to be modern, even futuristic. It is not running, he opens it, it is empty, the stale air carrying a faint but sharp tang of mould. On the bench there is a toaster, one of the ancient type that opens either side, and a pale green electric jug meshed with fine hairline cracks, black bakelite lid, dry as the sink. Some equipment for living, but where is the life? Sunlight flowing from the windows seems to pin down the various objects as though they are permanent fixtures. He has a ridiculous intimation that the house is watching him, waiting to see what he will do. The hangover again.

He ventures up a carpeted corridor, 'fifties floral, maroon, whoever designed these things? Musty. There are two bedrooms, one on either side and he pokes his head into both of them. The rooms are neat, again orderly, beds made with faded pink tufted-chenille covers, no clothes around, no bric-a-brac, presumably also unused. Beyond the bedrooms, at the front of the house on either side, are the living room and master bedroom. From the living room he can see through sagging venetian blinds over to his car. Shabby lounge, a single ornament on the mantelpiece. Incredible! It looks to be an exact replica of a Dresden miniature he bought for his wife on their honeymoon in London thirty years ago, now long lost. Memory plays tricks, but still, it looks uncannily the same. He turns it in his hands, a young girl in peasant costume, pointed black shoes, bright blue dirndl, and the face, yes, unmistakable. He bought the figurine because the face was so much like his wife's. And she was once like this, slim, bright, laughing. Another age. He had been so much in love; there had been nothing else. Impossible to believe. He realizes that for some reason while he has been holding the girl, examining her, he has also been holding his breath, and he now lets it out between his teeth with a long slow whistle. Upon which he finds he is on the verge of tears. Absurd.

He steadies himself and, model still in hand, enters the main bedroom. Here the air seems denser. Again, all is orderly and empty, except the covers of the bed are drawn back in what is comparatively wild disarray, and there is a large dark rust stain on the mattress sheet. He walks over and fingers it. Stiff. Old dried blood, although a strange discolouration at the edges makes it appear fresh, moist, where it blends into the cotton. He brings his fingers to his nose and for some bizarre reason smells his wife on them. A totally perverse olfactory illusion. Then from no motive he can credit, at that point or later, he places the figurine precisely in the centre of the stain. Suddenly the door knocker booms, scaring him half out of his wits. A surge of panic momently grips him. He races to the door and wrestles with the lock. How does the bloody thing work?

"Hang on!"

Finally it gives. The cold blows in. No-one on the doorstep, or in the yard. Kids probably. He quickly looks over to the car. Nothing. Unless they are coming around the back. He re-locks the door and retraces his steps down the hall and out the back door. No-one. He returns to the front. Better give it away. A prankster? Or something else. Something sinister? Something, definitely, but what? He pauses. It is there right before him, but he just cannot get a grip on it.

Silly nonsense no doubt. The westerly picks up, cutting through his coat. He walks back down the path and pauses again for a moment at the leaning gate, trying to think what, if anything, he should do. He waits, but nothing further happens and nothing comes to mind. If the call was genuine and the woman wants him, she'll ring again. Now the sun has gone and the pale winter light is dimming in the open sky with a bleak, brief radiance. He looks across to where that light is focussed, watches the broken shapes of abandoned buildings slowly blacken, coalesce, disappear, as the world itself slowly turns.

Queer business alright. The sealing kiss of the driver's door is comforting, final. Ignition, heater, radio. The car glides down the long street, takes the first corner and with a squeal of tyres accelerates away.

Over Your Head

Christopher Ringrose

Christopher Ringrose has lived and worked in France, Canada and the UK, and is now based in the Melbourne suburb of Newport. He writes poetry and fiction and co-edits the *Journal of Postcolonial Writing* and the book series *Studies in World Literature* for Ibidem/Columbia University Press. His poetry has won the Peterloo Prize in the UK, the Other Voices Prize in Canada and the 2014 Poetica Christi Prize in Australia, and been published in *Fiddlehead*, *The Human World*, *Australis*, *The Mozzie*, *Poetry Monash*, *Coolabah*, *The South Circular*, the *2018 ANU Prize Anthology* and *Award-Winning Australian Poetry*. His translations from Spanish of the poems of Ricardo Güiraldes appeared in *The Laurel Review* (Missouri State University) in 2018.

Chris's poetry about Melbourne was chosen for projection in Krakow, Poland, as part of UNESCO's "Cities of Literature" celebrations. His fiction was included in the *Melbourne Subjective* collection (2014) and in the microfiction anthology *Flashing the Square* (2014).

His poetry collection, *Palmistry*, was published by in case of emergency press in 2018.

Chris's poetry website is www.cringrose.com

Over Your Head

He adjusts his dog collar in the mirror. So neat and transformative, gleaming and white. He smooths down the black shirt, tightens his belt. Gives his reflection a quick smile of satisfaction, switches off the radio and picks up the slim leather briefcase before glancing round the apartment. The cat is asleep, or pretending to be.

As he walks down the busy street, he is intrigued by people's reactions to his clerical dress. The men who drop their eyes, as if at the memory of some childhood reproof. The pairs of girls who stifle giggles, and the older women who smile at him encouragingly. The sneers of teenagers. The shouts of mockery from across the road: "That's him who did it, Mummy, the man in black." That makes him blush. You could always cover up the dog collar, or not wear it in the street, but that would be pointless.

He checks his watch. Still half an hour to spare. He pushes open the door of Coffee Republic on Hall Street and approaches the counter. It's Alice today. She raises her eyebrows.

"Flat white, Father?"

"That will do nicely."

He flips his loyalty card onto the counter, and she punches a star into it.

He takes his cup to an empty table for two by the window, stretches out his legs and sighs. There is a newspaper on the table—yesterday's, but he flips though it anyway. He becomes aware of a young woman slipping into the other seat at the table. He smiles at her. Not a threat.

"Good morning, Father."

She is what you might call dumpy. Or stout. At least, some might call her that. Plain black T shirt, regulation jeans and sneakers. Her hair is a little greasy, in need of a wash. Fabulous eyes, though, with the merest slant to them—what used to be called almond eyes, with flawless whites and green, flecked irises.

"Good morning."

He goes back to his paper, but she is still studying him.

"Can I ask you something?"

He pushes the paper aside and looks up, signalling receptiveness. What else can he do?

"Of course."

"My sister has a little boy..."

His heart flickers slightly.

"Oh?"

"A lovely little boy. His name is Jayden. Olive skin and brown eyes. His Dad was... well, that doesn't matter. She loves him so much. We all do. But..."

Here it comes, he thinks.

"He going to die," she finishes. Water brims up in one eye. She blinks and the tear is released onto her round cheek.

"He's going to die," she repeats. "I can't believe I'm saying that, but it's the truth."

"Perhaps... there might be..." he falters.

"No doubt about it. Cancer. Can you believe it? What's that all about? Old people... "

"Die all the time?" No, that didn't come out right, he thinks.

But she didn't seem to notice.

"Yes, but a child... "

"Tragic. What's your name?"

"Tracy."

"And your sister?"

"Sandie."

"Tracy, Sandie and Jayden."

"Yes."

He is aware of Alice behind the counter, watching them. How much of this can she hear?

"And you are wondering how God can allow Jayden to have this disease?"

She just spreads her hands and raises her eyebrows slightly. Sad and angry.

"This is a question people have had to grapple with throughout history. There is a theological answer, and then there are my own ideas."

"Don't care about theology."

"It's just people thinking, like we are now."

"Don't care about them. What about your own ideas?"

"Life is sacred—a century of it or a second of it. A life lived for a few years has value. As much value as a really long life."

"So you don't mind if you drop dead now rather than in forty years' time? Or if I killed you now?"

"Of course I care. But if you did kill me now, my life would be what it is. Not better or worse than if it lasted longer."

"What about Sandie?"

"And you?"

"Yes, OK. And me."

"God created the world with laws—of physics, chemistry—and science can trace them. But there were things that were left to chance. That's a side effect of giving human beings freedom."

"God decides everything that's going to happen."

"But we don't know why they happen."

She looks up sharply.

"Don't tell me Jayden dying may be good."

"I don't know."

"Then what use are you?"

A wave of weariness floods over him.

"No use at all, perhaps."

They sit for a few seconds staring at each other over the plastic table. He notices that she has not ordered a drink. Her shoulders slump and she puts her head in her hands, while beating her heels in a curious pattern on the floor.

"We could pray," he suggests.

For a while she says nothing, then reaches out her hands. He takes them. They are warm and slightly damp. It's not unpleasant. He has to think of a prayer.

"Dear Lord… "

"Dear Lord… "

She is repeating his words a half-second after he has pronounced them. Disconcerted, he continues.

"… we ask for your care for Jayden, and Sandie and Tracy."

"Sandie and me," she says, adapting his murmured words.

"Help us to cherish Jayden. We thank you for his life and the joy within it. Guide us and others to help him in all the ways we can, trusting in your unfailing love."

He is sweating and his pulse is racing, but oddly he feels calmer now. Tracy's eyes are closed.

"… unfailing love," she concludes. She lets go of his hands, gets up without looking at him, then pauses near the door to speak, as if to the whole world.

"Thank you."

He nods. The door smacks shut behind Tracy. Alice comes over to collect his cup.

"That was kind," she says, "though you got in over your head there. What's the play?"

"Candida, by George Bernard Shaw. Rev. Alexander Mill."

"Any good?"

"No, rubbish."

"I'm sure it's not."

Then, as she walks away, she throws over her shoulder:

"But it really wasn't a good idea, you know."

The Dispatch Rider

Peter Newall

Peter Justin Newall lives in Thalgarrah, NSW, but has lived variously in Australia, Ukraine and most recently Kyoto, Japan, where he sang for a popular local blues band. He has been published in England, Hong Kong, the USA and Australia; his stories **The Luft Mensch** and **The Chinese General** were each nominated for a Pushcart Prize.

The Dispatch Rider

It was about six months after the end of the war. Nobody was quite certain it really had ended, and that German or Russian tanks might not yet appear on the plains below the city, despite what the radio and the papers said. But work had already begun repairing and rebuilding, and people had begun to think about having normal lives again, celebrating birthdays and going to church and falling in love and talking about having children.

It was in that strange indeterminate time I met Vesna. We hit it off immediately, and without even discussing it decided to be together. It's funny; a quarter of the city was destroyed, some streets still blocked by rubble, there was not much food, and men were still wearing their uniform jackets with the badges taken off, because they didn't have any other jacket to wear. Yet we felt so glad to be alive that it was like being in the Garden of Eden. And of course, it was spring.

Vesna was maybe twenty or twenty-one; I didn't ask. And I didn't ask what she had done during the last four years which had been the war, and nor did she ask me. You would assume that a man of my age had been fighting, and it was true, I had been with the partisans. But she never asked. Apart from the very few who were politically committed, nobody wanted to talk about what they had been or done. If your brother had been killed or the house you were born in bombed to rubble, you didn't say anything about it. What was the point? It was the war, another time altogether. So I didn't ask her if she'd been married or had a lover and what happened to him, and she didn't ask me questions like that. When I say it was like the Garden of Eden, I mean we felt in those days that we were starting out as the first man and the first woman, washed clean of everything, innocent. And absurdly, for people with only one room in an apartment building to live in and two changes of clothes and no butter or proper coffee, we were happy. And Vesna was very beautiful.

She was tall and wide-shouldered, with dark brown hair and hazel-green eyes. She had a round face with a strong chin, a typical southern Slav face, you might say, but it was a calm, pleasing, comforting face. Her neck and arms were tanned, but the rest of her body was white, a lovely smooth white like the ice-cream we'd had as children but hadn't seen for years now. I loved the smell of her skin, a warm fragrance like hay, and the faint salty-sweet tang of the sweat that trickled down from her armpits under her blouse, a smell and a wetness I loved.

Somehow she had kept a couple of blouses she had brought with her from the village before the war, white linen blouses with big puffed sleeves, frilled collars and drawstring necks. If you knew about these things you could probably tell what village she came from by the embroidery, but as a city-born man I didn't know that. All I know is the sleeves were bigger and puffier than any I'd ever seen. She wore these blouses with a modern skirt, short enough almost to show her knees. Like every other young woman in the city that spring she wore heeled sandals with white socks, but my Vesna wore stockings too, chocolate brown stockings that gave her legs between the white socks and short skirt a shapely, feminine look.

One day near the end of May, just before summer, we went out to visit my friend Tomas. He'd written to me that he had got married and was living in a suburb south of the centre. The trolleybus was working again over a part of its route, and we rode it as far as it went and then walked, following the directions he'd given me. It was nothing to walk a couple of kilometres; we were glad to be free to walk wherever we wished. The trees in this area had somehow been spared being cut down. I hadn't realised how much I missed seeing trees in the streets until we came upon a whole avenue of them, linden trees in fresh green leaf. The shade they threw on the cracked footpath was a mystery and a delight, dappled, shifting, cool. Vesna and I walked hand in hand the length of the street luxuriating in it. I watched the light and shadow dancing on her white blouse and her glossy brown hair. She wore the sunglasses I had got for her, good dark green glass in clear celluloid frames. She smiled a lot, even when we were just walking along without saying anything, and her teeth were very white.

Although the fighting must not have been heavy there for the trees to have survived, you could still see pockmarks in the façades of most buildings in the street from rifle and machine-gun fire. You couldn't go anywhere and not be reminded of the war. Yet in a couple of small plots bounded by bricks set into the ground, bright green spring grass had grown up where three months ago there had been only bare frozen earth and gutters of snow. This grass was new and fresh, it was this year's grass. It hadn't lived through the war and it knew nothing of the war. It was innocent. I loved the grass for its very newness; it was unsullied by all the things we'd gone through and seen and done during the last four years, it existed for today and tomorrow, not the past.

We found Tomas' building. It was a big old apartment block in grey stone that had once been quite grand. It had its bullet-marks in the façade, especially around the windows, but there was new glass in the window-frames and the street door had been rehung. Inside the building, the corridor, under a high arched ceiling, was laid with diagonal black and white tiles. A big staircase with a wooden banister led up to the floors above. Tomas had told me his apartment was on the third floor. Our hearts were so light that day that we ran up the stairs together laughing. Tomas was waiting for us at the open door of his flat, wearing a red knitted shirt like some Bohemian.

Because he was married, he had actually got a flat of his own—a bedroom, a kitchen and a living room. It was part of what had been a large apartment, now divided into small units. We sat in the kitchen. The window looked out onto the street; even only two storeys up, you could see a wide expanse of blue sky over the roofs of the buildings opposite. Below us the light green crowns of the linden trees quivered occasionally in the spring breeze. I've forgotten Tomas' wife's name now, but she was a pleasant woman with fluffy blonde hair. She wore a dress in dark blue with white dots, tied in tight at the waist. She'd certainly made a good lunch out of not much. There was dill soup, vegetable pie and a bowl of potato and cabbage salad.

Before we sat down, I took out of my satchel the gift we'd brought with us; half a bottle of slivovitz. Not the chemical-tasting spirit that had recently appeared in the shops, but real, pre-war slivovitz, the paper label so worn that you could hardly make out the fat purple plums that decorated it.

We had a small glass each; we drank solemnly, recognising the importance of the old bottle and what it stood for, spirit distilled unhurriedly from ripe fruit grown in the slow, peaceful, sunny days before the war.

Over lunch we talked not of the past but of the future, of books—Tomas was a budding writer, and called himself a socialist, so he railed against Krleza whom he said had lost touch with the people—and about art. I preferred mystical artists in the vein of Chagall, because I'd come to believe the only way not to repeat the war was for mankind to turn to the spirit, to God. Tomas, in line with his politics, was all for some sort of new realism; he thought men could fix their own fate on the basis of reason. We argued about this while Vesna and Tomas' blonde wife clattered about between stove, table and sink. Once lunch was cleared away, we decided to go out into the late spring sunshine. It was warm, almost hot, and I left my jacket in the flat. Vesna's puff-sleeved white blouse was exactly right for the weather; it radiated cheerfulness. Tomas said there was a park with a pond and benches not far away. We agreed to walk there and went out the back door of the building.

On one side of the enclosed yard was a sort of shed, like a bunker, concrete with a bolted metal door, orange with rust.

"What's in there?" I asked.

"You know, we've been here three months, and I've never looked," Tomas replied, "but there are a few keys on the bunch they gave me when we moved in that don't fit the apartment doors."

We watched as he tried several keys in the big padlock that held the bolt in place. On the fourth or fifth go, the padlock snapped open. We looked at each other. Tomas shrugged. "We live here, we can have a look," he said, dragging open the door.

Inside, the shed was dark, but it had obviously been used as a garage. The stale air smelled of dust and oil. The concrete floor was blotched with black stains. Rubbish lay around—crumpled rags, a few empty jerry-cans, their caps hanging open; sheets of flimsy paper that might have been military orders; some broken-up ammunition boxes. At the back, against the wall, a grey canvas cover was stretched over something waist-high and long.

Tomas stepped forward and peeled the canvas back. The front wheel and headlamp of a motorcycle came into view. He whistled, and heedless of dust pulled the cover right off. Astonishingly, given that transport of any kind had been worth more than gold in the last months of the war, the motorcycle was intact. It stood nonchalantly, leaning on its stand, its front wheel turned in slightly, as if it had been parked that morning. It was lean and racy, with swept-back handlebars and narrow, heavily-patterned tyres. I felt as if we'd discovered a hoard of buried treasure.

Tomas kicked the stand up, wheeled the cycle out into the spring sunshine, and stood it on the path outside the back door of the building. The four of us gathered around it. There was an Italian divisional sign stencilled on the olive-green paint of the tank. "Left behind by the Fascists when we threw them out," Tomas said. With difficulty he twisted off the petrol cap; the tank was bone dry.

The canvas cover had done its job; even the triangular brown leather seat was clean. "It's a Bellini, I think," said Tomas.

"No," said Vesna, "it's a Moto-Guzzi 250." Taking hold of the handlebars, she swung her leg over the bike and sat astride it, putting her feet up on the foot-pegs. She looked very much at home. Her suntanned hands gripped the handlebars confidently; if the bike hadn't still been on its stand you'd have thought she was riding it at speed. I still remember the warmth of the sunshine on my neck as I watched Vesna sitting on the sporty, low-slung motorcycle. She was smiling, and the sun shone on her broad forehead and glinted on her sunglasses. The puffed sleeves of her blouse floated like giant butterfly wings. I loved her very much in that moment.

Smiling myself, I glanced over at Tomas, but he had a very odd expression on his face, his brows drawn together, frowning.

Vesna climbed off the bike and came over to me, brushing her hands of imaginary dust. "A pity we don't have a camera. It would have been a good photograph," she said. I took her hands in mine.

"No photograph could do justice to how beautiful you look," I told her. I could just smell the perfume of her sweat in the sun. I turned to Tomas again.

"Finders keepers, it's yours now."

"Yeah, maybe you're right," he said slowly. "If I can get hold of some petrol I'll see how she runs, but I'll put her back inside for now." He wheeled the machine back into the shed, pushed the door closed and snapped the padlock.

"Well, let's look at this park, while it's still so warm," I said.

Tomas hesitated, seemed about to say something, but then took his wife by the hand and led us out the back gate.

The road behind the building was unpaved and covered in chalky dust that soon coated our shoes. The park was a few hundred metres on. Just as Tomas had said, it was green and had a small pond in the middle. A pair of ducks was sitting on the water. They must have been used to people, because although they swam out to the middle of the pond they didn't fly away. The male had a reddish head and cream wings; he paddled protectively in circles round the dun-coloured female.

Vesna pulled me by the hand down to the pond's edge. Her sandals half-disappeared in the soft green grass.

"See how he looks after her," she said. "They must be very much in love." The idea of ducks being in love hadn't occurred to me, but I grunted agreement.

We sat on the soft grassy bank and smoked. Tomas said very little, but his wife and Vesna chatted. The sun was descending the afternoon sky, and after half an hour it was noticeably cooler. We stood up to return.

The two women walked in front of us; Tomas touched my arm and held me back. Once they were twenty paces away he spoke to me in an undertone.

"Petar, how does your girl know the make and model of an Italian motorcycle when she sees one?"

"What? Oh, come on, man, people know all sorts of things. You and I know Fascist aircraft when we see them; we've shot at them. She saw a bike like this once, was told what it was called, and she's remembered."

"I just don't like that she sits on a Fascist motorcycle like she was born to it, that's all." I looked at Tomas. His shock of thick black hair stood almost straight up from his head, just as it had at school. His dark brows were knitted together doubtfully above his brown eyes. I could see he was taking seriously some conclusion he'd come to.

"Tomas, it's not hard to ride a motorbike. Forget it. You're just annoyed that she corrected you about it in front of your wife."

Tomas shook his head, but said nothing more. Soon we were back in his flat, collecting our coats and bags and saying thank you for lunch and good-bye. I left the slivovitz; a gift is a gift.

Out in the street it had grown even cooler, and before we set off for the tram stop, I put my jacket round Vesna's shoulders. She held the lapels together with one hand. It looked graceful to me, like a film actress, but to me everything Vesna did seemed elegant. "What was all that whispering you were doing with your friend?" she asked as we walked away from Tomas' building. I ducked my head under a low-hanging branch.

"Oh, nothing, he was just embarrassed that you knew the model of that bike and he didn't. I don't know what he's got to complain about; he has a motorbike he didn't have this morning; it's been a good day for him."

"No, I saw his face. There was something that angered him. And he was very cold when we were leaving."

"Look, I don't even want to talk about it because it makes me sound as silly as him, but he said it was strange you knew the make and model of that bike."

"Oh, that's not strange at all. I was a dispatch rider for six months. I rode a bike exactly the same as that one."

I didn't understand this. Without pausing to weigh it, I blurted out my question. "But how did you get a bike like that, an Italian bike?"

"Petar, we never talk about the war. I thought we'd agreed never to talk about it. What matters to me is that we're here now. I understand what you did, who you fought with. I was a dispatch rider for the Home Guard, that's why I had an Italian motorcycle."

My mind whirled. I actually felt dizzy. Yes, like most people we had instinctively agreed not to talk about the war. And yes, what mattered was that we were here now, and Vesna I loved very much, we were happy together, and I'd assumed our future would be together. But she had been with the Home Guard. They were allies of the Fascists. I'd fought the Fascists and I'd seen my comrades killed fighting them. I cursed myself for asking her, and I cursed Tomas for finding his bloody motorcycle that day of all days.

I realised I had stopped walking; Vesna stopped too. We stood facing each other on the footpath, under the leafy branches of the linden trees. The sun was setting behind a strip of cloud, and the sky had gone from blue to a pale purple.

"Why have you stopped here?" she asked.

I let out a long breath. "I have to think about this for a minute," I said.

"What is there to think about? We love each other. We are happy. In the war we did what we had to, to protect our country and our families. The war's over, thank God. Don't keep it going. Don't say everything has changed now because you found out something from back then. Do you think I didn't see any of my friends killed?"

I stood looking at her. I loved her, but I couldn't simply forget everything that had happened. It would be disloyalty to my comrades, men I had fought alongside, men who had died.

Vesna took a step towards me and looked up into my face. I looked away, trying to order my thoughts.

"No," she said slowly, "if you have to think about it, decide what to do, then you don't love me and there's no point in this. What a pity. What a shame." Her voice seemed to choke. Still looking at me she stepped back a pace, then turned and started to walk away, along the street towards the tram stop. After a few paces she broke into a run. My jacket fell from her shoulders onto the footpath. She kept running, a brown and white shape, into the evening gloom.

I opened my mouth to call out to her, but didn't. Of course I could run after her, catch her, take her by the shoulders and shake her, shout "Listen to me!" into her face, like in a film, but then what? Could I honestly say "I don't care about the past. You are all I care about"? In that moment I didn't know, and in that moment she went around the corner and out of sight.

Behind the Glass

Sam McAlpine

Sam McAlpine's work has appeared in journals, including the *UTS Writers' Anthology*. He holds an MA in creative writing and is currently working on his first collection of short fiction. He lives, works, and writes in Sydney.

Behind the Glass

Their shrieks hit me before I even part the blinds. When the cats fight they make sounds like babies being strangled. It gets me out of bed most nights, but what's worse is when I peer out into that shadowy, deserted cul-de-sac, there's no sign of them anywhere. No sign of anything. Just the wind in the trees and that awful shrieking. When I was my daughter Joanne's age my own mother used to say, you can get used to anything in life, given time and no other choice. But you don't get used to this. Not the sounds they make. My blood jumps every time.

I chose the area because it's cheap, close to a local high school. For the time being, it's all I can afford. But our unit's a shoebox and the building's falling apart. It's coming on two years now, but Joanne says she doesn't care. Mum, it's not even that bad, she tells me. I have friends here now.

It's enough to keep you up at night, only tonight it's something else.

It happened last week. Lugging groceries home, I had to sneak down the back lane because kids were blocking the walkway again. The same ones breaking into cars at night, four of them, on skateboards, waiting for people to walk past. I doubled back and slipped in through the courtyard instead.

Cats were sunning themselves on the dirty pavers. I had the night shift at the medical centre and wanted to tidy up and cook before Joanne got home from school. I raced upstairs, put the food away, and left a pot of water on the stove to boil while I got changed. I was passing Joanne's room on my way back to the kitchen, when I heard the *clack* and saw her door slowly swing open. She mustn't have closed it properly. I poked my head in. Dirty blond light speared in through the barred window. The heat smacked me, carrying with it that smoky odour of old acrylic carpet, slow rot, and mould. She'd be home from school any minute. Out in the kitchen, the water bubbled on the stove, and I hesitated and took a step inside.

I tried the window, but it wouldn't budge. Clothes strewn on the floor. Bed unmade. I had to fight the urge to straighten things. I stood for a moment by the dresser, its top busy with perfumes bottles, makeup, tins of hair-ties; everything cluttered and chaotic in the way only a teenager can navigate. I felt strange, almost like I was trespassing. Imagine feeling like a trespasser in your own daughter's room, in your own home, where your name is on the lease, where two-thirds of your pay disappears every week on rent.

Inside her top drawer, tangles of underpants which I gently raked aside. It was at the back, under an old photo of her father: a roll of fifties, secured tightly with a red rubber band. I heard the water hiss as it boiled over, and my stomach turned cold. I put the money back and left the room fast, shutting the door hard behind me.

I leave the window and reach for an empty glass beside my bed. I avoid looking at the alarm clock. I don't want to see the time again. I'm opening the surgery tomorrow. If I don't get to sleep soon, I'll pay for it. At least the cats have calmed down. A siren wails in the distance as I adjust the straps on my nightie and quietly leave the room.

Her door's closed—a sight I'm still growing used to. As I creep past, I think of that money stashed in her drawer. Wasn't long ago, when she was younger, that I used to wake to the sound of my bedroom door creaking open. I'd feel her crawling up the bed, under the covers, her doll-like hands prying my arms apart to be held. Even when we first came here, I kept my door ajar at night, waiting for her. Every night, I waited. Even in my dreams. I'd doze off like that, only to wake to phantom sounds—windows sliding open, the front door slamming—and I'd bolt upright, afraid. I stopped waiting and kept my door shut after that.

Now the hall is dark and silent save for my footsteps and the static hum of the refrigerator in the kitchen. I keep the lights off, padding quietly around the couch to stand at the sink. I pour a fresh glass of water. The refrigerator clicks, falls silent. It's cool at the sink with the lights off. The time on the microwave reads 2 AM and my mind is reeling. What the hell is she doing with that kind of money? Listening to the sound of the tap dripping, sipping cool, metallic-tasting water, I mull it over. She doesn't have a job, unless she got one without me knowing. But if she was working, I think I'd know. Maybe it's not hers. Maybe she's only holding it for someone. Or did she find it?

We have a small balcony that opens onto the street. I take the water with me and stand at the sliding glass door, gripping the handle with my free hand. My eyes scan the empty street. Streetlights cast cool ponds of amber on the road, leaving the block opposite ours draped in inky shadow. Out front an old Laser sits propped on stacks of red bricks, its wheels and number plates missing. It's sat there for months now, and I suspect it'll sit there for a long time to come. That's how it is out this way. Things get ruined, left behind, lost in plain sight.

I take a slow sip, watching as a car glides silently into view. It parks across the street. Clouds of exhaust burn volcanic in the glow of its taillights. The interior light blinks on. Inside a man and woman are having what can only be an argument. His hands grip the wheel, ten-and-two. He stares vacantly across the bonnet, slowly shaking his head. She's in her seat facing him. I watch as she punches the dash with one hand, clutching his arm with the other. I've seen my share of this, heard it through the walls. Loud bangs, things breaking. The woman climbs out, and he takes off with the door still open, leaving her there stamping as the lights peel away and the car tears off down the street. I've promised things over the years. We all have. But watching those taillights shrink, the only thing that matters is moving into a house again, and I don't care if I have to work two jobs to make it happen. A kid should grow up with a backyard, and I know Joanne's sixteen, but I don't think that matters. I don't think a backyard is too much to ask.

I rest my water glass on the coffee table, shifting to a window where the angle's better. I peer out through a kink in the blinds. She crosses, stopping under a streetlight like an actor finding her mark. Arms folded, shoulders hunched. She rubs her eyes before digging into her purse for something. I recognise her. From the block opposite ours, I think. I see her around sometimes, usually waiting to be picked up, always at weird hours. One of many faces. Working at the surgery I see these girls all the time. And I wonder where they come from, where they go?

Sending Joanne to a co-ed school in an area like this worries me. It's probably filled with younger versions of this woman I'm watching now. Working fifty-hour weeks makes it hard to keep your eyes open. But I'd know if she was involved in anything dangerous.

I made the mistake once of asking if it was a boy she was always texting.

No, Mum, she said, glaring at me from her phone, her eyes war-ready slits.

Why? What does it matter?

Before I could answer, she was off and the door to her room slammed shut.

The idea that she has to learn things for herself terrifies me. There's no way to tell her how easily things can turn. I picture her getting involved with someone like Craig, who I dated for two years after her father, and all I can think of is the little cards on the cheap bouquets of flowers he used to send. How quickly they changed from I love you to I'm sorry.

When I look up again the woman outside is gone. I turn to pick my glass up off the table, and in that same motion, hear the sliding door click as someone tries to open it. I spin and catch the silhouette of a person in the doorway, their shadow long across the floor.

We both scream as I see her face pressed up against the glass.

Jesus Christ, Mum!

I slide the door across—it's unlocked—and Joanne steps past me into the dark room. I turn on the lamp.

God, you scared me, I tell her. What are you doing?

Me? What are you doing in the dark, Mum?

The cats woke me, I explain. Why were you outside?

She drops her handbag, leans against the back of the couch, and folds her arms.

Sharni broke up with her boyfriend, she says, staring down at her feet. She kicks her black heels off one at a time, then reaches to pick them up.

Sharni? The name's only vaguely familiar.

Yes, Mum, she says. She comes around. You know her.

Her tone is sharp, questioning. It's enough to cut me from my initial shock.

I don't care who she is, I snap back. It's two-thirty in the morning.

What does it matter? She was upset, alright?

She turns away, and I feel every part of me start to tense.

Where does she live? I ask.

Not far.

Well, how'd you get there?

Walked.

In heels?

I took them off and walked. What does it matter?

Why are you dressed like that?

I've just noticed how short her skirt is, how much makeup she's wearing. It doesn't make sense. Everything's crooked and creased. I try to see her eyes, but she keeps looking elsewhere, avoiding me. She gathers her handbag and stands.

This is how I dress, she says, turning to leave the room.

Christ, you have school tomorrow. The edge is back in my voice. Do you know what time it is?

I'm going to bed.

I take a step forward.

We're not done.

She stops in the doorway without turning. I'm breathing hard. Ask about the money. I need her to tell me it's not hers. That she found it. She's saving it. She has a secret job. She's helping me save a bond, so we can get out of here.

How did you get home? I manage finally.

Told you. I walked.

Home?

Yes, I fucking walked home.

My legs and hands shake. I want to drag her into her room, tip the dresser, fling the drawers, and watch everything tumble out.

Instead she starts to sob. Just like that. The tears come, and she doubles over, sobbing, trying hard to breathe.

I take her in my arms without thinking, holding her as we both tremble. I don't remember the last time I held her like this. I can smell her sweet perfume mingled with smoke and sweat. That woman I watched through the window is a distant thought receding.

She lifts her head, her cheeks wet, glistening in the lamplight. Let's just … get out of here, she says. Okay?

Go?

Away. Tonight.

Tonight? We can't leave tonight, baby. Where would we go?

Anywhere.

Hearing this is almost too much. I want to cry too.

Soon, I tell her. I promise.

Why not tonight? she asks. What if … what if we could?

With that money you have in your room? I want to say. Only I don't, can't, for fear of losing this moment, of chasing her off.

How could we leave tonight? I ask.

Of course, we could.

But where would we go?

Anywhere.

Okay. Okay, tomorrow, I tell her, and I'm not sure I can get the rest of the words out. It feels absurd, almost irresponsible, to ignore the cold finality of our situation. But for Joanne, I'll do my best. I'll try. We'll just … pack our things then, I manage finally. Pack up and go.

Tomorrow, she says.

For a moment, I'm convinced she's going to say something else. I'm holding my tongue, waiting for it, hoping.

I'm tired, she says, voice cracking. All I want is to keep holding her.

Okay. Goodnight, my baby.

She pulls away from me and starts to head off. I pick my glass up off the coffee table. When I turn around again she's gone.

On my way back to bed I almost forget to turn off the lamp. Everything goes dark, and when I look up there's a cat sitting outside on the balcony ledge. I stand at the sliding door to see him better. He appears only in silhouette, one ear with a notch in it. His tail swishes back and forth. He's looking out at the street.

Sometimes the cats get run over or show up dead in odd places. Like the time one was stretched over the back fence, exposed like deli meat. Kevin upstairs said maybe it had been poisoned, but who would do something like that? I don't want to know. I've thought about leaving something out one night, a saucer of milk or some tuna. I think about the cats, even when they don't wake me. And I can imagine one, maybe this one, being won over gradually in time. Maybe one night I'll leave the door open a crack, and in the morning there he'll be, sprawled on the couch, his long tail swishing.

I place my forehand on the glass and outside the cat stiffens like he can sense it. He leaps down and with a blaze of moonlight on his fur, he's gone. I can only watch from behind the glass, wondering if he'll appear again. And when I'm sure he won't, I test the door to make sure it's locked, and slip quietly back to my room—but not to sleep.

Amanda

David Lloyd

David Grant Lloyd was born in 1979. He attended the University of Wollongong and received his Masters Degree in Literature in 2003. He worked for some years in Sydney before returning to his hometown Dubbo, where much of his writing is set.

Amanda

Amanda was a good woman. She was a few years younger than me and raising two boys on her own in a small drab house with bad piping over in Rosewood Grove (formally known as Gordon Estate) on the west side of Dubbo.

We met at the Amaroo one Friday night. I was sitting at a table outside on the balcony by myself drinking a schooner of Carlton and writing down some notes. She was alone smoking a cigarette. Our eyes met briefly and we smiled at each other. I went on with my writing, not thinking much of it, and pulled on my schooner. Next thing I knew she sat down next to me and asked, "What are you writing?"

I was a little startled. "Oh," I said, "nothing really. Just some ideas for some poems or something."

"You're a poet?"

"Not really. I just write shit."

She laughed. "You're funny," she said.

After a few drinks, smokes and some small talk she invited me back to her place. I told her I was an alcoholic. She said she didn't care. I said okay then.

We got a taxi outside the pub. She'd called for one on her mobile as we walked out the front entrance. We only had to wait a few minutes.

"Where we going?" the driver asked after we climbed in and fastened our seatbelts.

"Twenty-four Bunglegumbie Road," Amanda said.

He drove down Macquarie Street, past the library and under the railway bridge, and turned left onto Erskine Street. After crossing Serisier Bridge, he turned the taxi onto Thompson Street.

"I'll just drop you off at the corner," he said as we neared Bunglegumbie Road. "I don't like going down that road. One time a bunch of boong kids threw rocks at the vehicle and management took it out of my pay."

I wasn't sure how truthful he was being but he seemed adamant.

Amanda said: "Yeah, that's fine. I get it."

We got out at the corner and paid the driver. We went halves.

"That happens all the time," she said after the taxi drove off. "I can't even get a fucken pizza delivered."

"Seriously?"

"Yeah. They all got the same excuse. Abo kids throwing rocks at them."

"Do they?"

"Yeah," she said. "Sometimes."

The road was long. Like most houses in the area, the ones on Bunglegumbie Road were small and shabby and peeling. A lot of the front yards were unkempt, many with clumps of garbage bags and broken furniture and several windows boarded up.

Amanda pointed up to a pair of shoes dangling from the telephone wires. "They've been hanging there for nearly two years," she said.

"How long have you been here?"

"I've been here ages."

The street was unusually quiet for a Friday night. Most subdivisions around town would have had at least one party going somewhere. It was just past midnight but I expected there to be more noise. There were only a few houses with lighted windows. Most were dark.

"Is it always this quiet?" I asked.

"It depends," she said as she reached over and held my hand.

I gave her hand a squeeze. She squeezed back.

"You got rough hands," she said. "Are you a bricklayer?"

"No," I said. "I'm a cleaner."

"A cleaner?" she said. "What's that like?"

"About as good as it sounds."

She laughed. "I guess so. I work the cash register at Target. It's pretty boring but it's okay. And I need the money."

"We all do."

We arrived at her house. Her front yard was behind a slumping metal gate and had overgrown patches of weeds from the paling fence to the empty driveway. Her house looked much like the others in the neighbourhood: roofed with corrugated iron and walled with pale weatherboards, several brick pillars stood underneath the bulk, forming the foundation, and small concrete steps led up to the front door.

Amanda sighed as she took her keys from out of her purse. "Damn," she said, looking at the lighted window. "Those little shits are still up."

She unlocked the door and we went inside.

"Mum!" shouted Tim, the eldest of her two sons.

"Mummy!" squealed Joe, the curly-haired one still in nappies.

"What are you two still doing up?" she said in a deep, commanding voice. She placed her hands on her hips and scowled at them.

Unsure of what else to do, I went into the kitchen while Amanda reprimanded her sons. In her fridge I found a half-empty bottle of cheap chardonnay. I opened it and began drinking. In the other room, I could hear the kids struggling as their mother took hold of them and put them to bed. I sat at the kitchen table and kept pulling on the bottle. The kitchen was clean apart from the large, opened packet of CC's lying on the counter and a half-eaten Cadbury bar sitting next to the used ashtray on the wooden table. Dishes and glasses had been cleaned and placed on the drying rack near the sink. In the lounge room a DVD of Madagascar was playing and the well-worn carpet was littered with toys. It all seemed quite pleasant. But there was a strange rancid smell in the air that I couldn't get over. It wasn't overpowering but it was constant. And it seemed like it had been there forever and would remain forever.

After about ten minutes, Amanda came back. She watched me drain the bottle and said, "Help yourself, why don't you?"

"Sorry."

"It's okay," she said. "I've got a bottle of red under the sink if you want that too."

"Maybe," I said.

She lit a cigarette and sat down across from me, dragging the ashtray closer to her. She took a few drags and began talking a bit awkwardly. "Listen," she started. "I normally would've had a babysitter to watch over them. But… well…"

"I don't care," I said. "Don't worry about it."

She smiled. She kept smoking.

I went to the sink and opened the cabinet underneath. A bottle of Merlot was there among the bleaches and dishwashing detergents. I took it out and drank several large rapid gulps.

"You're drinking that stuff like water," she said. "You weren't lying when you said you were an alco."

"At least I'm honest," I said.

"True."

I sat back down. "So how old are they?"

"What?"

"Your boys."

"Oh. Tim's seven and Joe's two," she said. "Tim's father lives in Canberra. He wanted nothing to do with me after I… I was bad."

"What about Joe's father?"

"He's in Newcastle," she said. "He left a few months ago when the doctor diagnosed Joe with autism."

We sat in silence for a while. She smoked. I drank.

"Have you always lived in Dubbo?" I said.

"Yes," she said. "Have you?"

"Yes," I said.

The bottle was almost empty. I asked her where the toilet was. She told me it was down the hallway on the right.

I made my way out of the kitchen, around the lounge room and down the small hallway. Some of the floorboards under the withered carpet creaked and groaned as I walked over them.

There was one bathroom. Its walls and floors were a faded yellowy colour. In one corner was a rust-stained shower bath with an old shower curtain drawn back, on the other side was a toilet beneath a small window with a can of air-freshener on the sill. Between them was a sink and mirrored cabinet.

After using the toilet and flushing, I came out to the hall and noticed the darkness. The lights and TV had been turned off. It took a minute for my eyes to adjust.

"Come in here," Amanda said from her bedroom.

I went in, closing the door behind me, and could see her clearly despite the dark. We held each other. We kissed for a long time.

"You're sweet," I said.

"So are you," she said.

We kissed and fondled each other.

"Do you have to work tomorrow?" she said.

"No," I said. "Do you?"

"No."

I slid my hand down the back of her jeans and squeezed her arse cheek. Then I brought it back out and pushed it up under her blouse, caressing one of her small breasts.

"Do you want to make love to me?"

"I'm too drunk."

"Come on then," she said, taking her clothes off. "Let's go to sleep."

I watched her pull the covers back and climb over to the other side of the bed, her back to me. I took my clothes off and lay down close beside her, putting my arm around her waist.

We woke up still holding each other. We lay naked above the sheets on her bed by the window. A sliver of light shone upon us. We kissed.

The boys were in the lounge room. They were quiet but the sound of the TV carried.

"Wait a minute," she said suddenly, turning her head away. "Did you lock the door?"

"Um," I said. "I don't know."

"Shit," she said. "Come on. Get dressed."

We crawled out of bed and began putting our clothes on. She quickly went over to the door and checked it. It wasn't locked. She locked it.

"Sorry about that," I said.

"It's all right," she said. "I should've remembered."

When we were dressed she opened the door. The boys were sitting on the couch in front of the TV. I didn't know what they were watching. Some cartoon show. We stepped over the toys on the carpet and went to the kitchen. The boys followed us.

"Mum," Tim said. "Joe stinks."

Amanda sighed. "Okay, honey," she said. She lifted Joe up and smelled him. "Ugh!" she moaned. "We need to change your nappy."

Joe laughed.

As she and Joe left the room, Amanda said, "David, can you please put the kettle on?"

"Sure."

"And some toast?" she said. "There's bread in the freezer."

"Okay."

I walked around the kitchen, getting the coffee and toast prepared, noticing for the first time the stickiness of the linoleum under my feet. As the water boiled and the bread cooked, I picked up the near-empty bottle of Merlot from last night and started drinking from it. All the while I could feel Tim's eyes on me. I tried to ignore it and kept guzzling until the bottle was completely drained.

The two slices of toast popped up. I took them from the toaster, put them on a clean plate, along with a breadknife, and set the plate down on the table, where Tim sat. I went to the fridge and took out some margarine, honey, jam and Vegemite. Then I went back to the toaster and put in two more slices of bread.

Casually, I looked around in the cabinets to see if there was any more wine stashed about the place. There was nothing.

Amanda's pack of Winfield's was on the table beside the ashtray. I took a cigarette from the pack and lit it. Reluctant to sit down, I picked up the ashtray and took it to the kitchen sink with me as I waited for Amanda to return.

Tim buttered his toast with margarine and Vegemite, looking up at me every now and then, as if waiting for me to say something. I didn't open my mouth except to smoke.

He looked at me. I looked at him.

"Are you going to stay?" he said.

Marina

Gavin Mndawe

Moorish revivalist. Prince of the royal secret. One who breathes like tortoise. Mental health activist. Eleven embodied. Evangelist of the epiphysis. Owl incarnate. Modern-day Essene. Rising master faster. Angelo Soliman, Benjamin Banneker and Ziryab all wrapped up in one. Subject of the last absolute monarch in Africa and citizen of the Republic of South Africa.

Marina

There is a kingdom unbeknown to many. You could swear the buildings and streets are golden, the way they sparkle and dazzle. Rumour has it money is minted and printed down there. Many have mistaken this place for heaven.

Most of you have been to this kingdom and don't even know it. Others 'clock in' everyday and are not aware. This is no shock considering how quick it is to adapt down there.

Marina was lucky enough to learn of this kingdom, but not before it learnt of her. You see, Marina was dedicated at birth. Placed inside a disembowelled goat and trained in divination and potion production, she was to be a mighty subject in the kingdom.

She learnt a lot as an initiate under her mother; whose idea it was to have her dedicated. She was taught of the various spirits; the menacing monkey that hides your identity when you do wrong, the sensual snake that strikes down every counterpart in its path, the promiscuous dog that renders eye contact deadly. These were technologies Marina was to familiarise herself with. She learnt to identify them, to deal with them and to invite them. The monkey spirit for instance is inserted through incisions made by burnt monkey eyebrows.

Not only was she taught of spirits, she was educated in identifying the physical markers of a marine agent. Religiosity, skimpy clothing, 'profane' music, lack of manners, aggression etcetera are all indications of allegiance to the sea. If they love attention, they belong to the sea. If they 'zone out' often, they belong to the sea. If they fail to look an anointed one in the eye, they belong to the sea. You may think they are sleeping in church—not so. They are avoiding fire in their eyes.

Unless they are the result of recruitment, none of them has the same mission and yet there are some universal red flags. One of these red flags is 'zoning out'. An agent would be talking to you and he'd ask you about something you're passionate about. You would talk about your passion without realising no one is listening. It is only when you say something funny and pat the agent on the back that you'll realise you've been talking to yourself. It is also at this point that the agent would have to leave whatever marine boardroom and return to the body while it's still in the same position. A different position would spell death.

Another red flag is personality. A marine subject will change personalities when administering chaos. If it's music, their voice will change when singing. If it's fashion, they will be a different person in their Sunday best.

It is said "there is nothing new under the sun". Whoever said that didn't consider the oceanic threshold that exceeds the reach of sunshine. You see, where light fears to tread, lies thrive and mutation abounds, resulting in the "new".

Marina never doubted the power of her will, not after possibly witnessing it kill someone. Her one true friend Orphilia wasn't available suddenly. Who was she to share the wisdom with? Who would help her digest everything? Who was she to absorb from? The mother didn't trust Orphilia's siblings as much. She became demanding, always needing Orphilia to do something, to stick around the house or go some place. And so Marina purposed in her heart for Orphilia's mother to die. At first she balked at this malicious wish, later she grew accustomed to it, nursing it with every "she's not here" and "I've sent her to town".

Marina and Orphilia shared a bond so strong that a day without contact was like a day without fresh air and sunshine. Marina became completely consumed by the strangling thought of Orphilia's absence.

"Marina, write numbers one to ten for us, in order, thank you," decrees Miss Ekans, handing her the chalk. Up bounces the young lady with her trousers tucked into her boots. It is worth noting that girls that do not wear pants, nor do they wear boots in school. As she writes on the board the class erupts in laughter.

"Does that look like a seven to you?" snarls Miss Ekans. Unsettled, she turns to the madam who by now is standing akimbo.

"If I stand this way I am Marina, If I turn the other way, am I not still Marina?" she challenges as her audience ejects a barrage of chuckles, giggles and cackles.

Her mother used to say "peace implies war, power implies war and glory implies war". She could tell these were not her words because these words were stained with frustration. She was invested in indifference. Women and emotion are synonymous, but a dragged life of disappointment left her callous. It didn't help living in a land where the dams had dandruff, the function of rivers was reversed and the smell of rain was a distant memory. While kicking stones and mudcakes to or from her gig or what others call school, she would dip into the despair her mother wanted to feel.

There was a medicine woman in the village that Marina's mother was an apprentice to. It is said that all rains from the past fifty years were the result of her sacred dance. At seventy-four, and without anyone trained in this art and science, the village was in jeopardy. Guerrilla governments and mercenaries were closing in on this region and the rain and war goddess Aleeneh required appeasement. The rain dance was unlike any other. The shaman would have to camp on the bank of the river for five days. During these days the shaman would not eat or drink anything.

Candlelit dinners were the true reservoirs of knowledge for Marina. She often wore the tiara her mother received as Miss University, even at supper.

"Mama, why do we live in the desert?" asks Marina with feathery frustration.

"We live in the desert because we are poor; we are poor because Africa is poor and Africa is poor because things come easy here. You don't need air conditioning; you can sit under a tree. You don't need heated floors. You don't need to fertilize soil; you just plant a seed. The Sahara is cursed. I pray to Aleeneh, may this hell shed its rancorous skin to reveal the lush splendour our Moorish forefathers wrote of."

The ancestors have ways of calling the living into service. Marina's lack of attention at school wasn't due to her wanting attention. She was plagued by the sound of crashing water, visions of crystal crocodiles and the feeling she was not the only inhabitant of her body.

After vigorous evaluation, Marina took it upon herself to consult the old medicine lady to find out what the ancestors wanted. She arrived to a macabre display of freedom. Rare animal skins like that of leopards and pythons were draped on the walls as if to wean oneself off the wilderness. Elephant and hippo bones propped up the roof and were ignored by villagers, as if acknowledging some shamanistic immunity.

To enter a trance, the medicine woman had her assistant beat drums drunkenly as she eased into a limping dance. Incense smoke reminiscent of forest fog colonised the consultation room while the witchdoctor sought guidance from her bag of bones. A piece of broken mirror rolled out of the bag as she discarded its contents. "Makhosi" she grunted as she launched into convulsions and clapped her hands to welcome the ancestors. "Young lady you must answer the call of the ancestors or they will sicken you to death," she said while pointing at the mirror. "You are the only hope this village has. Perform the sacred dance. Know one thing however: you are replaceable." And she disappeared in a stinging storm of smoke before the assistant escorted Marina out.

Later that evening, Marina would set out for Lana River, carrying with her not a change of clothes nor food, but incense and other ceremonial devices. As she stargazed awe-inspired, she saw an array of lights zipping by as if to celebrate her journey. Prayer and chanting were the order of the night as she braced herself for this adventure. Hoots and howls fluttered in the air as Marina noticed a fig tree. She had never seen one this big, the fruit itself being of unprecedented proportions. Marina wrestled the craving, deciding to camp by the tree until she convinced herself. And surely she did, a few hours into the night. Five days will begin tomorrow, she thought comfortingly as she gorged herself on figs.

She awoke to an army of frogs encircling her. "What is this?" soliloquized Marina.

"You are pregnant," proclaimed a voice, seemingly coming from within her.

"But I've never… " shudders Marina.

"With desire," added the voice. "Sometimes willing and waiting are enough." And a cascading reassurance came upon Marina as she watched the frogs leap into obscurity.

Through a Child's Eyes

Jo Mularczyk

Jo enjoys writing in different genres for a range of audiences. Her stories and poems appear in *The School Magazine's* 'Blast Off' and 'Touchdown'; *Zinewest* 2019, 2018, 2017; *fourW thirty's* 'New writing: Pearl anthology 2019'; *Short and Twisted* 2017; Storm Cloud Publishing's *Short Tales 5*, *Short Tales 4*, *Open House 3*, *Open House 2* and *Christmas Tales 4*; *Wonderment* by Poetica Christi; *Love, Hate, Oceans, Sloth and Ancients* by Black Hare Press; *Daily Science Fiction*; a children's poetry anthology to be published by Bloomsbury UK; and other upcoming anthologies.

Jo has been highly commended, honourably mentioned and shortlisted in several competitions. She was one of the winners of the Australian Writers' Centre 'short short' story competition.

Jo loves to share the joy of writing through delivery of creative writing workshops and as mentor to a gifted and talented student writing group. Jo is an author with the Littlescribe student literacy program, providing story starters and writing tips to students who go on to co-author the stories (*www.littlescribe.com*).

Jo provides corporate writing services, having had an extensive background in corporate and strategic writing.

Jo lives with her husband and three children.

Website: *www.jomularczyk.com*

Facebook: *www.facebook.com/jo.mularczyk.author*

Instagram: *www.instagram.com/jo_mularczyk_authorpage/*

Through a Child's Eyes

Jim sat on his balcony, cocooned in his ageing wooden rocking chair. He leaned forward, willing his body weight to propel the chair along its arc. Momentum was the key. What would his students have thought if they could see him using physics in this way?

His strength and body weight were not enough these days to get any decent sort of motion going. The chair returned to its preferred inert state. The truth was that inert was also his preferred state. He cast his tired eyes around. The washed-out sky held just a memory of blue. His once proud garden stood overgrown. The stone pathway that led to his balcony seemed to regard him mockingly, daring him to navigate its uneven surface.

He used to go out walking every morning until he had stumbled on the stones. Now it was easier to stay on the balcony. Jim wasn't sure when *easier* had become his creed, but it had, and the balcony was a good spot to watch the world go by.

He heard the approaching footsteps of children on their way home from school. He knew what they called him. "Old Man Jim". It used to bother him but now he admired their honesty.

As he craned his neck to see the road, Jim heard the chair groan under his shifting weight. *My thoughts exactly*, he thought wryly. Glancing up, he saw that it wasn't school children he had heard, just a small boy walking with his mother. As he watched, the mother stopped to answer her phone. She started complaining about their train being late, about trackwork interrupting their trip, about being herded onto a bus with other passengers. Jim was so busy listening that he was startled to see the small boy leaning on his gate. The boy had a head full of blonde curls and one fell across his forehead as he tried to get a foothold on the gate. As he lifted his hand and impatiently pushed the curl away from his face the boy noticed Jim and waved. Jim waved back hesitantly.

Giving up on climbing the gate, the boy opened it and walked up the path. Jim noticed with a pang how deftly the boy mastered each step.

"You're Old Man Jim," the boy announced.

"That's what they call me," Jim answered. He cringed at how dry his voice sounded, like it had corroded from disuse. "And what do they call you?"

"I'm Asher. What are you doing?" Asher asked.

"Sitting… and watching," he answered.

"Watching what?" Asher asked, lifting an eyebrow.

Jim hesitated only a moment before answering with the jarring truth. "Watching life." Asher laughed. "You don't watch life. You live it."

Jim stared at the boy with a moment of awful clarity.

"Are you sad?" Asher asked. Jim wasn't sure what to say. He wasn't sure what he should say.

Before Jim had a chance to answer, Asher climbed the stairs. He reached out to touch Jim's chair.

"Is that a real rocking chair?" he asked. Jim nodded. "Cool!" Asher turned to look at Jim's yard. "Wow! I love your garden. Ours is so neat. But yours looks wild like a forest." The boy's random observation roused a memory of seeing the world through the eyes of his students, the everyday tinged with wonder. Jim smiled slowly; the movement felt alien but he let muscle memory take over.

Asher continued his happy patter. "Mum and I got to ride on a train and a bus today. It was so cool!" Jim looked up and saw Asher's Mum standing at the gate listening. In her eyes Jim saw the same awakening he felt. And just a hint of shame. Asher saw where Jim was looking and turned to face his mother. "I was just telling Jim about our amazing day."

Asher's mother nodded. "You're right darling. It was amazing."

Asher smirked at Jim, "I told you." Jim smiled more easily this time.

"The train was so fast. It was high velocipy." Asher asserted proudly.

"Velocity." Jim corrected automatically and he was surprised when he continued speaking. "I have a book about velocity. It has some great pictures of cars and trains."

"Can I see Jim's book Mum?" Asher asked.

Asher's Mum looked towards Jim who surprised himself again by nodding. "Maybe tomorrow," she answered.

Content with his mother's answer, Asher launched down the stairs. "Cool! Gotta go Jim. I'm going home to play with my trains. See you tomorrow."

Jim watched the boy skip to his mother, hair bouncing. He looked at his world, at Asher's world. He thought about life and how it was a collection of moments.

Jim leant back in his chair and then pushed forward. He started to rock.

First Steps

Sara Abend-Sims

Sara Abend-Sims was born in Poland and grew up in Israel. She lived in London for a short while and is now living in Adelaide, Australia.

She is a University of SA graduate who worked as lecturer and counsellor, travelled, wrote, painted, and exhibited her art in Australia and overseas.

In the last decade she has been using words instead of brushes, capturing moments and attempting to make sense of her own experience as well as others.

Sara is the recipient of two community first prize literary awards—2009 and 2015. Her stories and poetry have been published in anthologies, journals, and online in Australia and overseas.

First Steps

Weeding is therapeutic. Jason's words play a non-stop loop in my mind. "Therapeutic," I mutter and pull the weeds in my front garden, one at a time or whole clumps. "Jason didn't pull enough nightmarish-weeds though… should have," I groan. He would not have needed the bullet if he had. Wiping my forehead, I straighten and reach the bin to empty my bucket. I am in no hurry, knowing that what I will not do today will wait for another day.

Therapeutic, a process of pulling what is not needed in order to keep the mind and garden healthy and looking good. Words flap in the wind like Tibetan prayer flags: healthy and tidy, healthy and orderly, healthy with no harmful invaders, like weeds or the demons that have plagued Jason since returning from his last deployment.

I'm at Jason and Mel's place. Their baby is in a plastic bathtub. The baby is surrounded by warm water and bubbles. Mother Mel is stroking the tiny, wet limbs, and then rubs her nose onto the baby's chubby tummy. Their giggles mix with the scented steam.

I hear Jason's squeaking wheelchair through the open door.

"He needs to move in order to feel alive," Mel whispers.

"Yes, sweetie," I whisper back, "alive. Just."

Suzi and Johnnie are in the big bathtub. They laugh and wriggle; they throw soft toys and soapy splashes on the floor and mother's jeans.

"Nana," Suzi calls, "rubber ducky, gi'me Nana. P l e a s e."

"No, no," Johnny shouts. "It's mine, Nana, give it to me…"

Jason's failed suicide attempt, squeaky sounds and his limp body when the baby is placed in his lap, follow me on my way home. And no, I don't have a gun or know how to use it; yet thinking about Jason aiming at his brain and pulling the trigger, startles me again and again. "Thanks Jason," I mutter. "Thanks for the reminder that waiting for another day could be lethal."

Weeding is therapeutic, the weeding of hard feelings, of Jason's demons… it is the afternoon and I am by the River Torrens.

I am doing my therapeutic weeding by walking, by looking at birds and listening to my own thoughts. An early memory overlaps the image of Jason, of Mel and the bathing children. I'm about seven years old and in a new place. Mother and I have just moved into a communal house in the hills.

"You'll make new friends with the children who live here," mother says. She takes me by the hand to our new bedroom. We have a large mirror on one wall and two beds, a grey rug between the beds and a beautiful painting of ghost gums hung by the window.

"A lucky plant," she points at the potted plant that stands in the room's corner. The plant is almost as tall as I am, the leaves are dark and shiny. "It will be home-schooling from now on, shared meals and lots of fun," mum tells me, but her face is telling me something different. Her eyes have lost their spark, her lips are tight and I notice that her hands are trembling.

We walk along the corridor and pass closed doors till we get to the kitchen-dining room. We meet Val and she makes two cups of coffee for mum and herself and hot chocolate for me. They speak among themselves, hushed voices and serious faces; it's adult talk, not for me to hear. I get up and wander on my own.

Following the noise, I reach an open door and see terrazzo walls, timber benches and pigeonholes. My name is at the top row and above a pile of folded clothes. Standing on tip toes, I stretch my arm and reach my name—reaching me.

I look through to the adjacent room. Naked children are running around, laughing as they chase one another. The two showers on the far wall are squirting water, yet nobody is paying attention.

Mother startles me by sneaking from behind. "Go on, join in darling. Shower time. Be brave." I hear a fake note in her cajoling in spite of the noise. Still… I bury my head in her warmth, but not for long, as she breaks contact with a hurried 'must go.'

Shaking off this childhood memory, I pay attention to water and gum trees, to rustling leaves and rainbow lorikeets. On higher ground, I look at children on swings with parents watching them, protective.

And I am back to reflecting, back to questioning this early memory in the hills. Did my mother plan it, I wonder—this shower thing? Did she intend for me to go through with this on-the-spot rite-of-passage-transformation? Was I supposed to jump in and get wet together with these boys and girls, like it was a baptism of sorts; baptism for me and who knows, perhaps for mum through me? I feel silly thinking like that, magical thinking that is.

But how else can I understand mother's coaxing me to shower, to wash away the years of living together, just mum and me… to wash away the girl I have been, one in grey trousers and a pink top tucked in neatly, and to morph into a communal-house-kid, the navy blue T-shirt—my uniform, like the rest of them, with our identities blurred.

"A betrayal of the past, of us—the inseparable parcel," I whisper. "But a moment after her encouragement, the parcel is torn apart. She is gone."

And I try to imagine what a betrayal of the past looks like. Will it be twisted, maimed, deformed, like a shower in a house shuddered by an earthquake, a tsunami, a fire, where the metal pipe is drooping, where the showerhead has melted away? And what will happen to the story, to our story, to my story? Will it become a broken story, a deformed and maimed one?

And what will happen to Jason, Mel's husband, to his story, where will he bury the voices, the smells, the scenes… the fear… the past, his past?

Back at home I check my phone and Mel's message is the first one on my screen.

"Mum, Jason got out of the wheelchair a minute ago. He's standing. Now, he's taking his first step—
Jason not the baby!"

In the Beginning was Kitto

John M. Williams

John M. Williams retired from academia in 2015. He was named Georgia Author of the Year for First Novel in 2002 for **Lake Moon** (Mercer UP). He has written and co-written numerous plays, with several local productions, and published a variety of stories, essays, and reviews through the years. His and co-author Rheta Grimsley Johnson's play **Hiram: Becoming Hank**, about the formative years of singer Hank Williams, will be performed at the Monroeville, Alabama courthouse in October 2020. His most recent books are **Village People: Sketches of Auburn** (Solomon and George 2016), and **Atlanta Pop in the 50s, 60s, and 70s: The Magic of Bill Lowery**, co-authored with Andy Lee White (The History Press 2019). Previous publications can be found on his website at *johnmwilliams.net*, which hosts his blog, *johnmwilliams.net/blog*. He lives in LaGrange, Georgia, USA.

In the Beginning was Kitto

Leaf floating in mid-air.

Standing there, August 1952—rain-cooled, the air aching with the heartbreaking music of birds.

I will always remember this moment. And I have. It either is or as though I've been granted fifteen minutes to go back, and it's the *smell*—the moldy pine smell—I drink it, my eyes burning, and realize every age signs its name in scent.

Drips in the woods. Distant groan of machines. Thirty years old, home to take my half of my parents' estate (my sister the other), garden trowel, rather ridiculously, in my pocket—just as Kitto said, a survivor. Ah, Kitto. Saw it coming, and declined. Gone, but still there in spirit. Only, I know what that means now. Means gone.

Can't help it, can't help it, can't help it.

*

> *In the beginning was Kitto,*
>
> *And Kitto created the heavens and the earth. And Kitto said let there be light and there was light, And Kitto saw that it was good.*
>
> *All things were made by Kitto—without him was not anything that was made.*
>
> *And Kitto's light shone in the darkness and the darkness comprehended it not.*

My recitation hung in the air. Kitto, in his place—pieces of an old mantel, painted bricks, dolls' heads dangling on wires, coloured bottles, mannequin pieces around him in the dome of the candlelit fort—just looked at me. Bucky, Beetle, Chick, Tykie, and Dougy, in a semicircle behind me, kept a reverent silence.

Finally Kitto said, "Come receive the mark."

I hobbled on my knees closer to him; he took out pen and ink from a rusty strongbox in a tangle of vines to his side and drew the mark in the place destined, some years later, for a polio vaccination: K.

"Never wash there again," he instructed, then with his carved stick (so artistic to our amateur) knighted my shoulders and head.

An approving exhalation sounded from behind me. Weighed by Kitto and found not wanting. I was in.

The end of a process—and there had been nothing easy about it.

First: steal a model airplane from the Kress Five and Dime.

In any other store, this would not have been a particularly challenging task, but under the falcon-eyed surveillance of Mrs. Berman, it was almost impossible. It required, as Kitto knew, wits.

First, I asked to see school supplies, knowing she knew I knew she knew I didn't have any money—1934, who did?—but followed her, then looked studiously through the goods, worked my way up to the aisle, the models one counter away, Mrs. Berman stalking me like some kind of small-town Grim Reaper—what in blazes was *taking* them so long? *Finally*—a loud crash and wounded yelp sounded from the sidewalk out front, the few customers turning in alarm to look, jovial Mr. Berman at the front register bustling out the open door, Mrs. Berman clutching her sweater at her throat and craning her long neck in surprise, starting up the aisle leaving me the three-second gap I needed to suck in my stomach, slide the long flat box into my pants, under my shirt, and start away just as she caught herself and looked over her shoulder. But too late. I was sucking in my gut and engineering an innocent face, and we were in the flow, heading toward the excitement—out from the cool, fan-chopped store to the bright sidewalk where Mr. Berman was helping poor Dougy to his feet—Tykie picking up his bike, straddling the front wheel and straightening the handlebars—and she was on to me now as I walked stiffly away—*did you find what you were looking for?*

Yes mam! I limped a few more steps then broke into a crippled run. That afternoon, I presented the corner-crumpled box to Kitto.

Accepted.

Second: Tell a grown-up to shut their trap with two witnesses.

Had to call on the wits again. I finally decided on Barney the produce guy at the Jitney Jungle—borderline, only a year out of high school but married with a baby. Would that qualify? Kitto had to deliberate for several minutes—he scowled and didn't particularly like it, but finally approved.

In we went—Beetle, Dougy, and me. We loitered until there were no customers, dawdling around the apples as Barney glared from the potatoes, until finally he said *what do you little snots want?* We stood there, an odd little moment as the daring impulse rose in me; Beetle and Dougy like nerve ends about to fire, cut their eyes to me—and looking at just about Barney's shoulder I suddenly blurted out *Shut your tater trap!* and like lizards we exploded away. Heads turned as he pursued us in his green-stained apron out the front door almost to the alley, but we were faster. *You'd better not come back in here! I'll teach you little brats a lesson!*

Later, Kitto looked at us and squinted his eyes. "*Tater trap?*" he asked.

I nodded, Beetle and Dougy backed me up. Done.

Third: Take a crap in the girls' bathroom at school.

This one required mostly nerve, and some biological preparation. We stood under the high transom windows, looking for an unlocked one. There was always one somewhere. Oh God, nothing like the feel of the school at night—that sweet smell not out of place but of time, everything a ghostly version of its daytime self, that mystical feeling of rich violation, inviting the deep destructive part that comes out like a nasty little night animal. I slipped into Mrs. Abrams' room, looked through her desk, might as well have been her underwear drawer, fondled her red pencils, her whistle, the cool glass of her hand lotion, the confiscated tops and yo-yos, thumbed briefly through her gradebook with its spidery red hieroglyphics. *Come on,* hissed Dougy, my witness, but I took a few seconds to sit in Pamela Peterson's desk, the new girl, a mad feeling like wearing her clothes. Then at last we were slipping down the shadowy hall—the place was ours! made you want to *do* something—so I stopped at the bulletin board and started turning notices upside down, but Dougy hissed at me again and we entered that most mysterious inner sanctum of all, no urinals and the funny machine on the wall, a little light leaking through the frosted windows. I slid into the first stall, and sat trying to make out the graffiti, amazed that it was even there, neater, not as crude as the boys', but more personal and vicious. *Pamela Peterson Bitch Go Back Where You Came From*—I was sitting, straining—Dougy just outside the stall pacing, urging me to hurry up, but what are you going to do?—thinking he heard something every thirty seconds—not welcome news with your pants around your ankles, just froze me up more—finally it came, not spectacular but good enough. Dougy had an obligatory glance but it was too dark really to see—no question of flushing, the point was to leave it there anyway, and just at the door he claimed he *really* heard something this time. He cracked it open and holy cow! sure enough, a flashlight beam from outside slashed over the windows through Mrs. Dendy's open door. The bathroom door bumped to, and we froze, hearts doing a drum solo. Then holy bejesus the sound of the main door opening at the far end of the hall! Mad impulse to run, but that was suicide. Good thing I already shit. Footsteps slowly approached down the hall. We hurried into the far stall, closed the door, locked it, and balanced on the toilet seat like angels on a pinhead. The footsteps got inexorably closer, stopped, got closer, stopped—he'll see the bulletin board!—got closer—never been this scared in my life—the door opened! I swear I could smell him—sweat, tobacco. The light pawed over the walls, the ceiling, swathed the floor—maybe he was the funny kind, wanted to do it too! I was paralyzed, I hadn't breathed for five minutes, I was about to pee. Finally, ages later, the door closed and the footsteps passed on and finally melted away. We waited, standing on our crowded pedestal for an extravagantly long time as we imagined the sounds of closing doors a dozen times, then finally mustered the nerve to descend and I bumped into the toilet paper holder making a noise and breathing a just-verbal involuntary curse. Dougy jabbed his finger to his lips in earnest, and we slipped out of the stall. This window, said Dougy, and pulled the chain to open the high transom with a jarring grate and climbed up on the radiator to have a look. Then he turned to me and nodded, twisted himself up and wormed through. I heard him hit the gravelly ground outside with a crunching thud. I climbed up into the vacuum he had left and watched him dashing across the open, half-lighted drive to the cover of the pecan trees on the other side; and something about seeing him scot-free lit a fire under me and I was through the window and down and racing towards Dougy's whistle all in one long motion—then we were in the woods—our briar patch—the smell of the creek, the familiar paths. We saw a flicker of headlights out on the street, but they seemed remote. Later in bed: that *feeling*. That hot icy rushing wide-awake scared electric *feeling*. Who could know? You go through the rest of your life, never have it again.

Fourth: The church.

Same feeling as the school, but deeper—you felt it in the nerve cord under your scrotum. *A church is only a building*, Kitto always said, *like any building. Look at it: brick, wood, pipes and wires—just a building, no different*. Full moon night—the thrill running through you like some dangerous current. Dougy and me again—we went in through the little door to the bell tower, climbed the pigeon shit-encrusted ladder to the top open to the four compass points over the sleeping town—none of this elaborate ceremony necessary as the main doors below were never locked, but these things must be done in style—plus the rare view: the rolling moonlit panorama speared by two other steeples, the stores along the paved downtown streets, dominated by the bulky silhouette of Pitts Hotel, Main Street angling up to the tracks and the soft lights of the dozing depot—no traffic, no people—then we squeezed through the other opening into the sweltering attic, stepping our way like burglars across the rafters, emerging through the hole in the far back corner of the balcony. No desire to linger here—just do the mission and go. We took the stairs to the narthex, then padded down the centre aisle, up to the chancel, and I stood for just a few seconds behind the main pulpit looking over the big-worded Bible to the eerie sanctuary, the moonlight glowing through the stained glass windows. *Let's go*, wheezed Dougy urgently, and I walked back to the altar, looked all around me, hesitated for a minute, then worked up a mouthful and spit. *All right, let's get out of here*! Dougy whispered tensely, and I only thought about it as what Kitto said to do—nothing more.

And, later, he himself only nodded resignedly, not really interested in it.

Fifth: The Silo.

Remnant of an old dairy, long abandoned, whose history we never knew nor wondered about, with a big open-sided barn, lesions already opening in the roof, musty underneath, briars and vines snaking over the packed dirt floor, under the feed troughs, old rusty ploughs and harrows and rakes hanging, long removed from the last touch; next door, a concrete block milking shed with troughs and braces, long disused, windows busted out since the time of Noah; on the far end, a little room, must have been an office, where we held meetings sometimes, a little opening into the attic where we hid our cigarettes—all smothering in honeysuckle, privet, and a chinaberry grove that provided the green ammo for slingshot battles. Kitto had positioned the rusty bucket—it looked too far. Way too far. Just beyond it: the semicircle of expectant faces. Middle of the day—having drunk a quart of cold water, I took my shirt off, stepped out of my knickers and drawers, and then I was standing there with the inimitable sensation of being buck naked outside in broad daylight. The strange touch of the air on my body, the cool smell of the clumped feral pasture grass. Except for Kitto, a year ahead of us and just graced with the morning dew of manhood, and dark, single-eyebrowed Bucky, in whom it was a little freaky, none of them had been enhanced by Nature's brush yet either—so it was okay, even a little thrilling—and like all the rest it was just one of those things I had to do. Up the ladder I went, all the way to the scary windy platform at the top, wobbly it was or seemed, with the triangular opening into the creepy hollow dark cylinder a few feet deep at the bottom with some mouldy sawdust-like mush rumoured to harbor a giant coiled snake—and there I was, not a stitch on and addressing the world, faces below looking up like spectators at a fire: I gripped the shaky rail with one hand, tried to aim with the other, and it felt like it was going to take forever, and just about then I saw dust barrelling down Rock Mill Road heading our way and I almost aborted, but I wanted so badly to have it done, and I'd come this far—so watching the approaching dust I strained like Samson as the burning slowly inched its way down and the muscles at last obeyed with a little dribble that spattered feebly against the metal platform and stopped—the car was almost in sight, then another heave and thanks be to God it caught, and I was in full flow—like an artillery man I calculated the arc and it walked its way out to the bucket and then sent back to me the brief gratifying splatter—Kitto knew what he was doing, after all—he always did—I put everything I had into it, hitting in and all around it, drawing some cheers, until the arc lost its force and came hang-tail back to the house, and just then the car sped into the opening, slowed, and stopped. I instinctively dropped to a crouch, peeing on my leg and foot, and drew myself into a ball—nothing else to do—I couldn't see anybody at that distance but could feel them seeing me—then finally the car ground its gears and with a toot of its horn groaned away, kicking up a new trail. But by then this lizard was down the ladder and back in my clothes—and with the green sweaty breath of summer all around us, birds raucous in the privet, they surrounded me laughing.

And finally: The House.

An old abandoned two-storey homeplace on the far edge of our woods, on Bentley Road. Behind it sprawled the remains of a once orderly yard and garden: orchard, arbour, shrubs run crazy, an ocean of daffodils in early spring. We emerged from the woods on the dying trace of road and came up on the doomed structure from the side—a tall, vine-entangled chimney rearing starkly on each end. We circled around to the front door, permanently ajar and framed with panes of coloured glass—and entered the dog-trot hall. The staircase rose to rooms as empty and littered as the ones below—one, our gathering place, was leant an odd personality by a framed family photo mysteriously left on the mantel, and a rusted pistol on two nails above it. We came to light naturally in our semi-circle; and Kitto, presiding, brought out the liquor from a secret recess in a cabinet. I had dreaded this one above all, but tried to prepare mentally. Like everything else, no way out—they had all done it. Then Kitto had it in his hand: a quart Mason jar with rich yellow liquid—none of us knew where he got it though we all assumed from his father, the kook. He handed it to me, the glass cool in my hand. No hesitating, no sitting there trying to stoke up the nerve—Kitto hated that—only three deep breaths and I raised it to my lips, fought back a gag, then took a respectable mouthful—held it where it was even after all the dread and preparation unimaginably vile—I fought another gag, every instinct in my body wanting to spew it out, but I had no choice and so, fighting my own outraged will, *swallowed*—good God! it was paint thinner formaldehyde tractor fuel buzzard piss, a mouthful of toxic fire ants—it scorched a trail of molten lava down my throat and a lingering taste scarred into my sensate tabula rasa forever.

But it was over.

Only the ceremony back at the fort left. I looked up at Kitto, and as he looked back at me, I felt that razor feeling slice through my nerves, and my face grow hot.

*

Sporadic spatter from the trees to the wet leaves below—little shards of the grey sky showing through—summer, always summer—and there against a slice of sky floats the leaf—I watch it turning, trembling, slow-dancing for some unseen wizard.

The war, spent in England, then seven inconclusive years in New York behind me. The Siberian wind blows through my soul. Bulldozers—clearing lots. I already know the house is gone. I won't go there. *The Vanderbilt Man.* What? Fifteen years, 1937. A big black car came and got him as we watched from the woods. No one else. Kitto nowhere around. And for eighteen years a cider jar with candle wax dribbled into the seal has lain buried—holding a cache of our personal carved tokens, laboured over, sanded, varnished, and something on paper from each of us, wadded with twine—mine a map of all our places with illustrations around the edges. But the problem is, although I know the ridge easily, it all looks completely different, the lines of sight cut off in every direction by a new generation of growth, and the tree could be any one of a dozen, or none. I don't even take the trowel from my pocket.

Anyway, they're all gone—Dougy buried in France. I saw him only once, an odd October afternoon on furlough. Bucky blown out of the air over Austria, Beetle in Belgium, Chick in the Pacific, only Tykie alive somewhere, not here—and Robbie Moore running his father's appliance store. And me. Of course, on that December day in 1941 none of us had ever heard of Pearl Harbor.

*

Robbie Moore. Last day of school. He accosted me just off the back corner of the gym as I was starting home. We grew up three houses apart, used to be buddies. But now he had that look in his eye like a bad horse, breaking out into manhood all over, a locker room strutter, and all his ball friends. He stood in my way on the path.

"Pressy—where you been, Pressy? Haven't seen you much lately." I just shrugged.

"What are you planning to do this summer?"

I shrugged again.

"Play with your little gang? Oh, I know all about your little club, Pressy. Your little Kitto club. Everybody knows. You think it's such a secret."

He looked at me but I just stood there.

"Why do you want to go around with a girlie boy like him, Pressy? Are you a little girlie boy too?" He laughed. "Can I see your panties?" I stood there, waiting for it to be over.

"You know what my daddy says?"

I didn't answer.

"Do you know what my *daddy* says?" he repeated. He stared at me—I shook my head.

"His father's an atheist. Do you know what that is?" I nodded neither yes nor no.

"And his mother's an alcoholic. I don't want you going around with him, Pressy—you understand?"

"I'm not *going around* with him."

"Oh, don't lie, Pressy. Everybody knows. Your little fort—we know about that. And you know what? We're going to tear the hell out of it. Tear it to pieces. Your little percy-pants sissy club. See if we don't."

*

How could he know? We were invisible, and it was so perfectly hidden.

Woven into a tight-eye at the bottom of Pine Hill. Roof and sides formed of lashed saplings and bamboo and muscadine vines and sheets of tin and plywood and old signs and an assortment of other items from the ravine across Rock Mill Road that had for years served as an unofficial dump, which we'd hauled piece by piece like a file of ants—a beehive crisscrossed with a web of vines and limbs and smothered so thickly in pinestraw someone passing fifty yards away would not have seen it, we believed—that, and what Kitto told us: as long as we stayed together, we were invisible to everyone else.

Nine o'clock or so, Dougy and I got there together before anyone, crawled through the entrance tunnel and into the meeting dome, just enough light to show the note stuck on a nail between two bricks in Kitto's place. We took it outside and waited for the others—they were just behind.

"Captured by the Vanderbilt Man. Help. Come quick. P.P." Bucky handed out our sticks, and we were off.

Of course we knew where he'd taken her—to his lair of delights—way on the other side of the woods. We followed the sagging fence of the old pasture, crossed at the oak tree through the cactus field where we once saw a rattlesnake and the hair still prickled along your neck at the spot, skirted the dam end of Mr. Benefield's pond, then crouched in a group at the edge of the last strip of woods overlooking the sedge field and The Island.

"Let's split up," said Dougy, and he nodded to Tykie. "You and Chick and Beetle go around and wait for my signal."

"*You* go around," Tykie protested. "It's my turn to give the signal."

"No it's not."

"Yes it is. You did it the last two times."

"Who remembers?"

"It's *my* turn. You and Bucky and Preston go around to that side. We'll come in from over here."

He won. We got into position. Dougy peered across the field—and then we heard the whistle and saw them making a dash for it. We went flying out, sticks ready.

Just as we reached The Island I saw him—hands tied over a limb in the little clearing where a few times we'd found the remains of fires with charred cans—drooping stripped naked from the tortures he will later describe. We rushed in from every direction.

"Hurry," he panted. "Untie me. He's coming back. I know he's coming back—listen!—do you hear that? Hurry!"

We looked over our shoulders.

"Hurry!"

Bucky started fumbling at the loose knot, looked around panicky. Dougy took over.

When he was free Kitto said weakly, "Please get my clothes," and we brought them over and he got dressed.

"Let's get out of here," he said, and we surrounded him—Dougy and I got to help him—and made our escape across the field, perfectly aware we were not invisible to the Vanderbilt Man, whom we wanted to hear all about—but not until we were safe back in the fort where for the rest of the day he was P.P. Not to mention the things he told us.

*

Kitto at nineteen—well, we were *all* odd, weren't we? Sitting in that crazy filthy house, overrun with cats, little art-happenings of weed-speared junk in the never-mowed yard—his mother dead, his father permanently absent in a world of particles and nuclei.

Drinking whiskey? He looked funny. Chain smoking—he didn't smoke either. He gestured for me to get a glass so I poured some and held it—not sure if I could, but just sipping, wetting my lips, I could. Barely. I even took a cigarette myself. We've graduated; outside, a gardenia-soaked summer of '41 night pawed and snorted at the window. "Afraid of what?" he said.

"I don't know."

He took a sip of whiskey; I matched him. "Well, pick something," he replied. "God knows there's plenty to choose from."

"Just—I guess, everything."

He snorted. "Try hating it instead."

"I can't help it."

He exhaled. "Can't help it, can't help it, can't help it."

"I don't know what I'm going to do," I pleaded.

"It doesn't matter what you do."

"I don't know what's going to *happen*."

He laughed. "I do."

"What?"

"The same thing that always happens. They sweep down from the north."

I stared at him puzzled. The Siberian wind blew through me. I swallowed a lump of almost-panic. "I'm just afraid, that's all."

"Oh shut up."

"What are we going to *do*?"

"Oh," he laughed. "Now it's *we*. You're the survivor, the observer—*you* tell *me*."

I considered him, perplexed. He took a deep swallow of whiskey, which made me flinch. No more for me; and that picture—Kitto, blue eyes anchored to the floor, his smooth, almost hairless arms, and long fingered hands—disappearing in the closing door, was my last. No way to know that he wasn't drunk—but drunk enough.

*

Robbie Moore. The idea of him had infiltrated our midst like a rumour of pestilence.

In the Valley: we sat on our personal rocks, holding our sticks, around the bottom of the little boulder-strewn hill, facing Kitto on the huge flat lichen-splotched slab that would be the stage of this natural amphitheatre, ringed in wild plums. Here and there, like random sentries, stood the Rock-Men, on guard.

Kitto, deep in thought, gently rubbed his index finger on his chin. "Exactly what did he say?" he asked me.

"He said he knew about our fort and he—they—were going to tear it up."

I felt the slight fidgets and glances around me.

"You were friends?"

"Well," I shrugged, "we used to be."

Kitto reflected. "What do they say about me?" I demurred, with a shake of my head. He searched my face. "The truth."

"He says you're a girlie boy."

Kitto just listened. "What else?"

"Your father's a kook. And an atheist."

"What's an atheist?" asked Bucky.

Kitto silenced him with a glance. "What else?"

"Your mother's…"

"What?"

"Crazy."

Kitto nodded. "What else did he say—about me?"

"He said he wanted to beat you up."

Kitto just barely smiled. "Would you say he's the leader?" I thought about it and shrugged. "Yeah, I guess."

"You say he goes off with Pamela Peterson?" I nodded.

"You've *seen* them?"

I nodded again. "Yeah."

"Just him?"

"Yeah, I'm pretty sure."

"Do you know what they do?"

I shrugged. "He fingered her."

Kitto studied me. "He *says* he did."

"Well, yeah," I replied, "I'm pretty sure he did."

Kitto looked away in thought. "Who does he get into fights with?"

"Kenneth Meadows."

"Anybody else?"

"Not as far as I know."

"Who wins?"

"Neither one."

Kitto sat digesting it all. "Anything else you can remember?" I considered. "He says call him Rob now."

"Oh," Kitto said with a laugh. "I see. Big Rob, little Rob." He shook his head for a second. "And no doubt they talk about girls all the time." "Yeah," I answered. "And he's got some pictures."

Kitto's eyebrows went up. "Better than mine?"

"Kind of the same." Kitto frowned. "But not as good," I added. Postcards Kitto had gotten no one knew where, printed in faint colours—top secret and kept in his tin box in his hiding place, brought out sparingly, for rewards. I'd had two or three hungry glimpses—he gave you so many seconds, you tried to drink in everything you could. And a few of some kind of circus men.

"He wears good clothes," Kitto went on.

I nodded.

"He doesn't like to be made fun of."

I shook my head.

"Hm," Kitto concluded and drifted into reflection. We were momentarily quiet.

Then at last I got up the nerve. "I was wondering about Camille," I boldly asked.

He turned his head to me. The others were listening. "Camille?"

"I wanted to ask about her. She can do anything."

"She's a girl."

"Yeah, but she's different. Can she come to some meetings sometimes?"

He studied me. "She told you to ask me?"

I nodded equivocally.

"I'll think about it. She can't be *in*." He contemplated for a moment. "Will she take her clothes off?"

"I'm pretty sure."

He nodded, and you could see he was through thinking about that. "When do they like to go swimming?" he asked.

*

We waited three nights for a full moon, then orchestrated a mass sneak-out.

A warm cloudless night heavy with summer smells, humming and croaking with insects and frogs, drenched in moonglow from the fat orb just clearing the eastern treeline.

Camille, eleven, was not afraid or excited or anything—she was just Camille, unflappable, unawed, getting something she wanted. From the back of my house you could see the back of hers, a field and a little slice of woods in between. I had always known her.

We ducked into the woods at the pipeline and followed the moonlit creek to the dirt road, followed it, then angled into the tall pines and reached the fort. No one spoke—after all, we were sneaking out, but we were in ritual mode too. We kept quiet and grave.

We crawled through the damp pinestraw-smelling tunnel to the dome, cooler in there, and although the moon was finding its pallid way through cracks and holes, we lit the candles and brought the secret chamber into dancing life, obliterating all reality outside. Kitto sat cross-legged in his spot, and we fanned into a solemn and ceremonious crescent around him.

"You're the only girl who's ever been in here," Kitto began—but she and I knew it was not the first time. One late afternoon after relentless begging I in my new member status daringly brought her out for a sneak look. I didn't feel guilty exactly, just anxious at the thought of many-eyed Kitto finding out—risking the Belt Line, or, worse, the Horrible Mixture—but enjoyed the rush of power. "You can't be *in*—but if you do what I say, I will consider a provisional membership."

She had no idea what provisional meant and neither did we. "Can I come to the meetings?" is all she wanted to know.

"Yes," agreed Kitto. "Most of them."

"I want to come to all of them."

"Well, there may be some—not very many—when it's members only. Just a few."

"I want to go to all of them."

"Well, most of the time…"

She shook her head decisively.

"Okay," conceded Kitto, "but you have to do everything I say." She shrugged. "I want to go around with you too—everywhere you go."

"Yes—most of the time."

She frowned. Nothing doing.

"O-*kay*," Kitto exhaled. "But you're not an *official* member. Don't forget that. You are a provisional member."

"As long as I get to do everything *they* do." She nodded towards us. "Okay, okay." Because she had a high trump card and, duly rewarded in advance, now must play it.

Which, in her casual way, she did. She pulled her dress over her head, plucked out her arms, and it was just her panties. We surrounded her in breathless expectation, and I caught the familiar soapy and something else smell of her body and the bright leafy odour of her sweaty hair. She stepped out of her panties, amazingly at her ease, eyes fastened all over her like leeches, and, I imagined, secretly thinking "that's all?", leant herself.

Not long after, we did the same. Then we made our way to the Valley in the like-day moonlight, where we hopped about on the rocks, the warmcool air on our bodies—another sensation you never forget and never feel, just so, again.

Later, re-dressed, we gathered around Kitto in the fort once more. "Okay, here's the plan," he said, and turned to Camille. "I've got something very important for you to do. Can you?"

She shrugged. Let's hear it.

*

Four o'clock, four-thirty—somewhere in there—no one had or needed any kind of timepiece in those days of liquid no-time. We stood in a loose huddle waiting in the barn, the air uneasy with anticipation and fear.

This was our third try. The first time we had waited and waited until finally Kitto sent Beetle to check. About fifteen minutes later he and Chick, the lookout, had returned. No shows. "Okay," said Kitto, "somebody go tell the girls." The second time the same thing had happened. So today we felt especially touchy. Maybe they'll just never come, I privately wished.

Just waiting—I had drifted to the front corner of the barn, right there by those clumps of grass that lined the faded road and held back the briars, and all of a sudden I heard it—the thundering patter of bare feet sprinting up the road.

"Hey!" I cried—and just as they all turned to look, Chick came racing around the corner, panting—his expression screaming.

Then his voice. "They're there!" He leaned over, hands on knees, catching his breath.

Kitto walked over calmly to him. "How many?" Pant, pant. "Six."

Kitto nodded. "All right," he said, almost serenely. "Remember—wait till they're all out in the middle, and do it fast. *Fast.* You have to be fast. If you're not fast, I don't have to tell you what will happen. But if you are, they'll never catch you. Okay? You *fly* out of there. All right—go."

We had our fathers' turkey-hunting masks which we pulled over our faces after we crossed Rock Mill Road and circled through the swampy woods and stole up behind the swimming hole. Not our territory—outside the pale—an alien, enemy place, and it tightened your cods just thinking about being there. Good God, this was crazy. But Kitto—there was simply no question of not doing it.

I clung to a residual hope that it would prove a false alarm, but felt a surge of almost-terror as we began to just-hear, then heard their whoops and laughs and splashes through the woods. We got closer and closer, my heart beating like a hummingbird's—and I realized as we crawled sniper-like up the rise behind the thicket that we actually *were* going to do it because nobody would be the one to chicken out. Tykie, Dougy, and Chick elbowed the last few feet, evidently finding lines of sight, snickering and gesturing to each other. I couldn't stand it, so I pulled myself forward too, drawing an urgent quiet! signal from Tykie, but I found a spot. Well, there they were: Robbie—excuse me, Rob—Gordon, and four others. Six of them, six of us. The swimming hole pooled broad and deep just past a bend in the creek where a big sycamore tree held the swing. On this side, just before us, a sandy shelf followed the curve of the stream. I breathlessly took in the scene: the boys sailing, glistening, through the air, churning madly through the shallow water, tussling, tackling each other, engaging in wild splashing combats, coming out of the water and striding in that proud nonchalant way I never could, their wet bodies just curving into muscular definition, their miraculous patches of dark hair—all of which I stared at like a miser at someone's gold—and would have been content just to look—their clothes strewn carelessly over the rocks.

Maybe five minutes we just watched, eyes wide behind our masks—*actually do it?*—breathing in short little breaths, looking at each other waiting, waiting for Dougy to give the signal—but it was beginning to seem they would never be out in the middle all together. Several times Dougy tentatively raised his hand, then one would come out on the sand, and he would wave it off. So when it happened, the moment stood out so obviously—now or never—Dougy glanced quickly around at us, chopped the air, scrambled to his feet, and burst through the opening. From that point, I have no clear memory, except that somehow I was running too, adrenalin coursing through me in mighty waves, hardly believing it was me. The others, ahead of me, grabbed handfuls of the clothes and left almost nothing for me to get, just a shirt and somebody's dropped drawers which I scooped up on the fly, and it was that kind of running where you're scared and it's like you're about a foot above the ground and you feel no effort. Shouts barked after us from the distance I wished was ten times greater than it was—we came around the curve, exploded out into the open, crossed Rock Mill Road, and dropped the clothes in the middle of the clearing, then kept on flying into the woods—veering sharply off the path and circling quickly back where we slid up behind the trees, heaving with our mouths closed and necks craned—saw them as they barrelled out across the road, hands cupped over themselves looking both ways, and into the clearing just as Camille stepped out—and along with her, Margaret Farrow, Mertice Cooper, Lois Howard, Joanne Plummer, Marge Kinnebrew, Rachel Hollinger, Edna Keeble, Leola Hogg, and Joyce Creighton, cheering for their favourites.

No temptation to linger—we blew out of there. Kitto, waiting back at the Silo, heard our report, nodded, and sent us home. I flew like a shot arrow straight back to the house and up to my room where I had barely calmed my breathing when I saw Robbie out on the street, walking slowly and looking in my direction. I slid into full view in the window and feigned looking through some books; he stopped, stood there a minute, then headed home.

That night, having been drilled with the instructions, Bucky took the big piece of chalk Kitto gave him and a cue card, and wrote "Kenneth Meadows and Pamela Peterson" in big letters on the front walk of the school—and under it, "Poor Robbie."

*

Why that tree I have no idea—but Kitto had found some grace in it: a five or six foot blackjack oak on the ridge above the Valley. Late every midsummer afternoon, clouds permitting, at a certain moment the sun found its way through a series of opportune gaps in the trees and set it and a little magic circle of ground around it ablaze. A religious moment, for us, standing in silence like Druids. We buried the cider jar there.

Beetle missed the ceremony, but we met him coming for us halfway back on the road.

"Somebody's in the house," he reported.

We stopped. "What?" said Kitto.

"It's a man. He's there—in the house."

"What do you mean, he's there?"

"Staying there. Living there."

Kitto scowled. "Nobody could *live* there."

Beetle shrugged. "He took some stuff inside."

Kitto looked around, like the forest had ears. "Let's go to the fort." In the dome we sat keenly listening as Kitto drew pieces of information from Beetle: a man, not young but not really old, tall, dark-haired, driving a Studebaker—he had brought in some suitcases and several boxes and had stayed the night.

Kitto sat there absorbing this. "Are you sure?"

"I *saw* him," Beetle insisted.

"Do you know who he is?"

Beetle shook his head.

Kitto let out his breath. "We may be dealing with the Vanderbilt Man. Let's go see."

We froze. Kitto bestirred himself, crawled a few feet, then stopped and looked at us, riveted to our spots and gaping moonstruck at him. "Well?" he said.

No one budged. Then finally, *sotto voce*, awed, Bucky asked, "The *Vanderbilt Man*?"

"I don't *know* that," answered Kitto. "I don't *know* anything at this point. I said he *may* be. Let's go."

Twilight threatened. I was, we all were, in that dubious zone of parental displeasure—but the seriousness, the possible danger, of the expedition banished apprehension. We took our sticks.

At the edge of the woods we slid up, two to a tree, and knelt. The house and big oak tree stood in silhouette against the fading sky, and from our vantage point we had a good view of the one-time pasture and unruly grounds and wild orchard. In a little gap between the house and tree sat the black car, looking settled, and the kitchen window glowed yellowy, unnaturally.

We just crouched there taking this in, until we became aware, not suddenly but rather in gradual realization, that a part of this scene was moving, of a or the man walking slowly along the obscure path at the far edge of the orchard, taking a few steps, stopping, the smoke from his cigarette rising around his head and dissipating.

"It's *him*," Dougy wonderingly whispered.

Kitto grimaced, shaking his head for silence.

We watched a while longer. Then Kitto signalled, and we backed away, dissolving into the woods, I last and retaining a picture of the man standing there looking, I think, in our direction, but it was too far to know for sure.

I needed to go home, but Kitto stopped us in the fort.

I had never seen him agitated before; I guess none of us had—we looked at each other uneasily. "What's he *doing* there?" Kitto demanded to know. "What right does he have? He can't live there."

"Maybe he's not living there," said Tykie.

"No," Kitto decisively shook his head. "He is."

"Maybe he'll leave."

Kitto frowned and shook his head again. We watched him. "*The Vanderbilt Man*," he said with a resigned sneer none of us understood. I glanced around at all the bulging eyes, including Camille's.

"He *is* the Vanderbilt Man?" Bucky asked, almost in a whisper. Kitto, who alone had ever seen that mythical fiend, only narrowed his eyes and gave his head an ambivalent shake. "Who can get out tonight?" he quietly asked.

We stared at him in aghast silence.

"Who can get *out* tonight?" he repeated, louder.

"*He's* the Vanderbilt Man?" Chick asked.

"I'm asking who can help me tonight. If nobody can, I'll do it myself."

Tykie raised his hand. "I'm not afraid of him." He and Kitto stared at each other.

Then Dougy, Chick, Beetle, me, Camille. Everybody but Bucky.

"Midnight," said Kitto.

*

I met Camille on the path between our two houses, and we made our way through back yards from shadows to shadows, past Mr. Traylor's garden, stirring up the usual dogs as we went, but moving quickly. Kitto had it all planned.

The rocks would come from a half-tumbled wall at the lower edge of the yard. The kitchen light had been extinguished, when we arrived, but now a soft light wavered from a back upstairs window, where some kind of curtain had been hung. As we crouched there watching, a shadow passed behind it, and it felt like all the blood in my body froze. "We'd better get out of here," I pointed out.

Kitto shook his head firmly. "He can't see us."

So we started to work. Camille stuck close to me, her face wild with the thrill, having the time of her life—and maybe it wasn't *that* scary—because this was an odd Vanderbilt Man, not marauding in the woods, but moving into an abandoned house looking all too human. It's funny how a high purpose can unseat ordinary fears—such as of spiders and snakes—and we began heedlessly to dislodge several good thick flat rocks for the legs, and hustled them by turns to the little clearing Kitto had selected, hardly taking our eyes from the sinister window, where if anything moved, icy razor blades danced up my spine. The middle stone proved hardest to find, and it took three frustrating tries to get one to balance across the two leg columns. Then three or four more, and finally a more or less round one for the head.

The crowning touch Kitto had hauled in a paint bucket, having concocted it that afternoon: pokeweed berries, crushed and mixed to a bloody pulp with creek water. This maledictory libation he slathered over the head and we watched it, in the moonlight, drool down the rock man, streaking him in ghastly gore.

"Leave!" Kitto then hissed, spreading his arms like Moses commanding the sea. "And never come back!"

Then we hightailed it.

*

Naturally, the following morning, circumstances called for a spy expedition. We got our sticks and cut through the woods to the low side of the house once more, frogwalking the last fifty yards, sliding up into the cover of the privet.

There he stood, our most intimidating rock man, the bloody stain, which the night had dried to a purplish black, very menacing, I thought—just as we'd left him, but for a single odd touch: a bunch of wild roses in a rusty can at his feet.

Kitto stared, a curious, affronted expression straining his features, in silence, and we stared too, like little animals sniffing the air. Then I remember the faintest scent of tobacco smoke, and after that it became something that bypassed the senses and connected directly to the nerves, and I mustn't have been the only one because everyone's face screeched in silent alarm. We turned our heads in unison to see the man himself, a yellowish man, holding a cigarette, standing between two overgrown rows of apple trees, not twenty yards away.

We exploded like a covey of quail.

"Hey!" we heard behind us. "Don't go! Come back!"

Fat chance. We blew through the woods like something blasted from a gun, bounding over logs and ditches like deer, hit the road at a sprint, and not until we came around the curve to the side road that cut off to the Silo did I dare look back. Nobody. Well, except for Bucky—wheezing panic-stricken a good fifty yards behind. He caught up and we all gathered in the dim dingy barn panting like a herd of terrorized antelope.

"Okay, everybody just take it easy," Kitto said as we caught our breath.

"We need to get out of here! He can find us!" Chick pleaded. "He can't find us," Kitto replied, a little wearily. "He's not going anywhere."

"But if he's the Vanderbilt Man—" Dougy objected. "Maybe he is," Kitto cut him off. "Or maybe he isn't. Anyway, he's also a math professor. Or was."

We stared at him. "How do you know?" Beetle asked. "Because of your father. Right?" said Tykie, looking at him. "Yes. Because of my father. He knows him. Or knew him. Nobody talks to him—nobody likes him."

"Why?"

Kitto shrugged. "He's peculiar." We thought about that for a second. Then Kitto added, "He has cancer. He's dying."

We stared at him. No one knew what to say.

"His name is Redding Lang. It's his house. His family house." "The Old Lang Place," said Tykie quietly.

"Yes. The Old Lang Place. He doesn't work anymore. They don't get paid anyway. Just scrip. My father said he doesn't need the money." A strange little mantle of silence fell over us.

Then Tykie, in a tone that sounded some new note of sneer and disillusion, said, "So much for the Vanderbilt Man."

All heads turned to Kitto, but he let it pass, staring ahead of him at something we couldn't see. "I'm going to see him."

We gaped at him.

At last Chick asked, "Why?"

"To talk to him."

"Just you?"

"Yes," Kitto said. "Just me."

"Aren't you afraid?"

"Of what?"

"Of the Vanderbilt Man—of the things he does to you." Kitto only shook his head. "They're just things."

*

A wet day, dripping. It rained hard earlier and we stayed under the barn, dodging the leaks, watching it run off the edges of the roof—now, suppertime, it had fallen off to a dribble, its mission, of cooling the summer air, fulfilled.

Halfway home I realized I had forgotten my shoes—but I was hungry and kept going, with Camille, knowing I would have to retrace every step. Sure enough—but Mama let me eat first.

Then—trudging back, alone, and that *feeling*—like being in the school at night—everything so quiet, like something listening, waiting—nothing to distract it from just me, apprehensive, an intruder in my own world.

I reached the ridge and stood there, alone, feeling myself with strange lucidity, the water dripping from the leaves, and I thought: *I will always remember this moment.*

*

Even James, the delivery man at the drug store, was talking about the fight. Coach Howard, after enjoying it for a while through the door, broke it up behind the gym. Gordon's eye swollen shut, Robbie with a busted lip. Hard to say who would take who, if it came down to it—Gordon bigger but Robbie meaner. Just like their daddies, them two.

*

We didn't see or hear from Kitto for a week. All of a sudden—nothing to do. I moped around the house until my mother, threatening castor oil, ran me out—then went over to Dougy's until *his* mother, threatening kerosene and sugar, banished us as well.

"You boys go play—what's the matter with you—lolling about—a day like this."

Then finally, another wet day, a dire message went around and we hurried to the fort, all of us arriving together—Kitto already there—slowing our steps the last fifty yards in shock, then stopping, taking in the devastation. Bucky started crying. Kitto's expression was frozen ice-hard. He didn't say a word. Savage marauding glee still echoed around what was now only a debris-littered smear in the woods—a new junkyard, an eyesore. Dollsheads, broken bottles, showed through the pinestraw—the strongbox, we found out later, missing. The air reeked with befoulment. In the dairy office *Kitto Panty Club* had been painted on the wall with red paint, drooling down from the letters like blood.

"They'll be sorry," said Tykie darkly. "Oh God will they be sorry." He looked at Kitto.

But Kitto, self-absorbed, just shook his head, same expression. "They had no right to do it," said Beetle, blinking back tears. "Right?" Kitto laughed.

"I hate them," said Chick. "I hate their guts. I hate them so much I wish they would die."

"They will," Kitto replied. "So will you."

We had no spirit to do anything. We just got away from there, hardly even speaking. Kitto went home, then Beetle and Chick and Tykie. Bucky, Dougy, Camille, and I stayed around the Silo for a while—spy on somebody? build a dam?—nothing felt right. So we left too.

*

August was dying; September snaked its tentacles toward us—so little of the summer left, and for a couple of weeks we hardly saw one another. My forehead-feeling mother looked down my throat, checked me for ticks, brought out the castor oil. All the same, I stayed in my room and read, drew, drifted bored out of doors in the afternoons and did nothing with Camille, listened to *Amos 'n' Andy* and *Lum and Abner* in the evenings.

Finally one afternoon Tykie came over wanting to know if I had talked to Kitto.

I shook my head.

"Somebody needs to go over there. I've been sending messages but he won't answer them. It's time to *do* something."

So we got Dougy and went—but it was just his mother, whom I had seen maybe five times in my life, a sweet, quavering woman in a bathrobe who had no idea where her son was, and insisted on finding something to give us—finally coming up with some stale Graham crackers.

"Where *is* he?" Dougy asked angrily as we left, eating the mealy cookies.

"The house," said Tykie, and we looked at him amazed. "That's where he's going, I'm pretty sure. I vote we go see."

We snuck up in the usual place, feeling odd to be spying on *him*, but saw them clearly enough, the two of them, sitting on the back porch in the shadows, cigarette smoke drifting out into the afternoon. The next day Tykie came back and said he had talked to him. He would meet us in the Valley at four.

Full of hope, we went.

"I say we rebuild it in another place they can't find," Tykie defiantly proposed.

"They will find it," Kitto returned.

We waited—no one contested that—until Dougy said, "We can hide it real good—they won't find it."

Kitto shrugged. "*They*," he said, "never go away. And there's nowhere they can't find."

"We can paint over that in the dairy barn," said Beetle.

Kitto exhaled. "And what's going to keep them from coming back and doing it again any time they want? It's not our place anymore."

"It *is* our place," said Tykie.

"If it's *theirs* too," Kitto pointed out, "it's not ours."

Beetle was crying. "I *hate* them."

"So?" Tykie asserted angrily. "So—what then? That's it? They tear up our fort and we don't have a club anymore?"

Kitto shrugged.

"Let's *get* them. Come on—let's come up with a *plan*."

Leaning his head back Kitto closed his eyes and exhaled slowly. "Like what?"

"I don't know. We can think of something."

"Let's put a snake in Robbie's room," Chick suggested. "Okay—you go get the snake."

"I can catch a snake. If somebody helps me."

"I know," said Dougy, "let's steal their bicycles and bend the wheels up. And then dump them in front of the school."

"That'll teach them," replied Kitto.

"Well, *what* then?" Dougy demanded.

"Look," Kitto responded, with a little pulse of animation. "Say we find some place and rebuild the fort. What have you got? Same thing. A fort."

We watched him, waiting.

"Except not really a fort, because the only fort is really in your head."

We kept watching.

"And you can't rebuild that—not ever—don't you know that?" He made a sweeping gesture with his arm. "And they're here now. And they'll never be not here again."

No one said anything. His burst of energy subsided.

"Listen," he said. "This whole place—all of it—it's not something you have—not for good—you just have your turn, that's all." From us, silence.

"Professor Lang, and his sister—*they* used to play out here. They grew *up* out here. Their mother and their father died when they were little, and they grew up in that house with their uncle—then he died and they had to move away. And all of it—the same thing—happened to them."

"What?" I said—amazed, confused. "Robbie Moore?"

Kitto laughed. "Yeah—Robbie Moore." We marvelled at that. Then he added, "Okay, the name was different."

*

I was with Camille, going to get Dougy, when she told me. Her eyes burned sadly. Her mother had sat her down and explained it all—what to expect soon, what to do. I had never heard a more outlandish story in my life—something your first impulse refused to accept, but your intuitive suspicion knew was true.

That box in my mother's bathroom cabinet. "That's what that's for?" I asked incredulously.

Camille nodded.

"*All* girls?" I asked.

She nodded again.

That seemed surpassingly strange. The Jitney Jungle woman? The organist at church? Your grandmother? Pamela Peterson? I bombarded her with a hundred questions—I hungered for precise details—but she had few answers.

We got Dougy, but didn't tell him. Slowly the warm, inconsolable afternoon passed. We didn't do anything, just floated around. Every now and then someone would say, "Remember that time…?" Already there were two of her—the one *I* knew soon not to be.

*

September slipped under the door, when we weren't looking, and stayed. The muscadines were getting ripe; the old death march set in as *school* lay in ambush ahead. Tykie came by the house one morning and said he was starting a new club. The idea shocked me—I just stared at him at first. He said he already had Beetle, Chick, and Bucky—did I want to be in? Camille could be too—and would I talk to Dougy? We would still be invisible, just like before. He had found a perfect place for a new fort. "Not Kitto?"

"What Kitto? He's with that guy all the time."

I just squirmed, unable to accommodate this.

"Look," said Tykie, "can't you tell? He doesn't care anymore." "But—I don't know—"

"Well, this is the new club, that's all I'm saying. You can either be in it or not be in it."

"Don't you remember that time he gave you three dollars to buy that guy's bicycle?"

"So?"

"And Beetle and Chick—and he gave me his BB gun—and he took a paddling for Bucky. *And* for you."

"But what does that have to do with anything now? He's not coming out here anymore."

I sat confused, miserable.

"We're going to get Robbie Moore. We're going to get him good." "I don't know," I said, shaking my head.

That evening Chick and Beetle came by and tried to talk me into it. They showed me their new marks: T.

"We'll be invisible," Chick argued.

I just couldn't get easy in my mind about it.

"Well, it's the Club now," Beetle said impatiently—and they left. I agonized over it for a while, then went to see Kitto. Excited that someone had come, his mother tried to give us cookies or something, but Kitto barked her away. He was holed up in his chaotic room, where it felt like he was holed up a lot, books everywhere. He laughed at my fretting. "I don't care if they have a club," he said. "And I don't care if you're in it. If that's what you want to do, do it."

"I'm not sure," I replied. "It's not the same—"

He laughed. "Nothing's the same."

I was silent, then worked up the nerve to say, "He said you're with that man—"

Kitto laughed again, showing his teeth. I didn't recognize him. "Oh God," he said, and shook his head in some weary knowledge beyond my grasp. "Look," he added. "He's just a man who's about to die. That's all. Why don't you come with me and see?"

*

Hardly the Vanderbilt Man. The idea had simply died.

So it wasn't fear I felt—only something peculiar in my nerves. As Kitto said—just a man. Sitting on that rickety rose-smothered back porch in the old ragged stuffed chair that had come to rest at an odd angle there, smoke rising from his cigarette, not reading or doing anything, just sitting, as we approached through the apple orchard. He watched us, smoking, with an expression that proved to be a bemused smile as we got close enough to see it. I followed Kitto up the perilous back steps, and he just took a draw on his cigarette and peered with that half-smile through the smoke.

"This is Preston," said Kitto.

He held out his hand—I took the three or four steps to him and shook it. I couldn't have said how old he was—this tawny, surprisingly handsome—striking—man. Dark hair combed back, matinee-hero features gone a little heavy, piercing blue eyes, contaminated, like all of him, with yellow—eyes that sliced through me once, like an executioner's stroke. He wore a loose shirt with a low sagging pocket holding his cigarettes, baggy pants, and scuffed brown shoes, laceless.

"Hello Preston."

Then, oddly, no one spoke. We just sort of stood there, Kitto looking at him, I looking at Kitto, the man looking into the wild yard. You could smell, but not see, what he had been drinking.

Finally Kitto lightly sat down, on an old kitchen chair, and I mirrored his motion, and we made a silent triangle.

The man laughed. "You look at the same thing long enough, you can't get rid of it. It burns itself into your brain. That's why you'd better be careful what you look at. Same with what you think about." He pulled himself forward in his chair and got to his feet. "Excuse me." We watched him as he walked stiffly into the kitchen. We heard a few bumps and clinks, then he came back and eased himself once more into his chair with a long grunt.

"You ever have a red dream?"

I glanced at Kitto, who shook his head—then I shook mine. "Everything red—like that clay out there. Even the sky. Just you in the whole world—you'd get a good long look at it." He took a pull on his cigarette. "Same everywhere—one person to a world—scattered through all the galaxies. Finding yours would be like going into a library with a billion books and finding one—how long would that take? Maybe five minutes—if you got lucky. But of course you wouldn't. You'd need a system—you know what I'd do? I'd do the easy ones first—I say the *easy* ones, the ones you wouldn't have to bend over or climb to reach, and I'd run a string to show where I'd been, so if there were, say, eight shelves and you did the middle five you'd have what? a sixty-two point five percent chance of finding it the first go-round—which you hope you would because just imagine squatting down for that lowest shelf for a few hundred years—and what would be the probability of it being the very last book you checked? Same as the very first: nine hundred ninety-nine million nine hundred ninety-nine thousand nine hundred ninety-nine to one. Not real good. Of course—" wrinkling his brow—"the probability changes for each choice—say it was ten books—you're talking about the odds of picking wrong nine times in a row—nine-tenths the first time, eight-ninths the second, and so on—it ends up one-tenth." A little burst of silence. Then Kitto said, "It would have to be a pretty good book."

The man laughed. "Or written by a lunatic." He stabbed his cigarette into an overflowing ashtray and lit another. The smoke leaked out around him. "What would you do if you knew it would all come to nothing in the end?" He laughed. "Well, friends—you're doing it." His gaze sliced through me again—then over to Kitto, who looked up at him, then down. I shuddered.

"Tell Preston about how it used to be out here," said Kitto.

"Oh," he sighed, talking smoke. "I can't remember—I like this better. Reverting to a state of higher order."

He looked over the yard for a while, then emitted a little groan. "I don't like the days getting shorter, do you? I never have—I've always hated the dark—even though it's the natural state of things—we don't give people enough credit for just being conscious. You think of all the potential people—what would they be, spirits?—who never actually went through with it—they have no idea. Maybe we've chosen it somehow—because you know there's only a certain state of mind that lets you endure it—or a bargain you make with whatever powers may be—" he gestured toward the yard with his cigarette—"memory is a loan, you've got to pay it back—and the thing is, what you remember is nothing compared to what you don't. Nothing outnumbers something a trillion to one. Excuse me."

He got painfully to his feet again and went into the kitchen. I caught Kitto's eye. Then he came back.

"Ahh," he grunted, settling back into the chair.

And I knew that was all I could stand. His voice sounded like something that came through the air in coils, and I couldn't even look at Kitto, corrupted, lost—with my world. I remember the fetid breath of the dying house, the yellow glance of the dying man, and the scent of roses. I said "I've got to go," and hurried away across the wasted yard.

What were the chances I would ever come back here? Nil. And, in fact, the longer I stayed the more I threatened that old picture, that I realized I had to guard, no matter what. Certainly not let this new one, suddenly grown alien and tedious, displace it. The bulldozers groaned through the doomed woods. One last look at the leaf, just as a little wind nudged it into the light, and I caught a glimpse of silver filament. Always some old trick.

And some old lonely way.

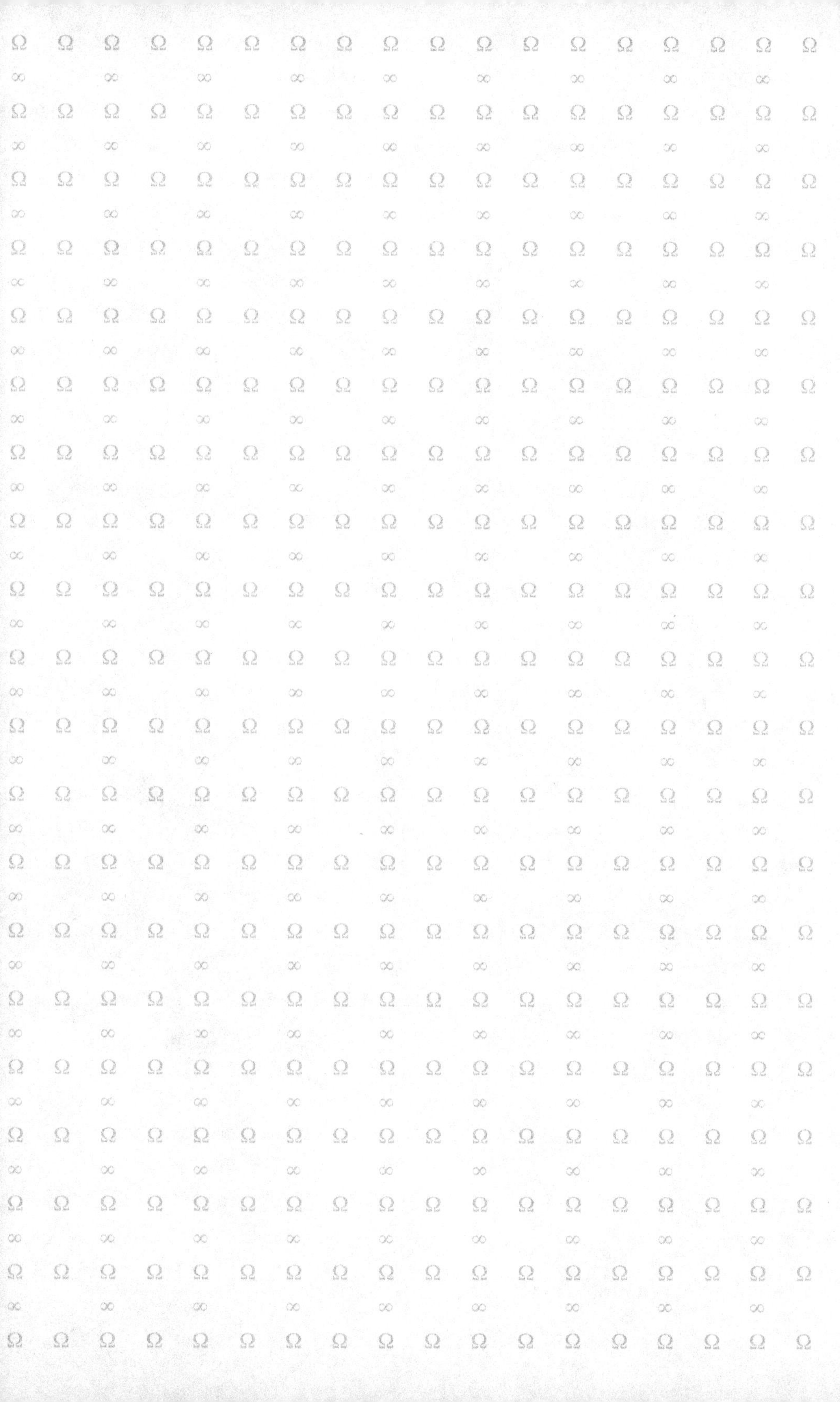

Ω Ω Ω Ω Ω Ω Ω Ω Ω Ω Ω Ω Ω Ω Ω Ω Ω Ω
∞ ∞ ∞ ∞ ∞ ∞ ∞ ∞ ∞
Ω Ω Ω Ω Ω Ω Ω Ω Ω Ω Ω Ω Ω Ω Ω Ω Ω Ω
∞ ∞ ∞ ∞ ∞ ∞ ∞ ∞ ∞
Ω Ω Ω Ω Ω Ω Ω Ω Ω Ω Ω Ω Ω Ω Ω Ω Ω Ω
∞ ∞ ∞ ∞ ∞ ∞ ∞ ∞ ∞
Ω Ω Ω Ω Ω Ω Ω Ω Ω Ω Ω Ω Ω Ω Ω Ω Ω Ω
∞ ∞ ∞ ∞ ∞ ∞ ∞ ∞ ∞
Ω Ω Ω Ω Ω Ω Ω Ω Ω Ω Ω Ω Ω Ω Ω Ω Ω Ω
∞ ∞ ∞ ∞ ∞ ∞ ∞ ∞ ∞
Ω Ω Ω Ω Ω Ω Ω Ω Ω Ω Ω Ω Ω Ω Ω Ω Ω Ω
∞ ∞ ∞ ∞ ∞ ∞ ∞ ∞ ∞
Ω Ω Ω Ω Ω Ω Ω Ω Ω Ω Ω Ω Ω Ω Ω Ω Ω Ω
∞ ∞ ∞ ∞ ∞ ∞ ∞ ∞ ∞
Ω Ω Ω Ω Ω Ω Ω Ω Ω Ω Ω Ω Ω Ω Ω Ω Ω Ω
∞ ∞ ∞ ∞ ∞ ∞ ∞ ∞ ∞
Ω Ω Ω Ω Ω Ω Ω Ω Ω Ω Ω Ω Ω Ω Ω Ω Ω Ω
∞ ∞ ∞ ∞ ∞ ∞ ∞ ∞ ∞
Ω Ω Ω Ω Ω Ω Ω Ω Ω Ω Ω Ω Ω Ω Ω Ω Ω Ω
∞ ∞ ∞ ∞ ∞ ∞ ∞ ∞ ∞
Ω Ω Ω Ω Ω Ω Ω Ω Ω Ω Ω Ω Ω Ω Ω Ω Ω Ω
∞ ∞ ∞ ∞ ∞ ∞ ∞ ∞ ∞
Ω Ω Ω Ω Ω Ω Ω Ω Ω Ω Ω Ω Ω Ω Ω Ω Ω Ω
∞ ∞ ∞ ∞ ∞ ∞ ∞ ∞ ∞
Ω Ω Ω Ω Ω Ω Ω Ω Ω Ω Ω Ω Ω Ω Ω Ω Ω Ω
∞ ∞ ∞ ∞ ∞ ∞ ∞ ∞ ∞
Ω Ω Ω Ω Ω Ω Ω Ω Ω Ω Ω Ω Ω Ω Ω Ω Ω Ω
∞ ∞ ∞ ∞ ∞ ∞ ∞ ∞ ∞
Ω Ω Ω Ω Ω Ω Ω Ω Ω Ω Ω Ω Ω Ω Ω Ω Ω Ω
∞ ∞ ∞ ∞ ∞ ∞ ∞ ∞ ∞
Ω Ω Ω Ω Ω Ω Ω Ω Ω Ω Ω Ω Ω Ω Ω Ω Ω Ω
∞ ∞ ∞ ∞ ∞ ∞ ∞ ∞ ∞
Ω Ω Ω Ω Ω Ω Ω Ω Ω Ω Ω Ω Ω Ω Ω Ω Ω Ω
∞ ∞ ∞ ∞ ∞ ∞ ∞ ∞ ∞
Ω Ω Ω Ω Ω Ω Ω Ω Ω Ω Ω Ω Ω Ω Ω Ω Ω Ω
∞ ∞ ∞ ∞ ∞ ∞ ∞ ∞ ∞
Ω Ω Ω Ω Ω Ω Ω Ω Ω Ω Ω Ω Ω Ω Ω Ω Ω Ω
∞ ∞ ∞ ∞ ∞ ∞ ∞ ∞ ∞
Ω Ω Ω Ω Ω Ω Ω Ω Ω Ω Ω Ω Ω Ω Ω Ω Ω Ω

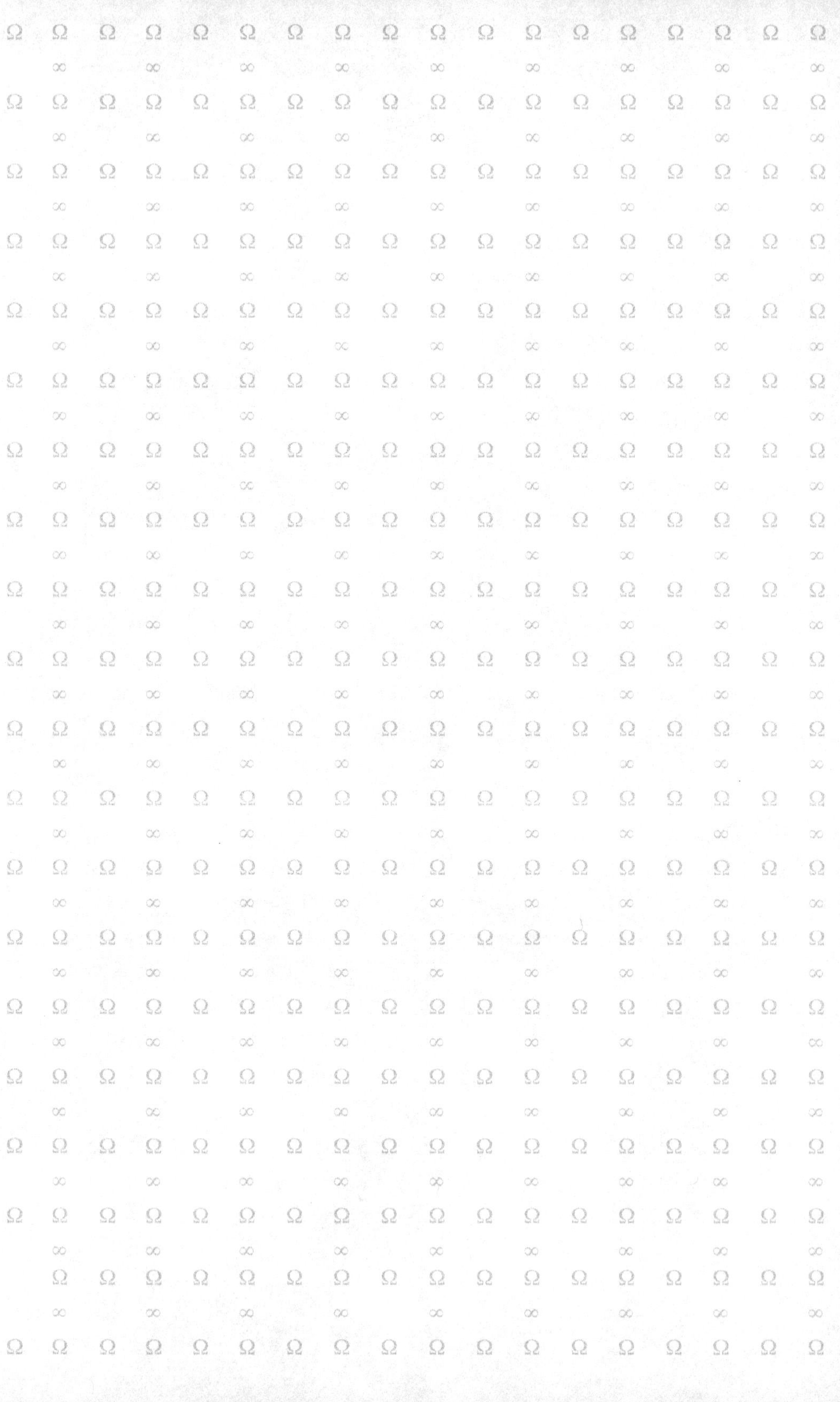

www.ingramcontent.com/pod-product-compliance
Lightning Source LLC
Chambersburg PA
CBHW021656110726
47902CB00007B/1948

* 9 7 8 0 9 9 4 3 5 2 5 7 6 *